Between Two Seas

Between Two Seas

MARIE-LOUISE JENSEN

OXFORD

UNIVERSITY PRESS

OXFORD
UNIVERSITY PRESS

Great Clarendon Street, Oxford OX2 6DP

Oxford University Press is a department of the University of Oxford.
It furthers the University's objective of excellence in research, scholarship,
and education by publishing worldwide in

Oxford New York

Auckland Cape Town Dar es Salaam Hong Kong Karachi
Kuala Lumpur Madrid Melbourne Mexico City Nairobi
New Delhi Shanghai Taipei Toronto

With offices in

Argentina Austria Brazil Chile Czech Republic France Greece
Guatemala Hungary Italy Japan Poland Portugal Singapore
South Korea Switzerland Thailand Turkey Ukraine Vietnam

Oxford is a registered trade mark of Oxford University Press
in the UK and in certain other countries

British Library Cataloguing in Publication Data

Data available

ISBN: 978-0-19-275530-8

1 3 5 7 9 10 8 6 4 2

Typeset in Meridien Roman by TnQ Books and Journals Pvt. Ltd.,
Chennai, India

Printed in Great Britain by Cox and Wyman Ltd, Reading, Berkshire

For Helle

Acknowledgements

Thanks to my fellow MA students and the staff at the Bath Spa University, especially Julia Green and Karen Saunders. Also to the helpful staff at Grimsby library and Erik Christensen of the Bangsbo archive for his valuable information about Skagen and Frederikshavn in the 1880s. And to Karl Taylor for a much-needed painting lesson.

ONE

Grimsby, July 1885

I'm heading for the privy across the yard, carrying my mother's full chamber pot, when they catch me. Three tall girls emerge from the passageway that leads out to the street. Two of them block my way forward to the outdoor privy, the third cuts off my retreat to the safety of the stairway. I turn to face them, my back to the wall.

'Where do you think you're going, Marianne?' demands one girl.

Her name's Bridget. She's hard-featured and scrawny and lives downstairs in the same tenement building as I do.

One of her skinny arms shoots out and shoves me hard. I'm not expecting it, and I fall heavily against the wall. The chamber pot hits the stone with a dull *thunk*, and shatters, spilling most of its contents down my dress.

'Oh, look what you've gone and done,' Bridget cries, malicious delight lighting her eyes. 'You've got it all down you!' She sniffs at me and then turns to her companions, holding her nose. 'She stinks like the kennel!' They all laugh. I try to slip away while her back is turned, but she pulls me back and slaps me hard across

1

the face. I lift my arms, covering my face, before she can do it again.

'And how's your filthy mother? We all know what she is!' Bridget's voice rings out, loud and confident.

I don't answer her. If I say anything at all, they'll mock the way I speak. I don't have their broad Grimsby accent.

'Speak up, Marianne,' cries another voice. 'We can't hear you.'

'Marianne?' taunts the third. 'Who'd want to Marry Anne?'

They screech with laughter.

'Marry Anne? No one marries a bastard!'

I stand still, waiting for the right moment to make my escape.

'Where's your pa then?' It's Bridget's voice again. 'Or doesn't your mother know which one he was?'

'Whore's brat!' the voices cry.

Their crude words ring in my head, but I'm past being upset. It's mostly lies, and I've heard it so many times before. I'm just desperate to get back to my mother.

She's lying upstairs, dying.

One of the girls is pinching my arm. I look down and see her filthy fingernails digging into my flesh. I slap her hand away and it works like a signal. They all close in, pulling my hair, pinching me, yanking at my dress.

I spot a gap and throw myself at it, tearing myself away from their cruel fingers. I knock the youngest girl flying into a pile of horse dung. I can hear the others scream with rage, but I'm free now, fleeing across the yard and up the stairs.

2

I slam and lock the door of our attic room behind me. Panting, I lean against it. My eyes seek my mother, lying quietly on her bed in the darkened room. Her rasping breathing is harsher than ever.

With trembling fingers, I wash my hands and remove my soiled dress. I only have one other, besides my best dress. Once I've put it on, I go to sit down by my mother. Her frail hands clutch the blanket. I take one of them in mine and hold it, hoping to comfort her. I can see she's in pain. There is fear in her eyes.

I can't even afford to get a doctor for her. It's always been a struggle for the two of us to manage, and now that she's sick, we have barely any money left. I haven't told her, but we are also behind with the rent. How shall we manage? I don't want to think about that right now.

'Can I do anything for you, mother?'

A small nod of the head.

'What can I do?' I ask.

Her eyes dart sideways to the slate lying on the chair by her bed. I put it into her hands and help her to sit up a little, propping her with pillows. She's no longer able to speak, and writing is becoming increasingly difficult. She grasps the slate pencil and begins to trace out a word. Her writing is shaky.

Sewing Box

I'm puzzled.

'I'd like to sit with you a little, mother dear, before I work some more.'

I can't sew by her bedside; the room is far too dark. I need to sit right over by the window to see what I'm

3

doing. My answer was not what she wanted. I can see her frustration as she slumps back on the pillows. I stretch out a hand and tenderly smooth back some stray strands of hair from her face. She clutches at my hand a moment, her eyes entreating me. Then her hand drops. She's exhausted even by this small movement.

'I'm sorry, mother, I didn't understand: my sewing box or yours?'

She jabs at herself with the slate pencil, and I go to fetch her sewing box. Sewing and embroidery is how we make our living, and our sewing boxes are precious possessions.

Mother gestures slightly and I understand I'm to open the box. I lift out the tray containing all her threads and needles. Underneath I find a small heavy package wrapped in waxed paper.

'Should I open it?'

A nod.

When I unwrap the paper, coins tumble out on the bedcovers, gleaming gold. Sovereigns. I'm speechless with amazement. Here is more money than I have ever seen together. I stare blankly, and then pick up a couple of the coins and weigh them in my hand. They feel smooth and heavy.

'Mother, we have been going hungry and doing without medicine for you, and all the while you had these hidden!'

There are two letters folded in the package with the money. One is sealed and addressed to Lars Christensen. That's my father. The other has my name on it.

4

'Do you want me to read this?' I ask, holding up my letter.

Her slight nod shows me that she does. I take it over to the window.

May 1885

My dearest Marianne,

I am writing to you before I become too ill to explain what this money is for. For many years I have been saving so that we can travel to Denmark together and find your father. I never saved enough. Now that I cannot go with you, there will be enough for you to go alone. Travel to Skagen and find him. Give him my letter. Please tell him I have loved him and waited for him through all these years. Seek a better life, Marianne!

Yours affectionately,

Your mother,

Esther.

This letter fills me with conflicting emotions. The mention of Denmark sends a thrill through me. Throughout my childhood it's been my fairy-tale land, the stuff of dreams.

But my mother's calm assumption that she's going to die appals me. I imagine her sitting down and writing this letter, months ago, accepting her fate, and tears prick my eyelids. I try to blink them back, but one escapes, trickling down my cheek and gathering on my chin. I brush it away quickly and return to my mother's bedside. I stroke her hands, her face, her hair.

5

'I love you so much,' I whisper brokenly. 'I want you to grow strong again, to get well, so that we can go together.'

Mother shakes her head very slightly and frowns at me. I realize, perhaps for the first time, that she lost the will to live some time ago. She's given up. Another tear slides silently down my face, and again my mother shakes her head. She doesn't like to see me cry. She wants me to be strong.

I take a deep breath, and count the money: it seems a fortune to me.

'Mother, let me fetch a doctor and buy some medicine for you with some of this money—I beg you!'

She shakes her head more vigorously than before and a spasm of pain crosses her face. She begins to write again. Slowly, tortuously.

Promise

'Promise what? That I won't get a doctor? That I'll go to Denmark?'

A father I've never met, I think bitterly. A wild goose chase. Wasting a fortune going to find a father who doesn't know I exist and might not welcome me when he does. I can't help thinking that if he had wanted to, he could have returned years ago.

Perhaps with my mother, it would be exciting to go, but how can I do a journey like that alone? I'm sixteen, and I've never left Grimsby. The very thought is terrifying.

But mother's eyes beg me, desperate. I drop to my knees and take her trembling hands in mine.

'Mother, I promise to go to Denmark and look for my father if that is what you wish me to do. I swear it if that will comfort you. But surely there is more than enough money here for the journey. Please, please let me get a doctor.'

Her face is set and stubborn. She won't give in now. And I've made a promise I must keep. My mother grows more peaceful.

It doesn't last, however. By the early hours of the morning she's no longer able to bear the pain. She is writhing and twisting in the bed, unable to make a sound, wild-eyed and sweat-drenched. I can't watch her suffer like this. Mother has been everything to me all my life; she needs help now.

'Mother!' I try to speak calmly and clearly, though my voice shakes. 'I'm not breaking my promise to you, but I am going to get a doctor!'

I can't tell whether she has heard me. Frantic, I run downstairs to Mrs Forbes. She is the only person in the building who has ever spoken kindly to me. One of the few respectable people who does not flinch at the sight of me, as though my illegitimacy were a visible stain. I hammer on her door.

Mrs Forbes appears, candle in hand, nightcap on her head.

'Is it your mother?' she asks.

'She needs medicine,' I tell her, and my voice is hoarse with fear. 'But I can't leave her alone.'

'Of course. I'll send my son for the apothecary at once. Go back to her, my dear.'

I turn and take the stairs two steps at a time. Mother has thrown off the bedclothes. I try to wipe the perspiration from her brow with a cool flannel, but I can't get her to stay still. I let out a cry of despair. But in a few moments Mrs Forbes joins me, and together we are able to restrain her.

It is the first time there has ever been a visitor of any kind in our room, but I'm glad of her company. It seems an eternity until the apothecary arrives. He examines my mother. She is so thin, and an unsightly growth has disfigured her throat. He takes me aside.

'There is little I can do for her but ease the pain. I would guess that she does not have many more hours left.'

I nod, blindly. This isn't news to me. The doctor at the charity hospital told us as much weeks ago. The apothecary administers a dose of morphine. I hand one of our precious coins to him. It's hard to part with it. But he pockets it almost casually, as though he sees such money every day, and then departs.

Mother's eyes glaze and lose their fear for the first time in days. Her frantic movements slow and then cease. Only her rasping breathing remains. Since yesterday she has no longer even been able to swallow, so I can't give her water. Mrs Forbes returns to her own rooms, leaving me alone with my mother. I sit, holding her hand, and watch her slowly fall asleep.

'I'm scared, mother,' I whisper quietly. 'I'm scared to lose you.'

She doesn't wake again. Towards dawn her breathing becomes harsher, more laboured, but then begins to fail. By the time the sky outside is turning grey she has gone. And I am left quite alone.

TWO

August 1885

I sit by the window, my embroidery in my hands. The afternoon sunlight slants in through the dusty window, lighting up the different colour threads. It's stifling up here under the roof, and I can feel my concentration wavering. Mrs Forbes is visiting, and sits by me, her own sewing in her hands. I can see beads of perspiration gathering on her brow.

'It's a hot one today, and no mistake,' she sighs, dabbing at her forehead and neck with her handkerchief.

'Yes indeed,' I agree sympathetically. 'I'm sorry I can't open the window today. It's the wind direction. I tried earlier, and was almost smothered.' We can both see the smoke pouring from the chimneys of the iron foundry behind us, and hear the relentless bangs and crashes of the machinery.

Our room is at the back of the tenement building in Riby Square, and as well as the foundry, I can see St Andrew's Church from the window. I think of my mother resting in the earth in the churchyard, and feel the familiar prickle behind my eyelids. I turn my face away to hide my emotion. It is a month since my mother was buried. I was the only mourner, but I wept enough tears for many.

The room is empty of all the things that made it home when my mother was alive. In preparation for my journey to Denmark, I've sold everything I can't take with me: the furniture, bedding, and kitchenware. Even my mother's clothes. I sold my own sewing box, choosing to keep hers to remember her by. I think I would have grieved to see the familiar things go, had I not already been numb with grief from my greater loss.

I've kept only mother's pearl necklace, which she brought from her parents' home in Mablethorpe, south of Grimsby. She brought very little, as she was given only an hour to leave the house when her father discovered she was with child. She was just sixteen. The same age I am now.

'You've been such a great help to me, Mrs Forbes,' I tell her.

She chuckles.

'Where did that come from all of a sudden?' she asks. 'I'm sure you've thanked me more than enough already.'

'I was just thinking that I don't know how I'd have managed without you since mother died,' I say. 'You've given me so much advice and practical help.'

'Pshaw! You and your fancy words!' she scoffs. 'You sound just like your mother. What did you expect me to do? Leave a chit of a girl to manage alone?'

'You've been a kind friend,' I tell her.

My first ever friend, in fact.

'Well, whatever are you doing travelling off to the ends of the earth then? That's what I'd like to know. My dear, you can't go all that way alone. You're just a child.'

I knew she'd mention this again.

'It was a promise to my mother,' I tell her. 'And what alternative do I have? The life that we led was bearable only because we had each other. Alone it would be no life at all. I couldn't face it.'

'I know your dear mother was a true friend to you, young as she was.' Mrs Forbes reaches out and takes my hand, looking earnestly at me. 'But it's possible now that you will make other friends. Not replace her, that can't be done, but so as you're not as alone as you think you'd be.'

'How would that be possible? We never made any friends in all these years.' I'm surprised. She must know how we were shunned, though she never did so herself. 'I even wrote a letter to my mother's family, as I promised her,' I remind Mrs Forbes. 'I explained who I was and that my mother had died, and gave them the date of the funeral. You know I haven't heard from them. I'm wanted by no one here.'

Mrs Forbes lets go of my hand and takes up her mending again. Looking at her sewing as intently as she had looked at me a moment before, she says, in a careful voice, 'Well, my dear, you'll forgive my plain speaking, I'm sure. But your mother was too proud and too ashamed of what she'd done to make friends even with those as would've been willing. She felt her situation more than she needed to. Especially brought up high like she was, in a grand house and all. She never got over the change. She turned to you. Inward-looking, like. You could live different if you chose.'

Her bright eyes are on me again, shining in her lined face. She means it kindly, I know, but I'm not used to anyone speaking to me like this. I feel resentment welling up inside me at this criticism of my mother. No one but me knows how hard my mother found it to live here among these people who despised her. I press my lips together and shake my head.

'No. It's better I go.'

I've looked into many ways of crossing to Denmark. I tried the larger ships first, which take passengers across the North Sea from Grimsby. The Danish company DFDS has a ferry called the *Esbjerg*. There are also a number of freight ships sailing regularly to Esbjerg. But none of these are within my means, as I also need money to travel to Skagen once I get to Denmark. I have a tattered map of the country on the wall and I can see the journey from Esbjerg to Skagen will be a long one.

I have been forced to go from one Danish fishing cutter to another in the harbour and beg a passage. Some of the men speak no English, and of those who do, most shake their heads at once and turn away when they understand what I want.

'We don't take women or children,' they tell me.

'Please!' I begged one gruff, bearded fisherman. 'I have no other way of crossing.'

'No. Not possible.' He waved me away, ending the conversation abruptly.

'I need to go to my father,' I pleaded with a kindly-looking captain only yesterday.

'Write him to come and fetch you,' he advised me, a strong Danish accent on his words. 'You are too young for coming alone on a boat like this.'

I walked home, defeated.

How can I write to my father?

He doesn't even know I exist.

I can see the light has begun to change now: my stitching is tinted with the gold of late afternoon sunshine. I lay it aside, unfinished. It's time to go down to the harbour; the fishing boats will be in. I feel the familiar lurch of dread in my stomach.

'I need to go out,' I tell Mrs Forbes.

She doesn't ask where I'm going. I always go to the harbour at this hour, but discussing it might reopen the argument.

'You're welcome to stay here and sew a while,' I tell her.

'That's all right, my dear, I got to get the evening meal on for the men.' Mrs Forbes's husband and son both work intermittently at the docks. She heaves herself out of her chair, and goes to the door, with a cheerful farewell.

As soon as she's gone, I brush my long hair, repinning it in a bun at the back of my head. It is a style my mother persuaded me to adopt a few months ago instead of my plaits. She said it made me look more grown-up, and that I would need that if I were to manage alone. My hair is golden. Like my father's, mother told me. She herself had lovely soft brown hair. Apart from our colouring, people always said we looked very alike. I remember her standing here where I am now, brushing her hair. I miss her so much it hurts.

13

I put my sunbonnet on and tie the strings under my chin. I look longingly at my cloak, hanging on its hook. I love to hide myself in it, but the day is much too hot. I sigh, and go down the stairs, out into the street. As I cross Freeman Street, the horse-drawn tram rattles by along Cleethorpes Road. I head in the opposite direction down towards the docks.

The streets are busy at this time of day, with trams and carts going to and fro from the harbour, and street sellers calling out their wares. There are some boys tormenting a dog at the corner, pulling its tail and throwing stones at it. I'm glad when a shopkeeper comes out and chases them off.

I've always hated going alone to the harbour. Sometimes my mother used to send me to buy fish. I would always hurry through the streets, my head down, avoiding the gaze of strangers. As I've grown older, I've come to dread it more, for now men sometimes call out or even try to speak to me. I always wrap my cloak more closely about me and hurry on my way, my face burning.

Mother bought fish direct from the boats as they brought their catch into harbour; it was cheaper and fresher that way. But I'm no hand at bargaining with the fishermen: I struggle even to understand their broad speech. When I pluck up courage to approach them at all, I can barely speak above a whisper. Mother always shook her head when she saw what small fish I had accepted. But she sent me often. I believe she thought I would learn the skill, as she had done. I never did.

And now, after her death, it is not the price of a couple of fish I'm negotiating, but the cost of a passage to Denmark. And it is deeply painful to have to ask.

The harbour, like the town, has grown out of recognition, even in my short lifetime. I walk along the quayside, searching the rows and rows of Grimsby fishing smacks, hunting for the boats that are flying the Danish flag. I have always liked that the Danish flag is simply the reverse of an English flag: a white cross on a red background. It's a link between the two halves of me.

At last I spot the flag on two blue-painted fishing cutters, smaller than the local smacks. I stand for a moment at a distance, watching the men on board, trying to summon up the courage to speak to them.

There are gulls on the quay, searching among the bundles of nets for pieces of fish. I watch one large gull tug a fish head from the net with its strong beak. It launches itself into the air. Two other gulls follow it screeching, and I watch them wheel and swoop in the clear blue sky.

I take a deep breath and approach the nearest boat. There is only one man on deck, sitting bent over his nets, mending them.

'Excuse me,' I say, but he doesn't even glance in my direction. Putting my hands on the side of the boat, I lean forward.

'Good afternoon!' I call out. The man, wizened and weather beaten, turns to look at me. His eyes are pale blue and rheumy.

'Do you speak English?' I ask him.

He shakes his head, but sits staring at me.

15

Do I continue speaking to him, or do I go away at once?

'I wish to go to Denmark,' I explain after a few moments' embarrassed silence. He puts one hand behind his ear.

'*Hvad?*' he asks.

He's forcing me to shout my business to half the fishing harbour. I can feel heat rising in my face.

'I wish,' I point at myself, 'to go to Denmark.' I make a wave movement with my hand, intended to signify a sea voyage, and point out to sea, to where I imagine Denmark lies. I feel so foolish. The old man stares at me a moment longer, and then shrugs, and turns back to his nets.

I take a step back and look over at the second boat; she has the name *Ebba* painted on the prow. To my mortification, there is a man standing smoking his pipe and watching me. He has obviously overheard everything. Should I walk up to him and repeat the ridiculous mime, or should I flee at once and spare myself the humiliation? But he's already beckoning me.

'You want to sail to Denmark?' he asks. 'How many people?'

'Only myself,' I reply. His sandy brows lift in surprise. I see him purse his lips, his bushy beard twitching as he does so.

'You travel alone?' he asks.

'Yes.'

He is silent a moment, looking suspicious. I wait for questions, but none come. He doesn't even ask my age.

'We sail to Esbjerg the day after tomorrow,' he tells me unexpectedly. 'If you can be ready you can come.'

'How much?' I ask anxiously. He names a price. It is more than I want to pay, but less than anything I've been offered so far. I should demur, and offer less, I am sure he expects it. But it is fish all over again, and after only a brief hesitation, I accept his terms.

He smiles and offers to shake hands on his bargain. 'Captain Larsen,' he introduces himself.

Now there's no turning back. I am almost elated as I hurry back through the streets to share the news with Mrs Forbes. At the same time I am deeply afraid: at that price, I'll have no money to return.

THREE

I take a last look around at the empty room, which has been my home for the last five years. Even by the grey light of the early dawn, it looks forlorn and shabby. I have folded the borrowed blankets I slept in for Mrs Forbes to collect later.

My trunk is already stowed on board the *Ebba*; I paid a porter to carry it down to the harbour for me yesterday evening. It has my name, *Marianne Shaw*, and my destination, *Skagen*, printed on the side. The things I will need during the journey are packed into the same carpet bag my mother left her home with some seventeen years ago.

I pick up the bag, gently close the door, and begin to creep down the staircase. But Mrs Forbes must have been awake and waiting for me, because as soon as the floorboards creak, she emerges from her rooms. She's wrapped in a faded pink dressing gown and has her hair twisted into rags. I can't repress a small smile.

'Goodbye, my dear,' she whispers, offering an embrace. I put my bag down and hug her tightly. She smells of tallow and cabbage.

'Thank you again for everything you've done for me. I'll write to let you know that I've arrived safely,' I offer

19

as we let one another go. To my surprise, she hangs her head and doesn't reply. I am confused for a moment and then I understand. She can't read, and she's ashamed.

I'm grateful to my mother, who though she couldn't afford to send me to school, passed on to me as much of her own fine education as shortage of time and money allowed.

'I shall send you a picture, dear Mrs Forbes,' I promise instead. Her face brightens.

'That would be a kindness, bless you,' she says. 'And here's a little something for your journey,' she adds, pushing a parcel neatly wrapped in brown paper into my hands. Then, without giving me a chance to look at it, she hugs me again.

'Off you go then. I wish you good fortune, and I hope you find your father,' she says briskly, and gives me a little push. There are tears in her eyes.

I want to tell her I'll miss her, but the words won't come. I pick up my bag again, and go to the front door. I linger a moment, looking back at her, and then step out into the street.

There are quite a number of people in town, even at this early hour. Everyone seems to be in a hurry. I cross the road, picking my way between the piles of horse droppings, and narrowly avoid a laden cart drawn by two scrawny-looking horses. Their load is fish by the smell of it.

It takes me only a few minutes to walk along Cleethorpes Road, past the Albert Memorial, to the docks, the route I have walked so many times before. I can't quite believe that this is the last time I'll walk it. I ought to feel sad, but my fear of the journey blots out all other feelings.

On board the *Ebba* the crew is busy readying her for the trip. Captain Larsen hails me as I approach. A younger man with the same sandy hair as the captain helps me climb onto the boat and takes my bag. He is a skinny, slight young man with an unremarkable face.

'I am Jens,' he says. He seems friendly. 'I show you the cabin,' he tells me, in strongly-accented English. 'You need to stay there until we are coming out of the harbour—not get in the way.'

So there and then I look back at Grimsby, and bid England a hasty and silent farewell. All my memories are here on these shores, but my hopes for the future lie across the North Sea.

I follow Jens across the sloping wooden deck to a small hatch, and watch him climb down a ladder. Wrapping my skirt tightly about my ankles, I struggle down after him.

I have never been aboard a boat before. I had no idea how dark and cramped it would be below deck. Or how strong the stench of fish and slop buckets would be. The prospect of sharing this space with four men for several days and nights appears suddenly indecent. I blush to think I proposed it. The sleeping quarters are merely low bunks tucked into odd spaces around the living area, which in itself consists only of a table with benches.

Jens shows me that he has hung a blanket before my bunk, so that I have some degree of privacy. He has hung another blanket across the corner where the slop bucket serves for a lavatory. But a blanket offers no protection from sounds or smells.

'I need to help now.' Jens points up on deck and then disappears up the ladder again. By the sound of it they are losing no time in casting off from the quay. Ropes grate against the side of the ship and thud as they land on the deck. As the men thunder about above me, calling to each other in Danish, I sit down and open the package Mrs Forbes gave me. There's a seed cake and some home-baked biscuits inside. She's kind. I shall save them. I'm too nervous to swallow even a mouthful this morning.

The boat sways as we leave the quayside. I feel strange almost at once: light-headed. As we leave the harbour and head out to sea, I have a shock. I was entirely unprepared for the effect of the motion of the boat. It is a bright, clear day with a brisk wind, not stormy. But as the boat begins to plunge in the swell, my head begins to ache. It becomes more difficult to sit up. It doesn't take long before I crawl into my cramped bunk and curl up. The relief is only temporary.

I'm shivering and suffering cold sweats. At every lurch or roll the boat makes, my mouth fills with saliva as fast as I can swallow it. My stomach begins to heave. I hear Jens quietly placing a bucket by my bunk. I'm vilely ill. Time passes in a haze of endurance and sickness. I notice at one point that the bucket has been swilled clean with seawater. Jens makes no comment. I'm too ill and too embarrassed to thank him, but I shall never, ever forget his kindness.

The men come in and out of the cabin, sometimes to sleep, sometimes to slice bread, fry fish, and smoke their pipes. The smell is unbearable. At night I drift in and out of sleep, but never for long.

When daylight comes, the boat seems to move less. Jens tells me we've arrived at the fishing grounds, that the nets are now out, and invites me on deck. At first I decline, not daring to rise from my bunk.

'The fresh air will help,' he insists.

It takes courage to leave the bunk. The walk across the swaying cabin and the climb up the ladder are almost my undoing. Once on deck, however, the clean sea air revives me. It helps to see the waves as well as feel them. With Jens's help I find a seat on some coils of rope just before the main mast. Captain Larsen greets me with a cheerful 'Good morning!' and then returns to checking his nets. Jens is attentive, however. He goes below, and then returns a few minutes later with a mug of tea and food for me. I refuse the fish hurriedly, but accept the rest. As I sit nibbling the bread and sipping the tea, I'm surprised how much better I feel.

Occasionally I catch a baleful stare from the first mate, Johannes. He's as shrivelled as a prune and has a sour face. I can hear him muttering to himself.

Worse than this are the stares of the man Torben. He's unkempt and filthy, with broken front teeth. I feel his eyes on me and it makes me uncomfortable. It's not dislike he shows, more a penetrating curiosity. He comes over and tries to speak to me. The only English words I can catch are 'fish' and 'gin'. I shake my head at him and

23

turn away. I can't bear the stench of spirits and unwashed body that hangs around him like a cloud.

It's cold in the sea breeze, so after a while I go back down to my bunk. Torben is standing in the middle of the cabin watching me. The living quarters are very cramped but Torben makes no effort to move out of my way at all. I have to push past him in my rush to lie down before sickness overcomes me again.

The air in the cabin is fetid and stinking. As soon as I'm thoroughly warm again, I decide to go back outside. I check that Torben is not in the cabin before I crawl out of my bunk. To my horror, he is at the top of the ladder as I climb up. He takes hold of me round the waist to help me up. I pull away from him and go to my place on deck. Only a moment later, I make the mistake of looking in his direction. It gives him the opportunity to leer at me. Repulsive. He makes me feel unclean.

I try to put him out of my mind and concentrate on breathing the bracing air. To distract myself, I think about my father. I wonder how easy it will be to find him. Whether he will be pleased to see me.

My mother often spoke of him. When I was little, he was always my favourite bedtime story. I know that he returned to Denmark before I was born. My grandfather, who was one of the Mablethorpe gentry, didn't approve of him as a prospective husband. But he and my mother promised to love one another always. He went back to Skagen to earn enough money to come and take her away.

24

This, of course, was before my grandfather disowned her. By the time her condition was discovered, my father was long gone.

It's a terrible thing to be with child when you're not married. You could say I ruined her life. Poor mother. I'll never let that happen to me.

My mother always told me what a good man my father was. I learned, while still very young, not to ask *why* he never returned as he'd promised. Such a question would signal the end of our happy story time, and drive the smiles from my mother's face.

I hope my existence won't come as an unpleasant shock to him; I prefer to think that he'll be happy to know me and to help me. But I wonder how he will explain why he never came back.

FOUR

The wind has increased considerably while I have been sitting on deck. Dark, ominous clouds are rolling across the sky towards us. All four men are busy, working silently, glancing at the sky. I'm chilled to the bone and beginning to feel seasick once more. I urgently need to lie down. I stumble along the deck towards the hatch, clinging to the steering house in order to keep my balance.

When I'm at the bottom of the ladder, a shadow falls on me. I look up and see boots appear at the top of it. A particularly violent roll forces me to cling to the table halfway across the cabin to my bunk. And it's here that Torben catches me, his arms tight about my chest, squeezing my ribs, his breath on my cheek, stinking of fish and spirits.

I cry out and try to thrust him away. I'm surprised how strong he is. He pulls me round to face him and for a moment I see his filthy, rotten teeth and cracked lips close to me before he clamps his mouth down upon mine so that I cannot make a sound. I twist my head and cry out, but he forces his mouth over mine again, poking his tongue into my mouth like a slimy raw fish. He has my arms pinned tightly to my sides, and I can't make a sound. But I can move my legs, and I bring my right knee up sharply, and feel it thud into his groin. It was an instinctive move and for a moment it seems to have worked. He releases me and bends over with a groan. But as I start to back away, retching with disgust, he straightens up. Now his face is contorted with pain and rage, his lips curling back from his brown teeth. A wave of terror washes over me. He grabs me by the hair, yanking me towards him, and this time I scream, as loudly as I can.

'Help!' I yell. 'Help me, please!'

He twists my hair in his fingers, and slams me against the cabin wall. There is a singing in my ears. His free hand is on my breast, squeezing and pinching me painfully through the fabric of my gown. I try to scream again, but he pushes his mouth against mine to stop the sound, his teeth bruising my lips.

'Torben!'

I'm released so suddenly that I fall heavily against the table. Gasping with pain, I look up to see Jens's furious face glaring into Torben's. They stand facing each other, fists clenched, each trying to outface the other. It's Torben who backs off, shuffling across the cabin to the ladder, with a shifty, backward glance. Jens barks an order at him. I don't know what he is saying, but he's making him leave and I'm thankful.

Jens turns and offers to help me up, but I can't bear to be touched at all now and shrink away from him. His freckled face looks sombre as he stands back.

I drag myself to my feet, only to stagger as the boat lurches once more. Ignoring my protests, Jens grasps my arm and helps me to my bunk before I can fall again.

'What did I do?' I am asking myself more than Jens. 'To make him think he could treat me like that?' In my heart I already know the answer. I've come aboard this boat alone. I'm surrounded by men; no longer young enough to be seen as a child, but not yet adult enough to understand the dangers. So now he thinks I'm a whore. They said that about my mother too.

'He's disgusting!' My voice shakes with loathing. I can taste blood on my lip where his teeth cut me.

'Try to rest,' Jens tells me. 'I not let him trouble you again.'

He turns to go, but then hesitates and turns back.

'Bad storm coming,' he tells me. 'Stay here.'

I nod, and lie on the bed racked with sobs. I weep for shame and anger. I weep for myself and my life and I weep for my mother. Eventually my sobs still. Fear takes the place of grief. I thought the motion of the boat had been dramatic during the past few days, but I now realize I was mistaken.

The boat is being flung this way and that, shuddering violently as waves crash against her. The wind has risen to a howl above which I can hear the shouts of the crew only faintly. I wrap my blankets about me, shivering. There's a particularly loud crash and the boat pauses and shudders violently before pitching forwards and then rolling so steeply that I am flung into the wall next to my bunk.

Bracing myself against the pitching of the vessel, I remember my mother telling me the story of how my father came to her home.

29

He'd been working on a freight ship in the North Sea and was heading up the Humber estuary for Grimsby when his ship met a storm. The ship was blown off course, to the south, and was wrecked on the coast at Mablethorpe. My mother's father, my grandfather whom I have never met, found my father crawling out of the sea onto the beach. He was in a dreadful state: sick and injured. My grandfather had him carried up to his own house to be nursed. It was many days before he came out of his fever and began to recover.

But the other crew members were all drowned.

Silently, I begin to pray.

FIVE

The crew is on deck, battling to control the boat in the heaving sea. All the while the wind howls and the boat pitches and shudders. The timbers groan with the strain. A frying pan someone has left out is flung across the cabin, rattling against the wall. Each time the boat crashes into a wave, I hold my breath, thinking this time it must have been a rock, and any minute now I will hear the boat splitting open, and see the water rushing in. And then as we lurch on, I let my breath go in a sigh of relief. But the relief is short-lived. There's always another wave ready to break upon us.

When any of the men come down into the cabin, to eat or to take a short rest, they are drenched and exhausted. Even Jens has no word for me, only an anxious smile. They are battling for our survival. Each time one of them unbattens the hatch to come down into the cabin, water pours in with them, and then lies swishing back and forth on the floor. I can hear it in the darkness, and it makes me think of the whole sea trying to tear the ship apart. Terror sits like a hard knot in my stomach.

I listen to the sound of the men's boots above me, and the shrieking of the wind, and I long for it to end. I can't sleep for the many hours that the storm rages, only lie and wait.

At last it seems to lessen. The boat begins to move more purposefully again. Exhausted, I fall asleep.

When I wake, the hatch is open and light is streaming into the cabin. The creaking of the ship sounds friendly once more. Two sounds tell me all is well: on deck, someone is singing; and closer at hand, there are steady, rhythmic snores.

I sit up cautiously and climb out of my bunk. The captain is stretched out, fully dressed, in his bunk, asleep.

The singing stops, and Jens climbs down the ladder. He gives me a tired grin and says, 'The storm is over now.'

Weakened beyond belief by seasickness and lack of food, I drag myself across the cabin. When Jens sees me trying to climb the ladder, he comes to help me up onto the deck. The sea is an angry boiling grey, the sky overcast. To my great joy, there's land on the horizon.

'It's *Tyskland*,' says Jens. 'Germany.' I must look startled, because he laughs. 'We come too far south in the storm,' he explains. 'But we'll be soon in Esbjerg now.'

As I look at the land, I feel a deep excitement rise unexpectedly within me. I had never left Grimsby and here I am looking at Germany. I imagine all the people there, living their lives, speaking their language.

'Is it very different to England?' I ask Jens. He is still standing next to me.

'Germany?' he asks. 'I never went there.'

'What about Denmark?'

He smiles at me. 'Yes, quite different.'

I think how much I've grown to like his face these last few days. When I first saw him, I thought he was quite ugly. Skinny, with sandy hair and pale freckled skin. But now I find his face familiar and friendly. I find myself smiling warmly back at him.

'Why go you to Denmark?' he asks.

I feel myself closing up at once. I'm not going to share my story. I'm afraid of seeing him turn away from me in disgust. That's what most people do when they discover I'm illegitimate. A whore's brat, they call me. But I've seen whores with their painted faces and their shameless, flaunting ways. My mother was nothing like them. She was a lady.

A half-truth can do no harm.

'I'm going to see my father,' I say. 'He came back to Denmark, and he doesn't know my mother has died.'

Jens looks slightly puzzled. I don't want to give further explanations, so I hurriedly add: 'He lives in Skagen.'

'Skagen?' Jens whistles. He pronounces the name *Skayen*. 'You have a long woyage. Someone is meeting you?'

I can't help smiling at his mistake, though I wish I spoke his language half as well as he speaks mine.

'No. I don't know yet how I'll travel.'

Jens looks at me, and I think I see some admiration in his eyes. For the first time, I'm slightly less afraid of my journey. I feel instead a little like an intrepid explorer, setting out alone to undiscovered corners of the world.

'There's a train,' he tells me. 'From Esbjerg. But I think it cost a lot of money.'

I'm about to ask him more, but Jens is watching his father loudly reprimanding Torben for some ill-done piece of work. Torben has been sullen since the incident in the cabin. Jens scowls as he watches him. He leans towards me and speaks in a lowered voice.

'It's the first time he fishes with us,' he tells me. 'My father says the last. He's lazy, and not a good fisher.'

I want to thank Jens for continuing to shield me from Torben, but I don't know how, and I can feel myself blushing as I try to find the words. Even as I draw breath to begin, he moves away from me to help his father with the sail.

I lean back against the mast, wrapping my cloak more closely about me, and take a deep breath of the fresh air. It fills me with courage.

SIX

Esbjerg, September 1885

Idon't know what I expected Denmark to look like. Beautiful and magical perhaps, as it does in my dreams. But at first sight it's not so very different to Grimsby. There are sand flats outside the harbour with wading birds and seagulls. As we come closer, I see the houses look unfamiliar. They are lower, and mainly thatched.

What strikes me as most different is an indefinable change in the quality of the light. It is stronger, bluer, and the sky looks bigger somehow. I tell myself I'm being fanciful, but the impression remains.

Captain Larsen hands me off the ship and onto the quayside. My legs tremble beneath me as I stand on solid ground at last, waiting for Torben to carry my trunk off the *Ebba*. The boat looks battered by the storm: her paintwork has suffered and her mainsail is torn.

Torben dumps the trunk ungraciously at my feet and climbs back on board without so much as looking at me.

I'm glad to see the last of him.

'Where shall you go?' the captain asks me brusquely.

I've been wondering the same thing myself.

This is a busy harbour, much like Grimsby. There is a huge amount of building work being done. I've seen them extending the docks in Grimsby over the years, and the same thing is happening here.

This part is the fishing harbour, and mainly filled with boats similar to the *Ebba*. In the distance I can see freight ships being unloaded, and I can hear the clang of metal on metal, drowning the nearer sound of the seagulls. I'm aware that I'm in a country where I don't speak the language. I feel small and alone, but don't want to show it.

'I need to find an inn,' I tell him firmly. 'Can you recommend one? Not too expensive . . .' I add self-consciously.

The captain calls out something to Jens who is helping the other men unload the crates of fish packed in ice, and then he nods in my direction.

'My son will show you,' he says.

Jens steps off the boat, lifts my trunk onto his shoulder, and begins to walk along the quayside. I pick up my carpet bag and turn to follow him. To my horror, what I had thought was firm ground beneath my feet suddenly sways and lurches and I stagger. The three men on board the *Ebba* laugh. Jens turns to see what the joke is and grins to see me attempt another unsteady step.

'It strange on the land again,' he says. 'You soon be used to it.'

I struggle after him, swaying on my feet. I've barely eaten for days and the effort of walking is making me shake. I look around me at the buildings, the boats, and the people, and it all seems so real, so solid. I can smell fish and machinery. Gulls are fighting over discarded fish heads on the quayside, just as they do at home. I can feel a sense of disappointment nagging at me. Surely it should all be far more beautiful than this?

I have to hurry to keep up with Jens.

'Is my trunk not too heavy for you?' I ask anxiously.

'No,' he assures me. 'It's not far.' And indeed, as we turn a corner, there's a small inn on our right. It's a low building, just one storey, with big wooden beams in the walls, and the stonework painted red. Jens places my trunk carefully just inside the doorway, and then turns to face me. We look at each other uncertainly for a moment, and then he wipes his hand on his trousers and offers it. I shake it. When he leaves I'll be alone again.

'You'll be all right?' he asks.

I nod, trying to recapture the feeling of bravery I experienced earlier.

'Thank you. For everything,' I stammer.

'You're welcome!' He winks, grins, and saunters off.

A large, motherly-looking landlady has appeared beside me, looking a question.

'Do you speak English?' I ask tentatively.

'*Nej*,' she replies, shaking her head. It's a bad start.

'I need a room for the night,' I try again.

The warmth is fading from the afternoon sun, and I'm exhausted. She speaks to me in Danish again, and then disappears, returning a few moments later with a thin, stooped man I take to be her husband.

'English?' he asks. 'Room?'

'Yes,' I agree gratefully. I'm relieved, but in fact his English is very limited and we struggle to understand one another. Neither will he accept my English money, directing me to the bank to exchange it for Danish *kroner*. Of course, I should have expected that. But what I need more than anything in the world right now is to lie down on a bed that will remain still beneath me.

'Tomorrow,' I beg.

He nods.

'*I morgen*,' he agrees. 'Tomorrow.'

At last he picks up my trunk and carries it into a small bedchamber at the back of the house. It is sparsely and simply furnished with a bed, a chest, and a washstand, but light and clean. A wonderful contrast to the boat. The landlady brings me a jug of water and a candle. I can relax for the first time in days. I take a deep breath and let it go in a sigh of pleasure.

I drink a little water, then wash my face and hands, and lie down on the bed. I listen to the noises of the inn and, further away, the harbour, so different to the sounds at sea. In only a few moments the sounds fade and I fall into the first real sleep I've had since I left England.

When I open my eyes it's early morning.

The inn is bustling with noise and activity. There are noises from the kitchen. Breakfast being prepared perhaps. It sounds comfortingly ordinary. But then I hear someone speak Danish. I'm in a foreign country now. Nervous butterflies flutter in my stomach. My father's language. It is a strange thought that it may become a familiar language to me. I know how hard it is to learn a language: my mother taught me a little French.

I lie in bed for a while, savouring the stillness after the days and nights on board the *Ebba*. I stretch and yawn luxuriously in the clean sheets. I'm so comfortable I'm soon in danger of falling asleep again.

'I need to move on,' I say out loud to myself, and I sit up. I can't waste this day; I don't have the money for many nights lodging. In any case I'm eager to get to Skagen. I feel better for my sleep, but I can see in the looking glass that my eyes still have dark shadows etched beneath them.

Timidly, I seek the landlord. He speaks to me at great length in a mixture of Danish and English, and I understand perhaps a quarter of what he says. I keep smiling. I ask him about the bank and the train station and get some directions which I am not clear about: 'You goes up the *bakken*. Up, *ja*. Until you get to *by*. Many *huse*. Yes, then you turning to right to find bank.'

I'll just head for the town and ask again.

Meanwhile his wife fusses about kindly, setting breakfast before me. She gives me weak ale, to which I'm not accustomed. We drank tea at home. The bread is dark and bitter, like nothing I've ever tasted. I don't like it at all. I hope they have proper bread here as well as this sort.

Once I've eaten what I can, I thank the landlady and she teaches me the word in Danish. *Tak*.

'*Tak!*' I imitate. She smiles, and pats me on the cheek.

It's my first word of Danish and it will be useful. I'm still weak and shaken from the sea crossing, but the ground is firm beneath my feet now, and I'm able to walk up the hill to the town.

SEVEN

Frederikshavn, September 1885

I shiver as I climb down from the train into the smoke and steam on the platform: the temperature has dropped at the end of the day and I'm stiff and cold. A porter hurries forward to take my trunk. I'll have to pay him. More money gone.

Large signs announce that this is Frederikshavn, the last station on the line north. I am only some thirty miles south of Skagen now. Nearly there!

I have travelled up from Esbjerg in just one long day. The train was comfortable and swift, and I enjoyed the journey. But it was an expensive luxury. I only have five Danish kroner and a few øre left. The coins are wrapped in a handkerchief, carefully tucked into my pocket. I've counted them over and over again.

As we walk up the platform, I look for a railway official. When I see one in his dark suit and cap, he is surrounded by passengers. I must wait my turn to speak to him while the porter taps his wooden clogs impatiently. I feel flustered. Queuing is not much respected here, it seems, and I am left standing stupidly as other passengers push past me to speak to him.

'Excuse me!' I say at last, when there is a moment's pause. 'I need to go to Skagen.' I've written the name on a piece of paper. He says something and gestures, but of course I don't understand. I'm so tired I can't think of a way to explain. In the end he shrugs and turns away as someone else claims his attention. My heart sinks.

'Problems always look smaller in the morning,' my mother used to say. I settle for miming to the porter that I need to find somewhere to sleep, somewhere cheap.

As I follow him out of the station I can smell the sea and the fish from the harbour. We are right by it here; I can see cranes and warehouses on the quay, and here too, they are extending the harbour.

We pick our way through a maze of narrow, filthy alleys. Either side of us are hovels and drinking houses, from which men emerge from time to time, reeling with the effects of drink. Outside one, two men are attempting to fight, but are almost too drunk to stand upright. They slip and stagger among the refuse that's lying in the street. We give them a wide berth. I've never been out this late, though I've heard the sounds of drunken men often enough.

The place the porter takes me to is neither clean nor friendly, but it is cheap. The name on the front of the building is *Cimbria*. It's a huge, many-storeyed building on the harbour front, and stinks of fried fish, stale spirits, and pipe smoke.

I thank the porter, and impulsively press a fifty øre coin into his hand. That's half a krone. I can't afford so much, but he's carried my trunk a long way. He touches his cap and smiles as he leaves. I'm glad I gave him the money.

A hard-featured woman with a dirty apron slaps some fried fish, bread, and ale on a dirty table for me in a busy public room, and then ignores me. There are shouts and bursts of raucous laughter from the men and women at the other tables around me. They too are drinking. My mother would not consider this place respectable. I feel conspicuous sitting alone.

I eat quickly and flee to my room. It's right up on the attic floor under the eaves. The room is tiny, just space for a bed. By the sound of it there are whole families squeezed into the other rooms around me. I can hear the sounds of children crying and voices. I don't recognize the sing-song language: it's not Danish.

Even up here I can hear loud drunken voices. There's a particularly loud shout and a bang, as though someone has overturned a table. I shiver with fear, and look for a key in the lock of my door. There isn't one. I drag a small chest across the floorboards and push it against the door. It will have to do.

I climb between the grey, musty sheets and blow out my candle. I feel empty and numb with tiredness. Footsteps go back and forth along the corridor outside my room. I hold my breath each time until they pass. In the next room a baby wails. As I lie sinking into sleep, I push away the anxiety I have about tomorrow, and remind myself instead how far I've come. How well I have managed by myself.

The next thing I know, sunshine is pouring into my room and I can hear the familiar cry of gulls in the distance. A thrill goes through me, and I jump out of bed. Today I hope to reach Skagen.

EIGHT

'I need to go to Skagen, *not* America!' I say again.

The landlady of this dreadful place seems to be taking it as a personal insult that I don't wish to board the ferry to America. She repeats the word indignantly over and over again.

'*Ja, ja! Amerika!*' She points out to the harbour again, where a large ship lies at berth. Most of my fellow lodgers, who are from Sweden, I've discovered, are already heading down there. They lug suitcases, bundles, and in some cases, children.

They are like me, I think. They are seeking a new life.

'No! Skagen,' I insist.

I show her my piece of paper with 'Skagen' written on it.

She squints at it briefly, and looks back at me. I suspect she can't read it.

She sighs however, and flounces out from behind the greasy counter, beckoning me to follow her.

The back door hangs crazily, half off its hinges. We go through it into a stinking backyard. Piles of refuse and horse droppings lie rotting on the cobbles. A man is unloading peat from a rickety cart. A scrawny-looking brown horse stands wearily in his harness, resting one foot.

The landlady speaks to the man and their conversation rapidly escalates into a heated argument. I never heard such a strident voice as this woman has. She stands, feet planted firmly apart in her wooden clogs, dirty apron flapping in the wind, her hands on her hips, except when she wags a finger in the unfortunate man's face. Half the town must be able to hear her.

Whatever the argument is about, she clearly wins it. She turns to me with a triumphant smile, revealing two missing teeth.

'*En krone!*' she says, holding up one finger, the nail torn and filthy.

'One krone?' I have that much. Relief floods through me. I don't know why she's suddenly decided to help me, but I'm glad of it.

The man, muttering darkly, stomps into the inn and comes back out with my trunk. He slings it roughly into the cart, where it picks up a generous coating of peat. Seeing this, the landlady boxes him on the ear and tells him off loudly. I'd love to know what she's saying.

She waves me enthusiastically towards the cart.

'Skagen?' I ask.

She shakes her head, takes a stick and draws a line in the dirt. She points to one end and says *Frederikshavn*. That's where we are now. 'Skagen,' she says, pointing to the other end of the line. Then she draws a mark midway between the two and says, 'Ålbæk!'

I nod my understanding. Halfway to Skagen. Well, that's something.

'*Tak*,' I say to her, and she nods at me and disappears back into the building. I hand over the coin to the driver, wondering how he feels about having been forced into giving me a lift. He pockets my coin, without looking at me. Pulling his cap low over his forehead, he hoists himself up into the cart, leaving me to scramble up beside him as best I can.

He slaps his reins on the horse's back. The cart, empty now, but for my trunk, rattles over the cobblestones and out into the road.

The land looks very flat as we take the road northwards out of the town. We're following the coast, and I can see right down to the sea on my right-hand side, and in across farmland on my left. It is a patchwork of well-tended fields dotted with small farmhouses.

I wonder again what Skagen will look like. My mother repeated the tales my father had told her about it. Wooden houses, golden beaches, blue, blue skies, and the merry life everyone led there. He had described to her how the seas were so full of fish, one only needed to throw in a net to be sure of a good catch. Midsummer festivals, where fires were lit on the beach. In the confinement of our dark room in Grimsby, in the smoky streets where we saw the sky only in snatches, I dreamed of open blue skies and beaches and grasses waving on sand dunes.

I'm so nearly there now. I'm quite sure that Skagen will be beautiful. I can't wait to be there. I seem to have been travelling for a lifetime.

We pass a low stone-built farm. It is built on a pattern

I've seen many times on my journey: three sides of a rectangle. The central building is the house; the two side buildings are barns. The courtyard, enclosed on three sides, is orderly and well tended. The buildings are all whitewashed, and there are red flowers in window boxes. A dog basks in the sunshine in front of the door, too lazy to get up and bark at the cart as it passes. I wonder if my father lives in a house like this. I imagine myself in such pleasant surroundings, and my heart misses a beat.

We round a corner, and move out of a small stunted patch of trees all bent by the wind, onto a long, straight stretch of road. I catch my breath at the openness of the landscape. The sky seems endless, low above my head, like a vast blue roof. It's breathtaking.

It's not long before the road deteriorates. It becomes a deeply rutted track, swimming in muddy water. The cart slips and slides, often tilting at such steep angles that I have to cling to the seat in order not to be thrown out. It's exhausting. My dress, already travel-stained, becomes splashed with mud. Every now and then we sink into a deeper patch and the horse strains in his harness. Then we lurch and splash forward again.

We meet other carts coming south. They are faring no better than us; the ones that are laden are struggling more. We come to one cart which is stuck, one wheel deep in a rut. Some men have already stopped to help push it out, and my driver halts too. Handing the reins to me without a word, he climbs down and wades through the mud to help. He and the other men push from behind while the owner encourages his horse forward.

48

My horse is easy to hold, though I've never done it before. I think he's glad of the rest. On a better road, it would be fun to try and drive him.

There's a lot of good-natured shouting and laughter among the men as they push, and when the cart eventually pulls free, a great cheer goes up. The horse stands sweating and blowing, his legs plastered with mud.

My driver returns, muddied, but in a visibly brighter mood. He even gives me a broad grin. Then we're slipping and slithering from one puddle to the next, our progress painfully slow. I wish I could ask how far it is. It's frustrating not speaking Danish. I need to learn it as soon as I can.

I've met so many friendly people on my journey, and haven't been able to speak to them. Perhaps they wouldn't have been so friendly if they'd known my background. I wonder what the Danish word for *bastard* is. I hope I never find out.

The wind is strengthening. The weather is still clear and bright, but the temperature is dropping. The road is getting worse, if that's possible. There are several deep streams with no bridges. The driver simply urges the horse straight into them, so that the cart plunges in, water splashing up on either side, spraying us both.

It's well past noon when we pull up at a large thatched building with *Ålbæk Kro* in lettering on the front. The driver lifts my trunk down, more gently than he lifted it up. My lift is at an end. I get down; the driver nods to me, smiles, and departs.

My cloak flaps in the wind and my sunbonnet tugs on its strings. No one comes out to meet me, so after a moment's hesitation I walk into the inn.

A severe-looking woman in neat, dark clothes, her hair scraped back tightly into a bun, is standing behind a spotless counter.

'Do you speak English?' I ask.

She shakes her head. I'm disappointed, but not surprised.

'I need to go to Skagen,' I say slowly. 'With my trunk.' I point at it through the open door.

I point at myself.

'Skagen?' I repeat.

I know I'm saying it right now: *Skayen*.

The woman nods, but seems at a loss for what to say.

'*I morgen*,' she says at last. I know that means tomorrow, but I don't have the money for another night's lodging. I shall be arriving in Skagen practically penniless as it is. Krone-less.

I carefully place my few remaining coins on the counter. I spread them out and look at her. There is a one krone coin, a fifty øre and a number of one and two øre pieces. I see understanding dawning on her face.

She calls a girl from the kitchen and sends her running across the yard. We wait in embarrassing silence until she returns with a formally dressed, grey-haired man in tow.

'I am schoolteacher,' he announces. 'You are English?'

'Yes!' I'm overjoyed to have found someone who speaks my language. 'I'm travelling to Skagen.' My voice feels husky with lack of use.

50

He nods.

'There's no more road,' he explains.

'There's no road?' I echo, bewildered.

'Carts . . . go . . . on the beach,' he tells me, with pauses while he searches for words. 'But by fine weather. Not today.'

'The weather is fine today, surely?' I ask.

'No. Too much wind. The sand is blowing,' he says. 'Better . . . stay here.'

'I have no money,' I tell him, my voice low. I'm ashamed to admit it.

He looks at me for a moment.

'Walk!' he says, walking his fingers on the counter. '*På stranden*—on the beach. It take you less than one day. But not today.'

I could walk, of course. One day's walk isn't far, and it would cost me nothing. But there's my trunk. I can just about lift it, but not carry it ten miles or so. The landlady has already anticipated this. She is talking to the man about it now.

'The box go soon, maybe Friday. To the hotel in Skagen. Fifty øre,' he relays the information to me.

Two days' time.

'Thank you. I accept. But I shall go now,' I announce, wanting to make the most of the afternoon. I give the landlady my fifty øre coin from my pile.

'Can you tell me the way? And I need to buy some food to take.' When my request is translated, the landlady disappears to get food. The teacher accompanies me outside to explain my route.

First he pauses, frowning. He looks as though he's searching for a word.

'Today is *farlig*,' he says at last. 'I not knowing the word in English. But too much wind.'

'Tell me the way,' I beg him again.

'That way to beach,' he points east, 'then . . . left to Skagen. Follow the beach.'

That sounds simple enough.

'Thank you very much,' I say. '*Tak*.'

He throws his chest out proudly and shakes my hand.

'It was so little,' he says, and strides off, presumably back to his classroom.

The landlady accepts only a few øre for the packet of food she brings. She also gives me a large glass of water, which I drink thirstily. Then I set out for the beach. As I leave the inn, I see a man carrying my trunk into an out-house, and I fear for a moment that I'll never see it again.

I have no reason not to trust them, I tell myself firmly.

It makes me feel free to be moving on, unburdened by my trunk and under my own steam. The wind is strong, but exhilarating. I need to walk on the edges of the track and to jump muddy patches. By the time I reach the coast, the bottom of my skirt and my boots are plastered with mud.

The sea, when I reach it, is blue and sparkling in the sun, the waves topped with white horses in the strong wind. A handful of fishing boats are pulled right up onto the beach, their sails furled neatly, their oars stowed. I stand for a moment and watch a large rowing boat being hauled out of the sea. There is a bustle around her as crates of fish are unloaded. A cloud of gulls circle the boat, screeching, hoping for scraps. The men call out a friendly greeting to me. I've learned to answer with *God dag!* It's fun thinking that they don't even know I'm not Danish. Almost reluctantly, I move on.

The sand is palest gold, and very soft. My feet sink down into it at every step. As I turn to walk north, the wind hits me full in the face.

NINE

Ålbæk Bay, September 1885

The wind tears at my clothes and my hair. I turn my back to it for a moment and pull my shawl out of my bag. For a few moments the wind fights to snatch it from me, before I succeed in wrapping it around my head and shoulders. I walk on, bent into the wind. It's a shock to find it so much stronger on the beach.

The sand is soft and yielding underfoot. It's pleasant at first. There are seashells everywhere. I stoop to look at them, picking up a few of the prettiest and putting them in my bag. I soon stop. There are so many of them, and each time I bend down, the wind blows sand in my face. It's swirling in fierce clouds across the beach.

I can't see many ships on the sea. The waves are white topped and I wonder whether the shipping has sought shelter.

I haven't walked far before I come across a wreck. The rusting remains of an iron hull lies on its side, half in, half out of the water. The waves hush against the metal and the wind howls through the broken hull.

As I walk, I come across more and more wrecks. Some show above the waves, others are right up on the beach. The skeletons of wooden hulls lie exposed to the elements, their planking long since removed or rotted away. The beach gradually comes to feel as forlorn as a graveyard to me. All those journeys ended in terror and perhaps death. The thought lowers my spirits and makes walking harder.

My legs begin to ache, and the sand that has found its way inside my boots is rubbing my toes. I'm already growing tired, and there must still be a long way to go. I stop and empty my boots and try walking on the firmer sand right by the water's edge. It's easier, and this helps me summon up reserves of strength.

All at once, I come to a place where I can't walk on. The sand is soggy and wet, and when I step out into it, I quickly sink up to my ankles. I hurriedly draw back. Shifting my bag into the other hand, and pulling my shawl over my face, I turn into the wind. It scours sand across my forehead and into my eyes and whips my hair in my face. I trudge towards the dunes. Every now and then, I venture too close to the patch of bog or whatever it is, and sink a little, before struggling out.

I claw my way up the dunes, gasping for breath under my shawl. They're steep, and the sand keeps sliding away from under me. At the top, I'm up out of the drifting sand, but the wind is stronger than ever. It tugs at my clothes, screams in my ears and numbs my senses.

I'm exhausted now. I scan the land, desperately look-ing for some signs of human habitation. Perhaps a barn or a house I could shelter in. I'm ready to give up the journey for today.

But there's nothing.

Just rolling dunes with waving grasses, patches of heath and pools of water as far as the eye can see.

Disappointed, I make my way slowly along the top of the dunes for some distance before I venture back down to the beach. The sand is normal again now, and I make my way to the water's edge. I concentrate on putting one foot in front of the other. The wind is like a solid wall, pushing against me.

Time crawls by while I struggle northwards. Eventually I sink down onto the sand, exhausted, my back to the wind. I hug my bag, and quickly begin to shiver. I wonder what the man at the inn meant when he described the beach today as *farlig*. At first I thought it might mean tiring. Now I'm beginning to wonder whether he meant dangerous.

I consider going back there and offering to work for a night's lodging. But it would be as far to walk back as to go on. I have to reach Skagen.

I struggle to my feet and pick up my bag. It feels as though it's filled with rocks. As I turn and try to walk, the wind slams into my chest, knocking the breath out of me for a second. I'm stiff and aching all over. I can feel tears of self-pity streaking my face. The wind chills them, so that they run cold and gritty down my face.

I force myself to take another step. And another. How far is it? I feel as though I simply can't go on. Sobs make my chest heave, but I can't hear myself crying over the gale. The daylight is beginning to fade.

A dark shape rears up in front of me, lessening the force of the wind. Another wreck. It gives me an idea. It would be shelter of sorts if I could climb inside it. But there is too little left of this wreck to offer decent shelter.

I push myself to keep going, perhaps to find a more complete wreck. I lose all sense of time. Perhaps five minutes or perhaps five hours later I come to a stream. The water flows, brown and peaty, from the dunes. I unlace my boots, my back to the gale, and sling them around my neck. Gathering my skirts tightly in my free hand, I step down into the water. The unexpected cold makes me gasp. The sand has a slightly slimy feel underfoot, and I wade across as quickly as I can. As I step out of the water on the far side, sand whips around my legs, burning them.

I can see another wreck ahead. Without bothering to put my boots back on, I fight my way towards it. I'm breathless and exhausted when I reach the shelter it offers. I can breathe! I hear myself panting and gasping for air in the relative quiet.

This is a steam ship, a massive iron monster. It's lying on its side, twisted and broken, the sand drifted into huge silver mounds around it. I'm almost hysterical with relief, as I throw myself down on the sand in the lee of the hull. I rub my face with my hands: it feels numb. But even here it is too windy. It's also getting dark, and I've never been out alone at night. The thought terrifies me.

I walk around the vast bulk of the wreck, looking for a more sheltered spot. At the end that faces the sea, where the propeller must once have been, there's a gaping hole. The metal has been torn wide open, leaving a jagged entrance to the hull.

I peer inside. It looks sheltered and reasonably dry. But it's dark. And it stinks of rotting seaweed and rusted metal. I stand, trying to gather the courage to go in. Who knows what may be inside?

Holding my breath, trying not to touch anything, I crawl in. It's warmer in here. I can hear the wind still screaming and scraping sand against the outside of the hull. Gradually as I get used to being in the ship, I begin to relax a little. I can wait out the storm, tucked away in here. The relief is still intense. For a short time, I became afraid I might die out there on the beach.

Darkness falls. It's so black inside the wreck that I feel blind. I sit shivering, whether most from cold or fear, I'm not sure. My eyes are stinging with tiredness.

Every now and then the hull groans and creaks in the wind. Every sound echoes around it. I sweat with fear. I can't stop imagining the drowned crew. They walk, grey and rotting, out of the sea towards me. Seawater streams off their ragged clothes. There is seaweed tangled in their hair. Their eye sockets are blank and empty, their hands reach out blindly towards me.

Shivering uncontrollably, I stuff the end of the cloak into my mouth and bite down on it hard to stop myself from screaming. I wait, breathless, for their hands to find me. Minutes draw out into hours. Sometimes I think I can feel their ghostly hands on me, their rotting breath against my cheek. My whole body is rigid and shaking. Don't be stupid, think about something else. I can't say it out loud in case it draws the ghosts to me. I do try, but no other thoughts can keep my fears at bay for long.

Not until the first grey light of dawn signals the start of a new day, do I begin to relax. This has been one of the longest nights of my life.

I must have fallen asleep after all. I'm twisted uncomfortably, my head on my bag. As I sit up, I'm stiff and aching all over. Bright sunshine is pouring in through the hole in the hull.

I crawl out onto the beach and blink in the bright light. The wind has almost gone. The sand is still, and the sky is a clear, clear blue. I'm dazzled for a moment. And then I smile at the beach, beautiful in the morning sunlight. Holding out my arms, I spin around, laughing with joy and relief, and then fall onto the sand, smoothing it with my hands. I'm still alive. I've done it. Now I can do the rest as well.

I'm starving. When did I last eat? I can't remember. A day ago perhaps.

I pull my parcel of food out of my bag and fall upon the bitter dark bread, the juicy yellow plums, and even the raw pickled fish. I would normally push it aside and leave it. It's slimy and tastes of vinegar, but I'm so hungry I don't care.

Sand has got into the food; I can feel it crunching between my teeth, gritty and salty. Nonetheless, I eat every last crumb. Now I'm thirsty, but I don't have a drink. Time to move on.

TEN

My feet are hurting. I stop and remove my boots and peel my stockings off painfully. I have blisters all over my feet and toes, and they are weeping and bleeding. I hitch up my skirt and step into the shallow waves. The salt water stings. My breathing is ragged as I grit my teeth.

I walk up and down, swishing my feet in the beautifully clear water. There are a few brown jellyfish floating in the small waves, but I take care to stay away from them. After a while my feet stop hurting and feel better.

I walk on barefoot. Now I'm leaving footprints and toe prints in the soft sand instead of boot prints. I turn and walk backwards a few paces to see the prints appear.

When I come to a stream, I walk inland a little, and then lie down on the dune grasses and scoop water into my mouth with my hands. It tastes earthy, but it's cool and refreshing. I drink and drink until my thirst is quenched.

I climb onto a tall sand dune to get a view inland. Only rolling dunes as far as the eye can see. I sit down and slide back down the dune, the sand cascading around me. I dig my hands into the pale gold, and trickle the grains through my fingers. It reminds me of when I was little, when mother took a day off work and we walked to the beach. Those are happy memories, and I smile to myself.

Quite by chance I look behind me. There is movement. I scrunch up my eyes, trying to make out what it is. I can feel my heart beating faster, whether with hope or fear I hardly know. It looks like a horse and cart, but I can't be sure. I keep looking back as I walk. I feel as if I've been alone for months.

I can see it properly now. Definitely an open cart, like the one I rode in yesterday. It has huge wheels, and I can see the driver sitting straight, holding a long whip. He's driving it with two wheels in the sea and two on the beach. Why? Oh, of course. The sand is so soft. I've discovered for myself it's easiest to walk right on the water's edge.

Hurriedly, I force my sore feet back into my boots, and then walk on, full of hope.

They're catching me up now. There are two men, besides the driver, and I can hear them speaking Danish. I slow down, limping more than I need to, hoping for a lift. Surely they will stop?

The cart draws alongside me and begins to pass me. Disappointment courses through me, and without quite meaning to, I look up reproachfully at them.

One man catches my eye. Immediately he calls to the driver:

'*Holdt!*'

The cart pulls up just ahead of me. Now that they've stopped, I'm suddenly shy, but both the passengers are smiling down at me in the friendliest way. They are smartly dressed. One is an adult with a full beard, twinkling eyes, and smile creases. The other is a young man, just a few years older than me, I would guess.

The older man speaks to me.

'I'm so sorry,' I say. 'I don't speak Danish.'

His face falls.

'*Engelsk?*' he asks. '*Nej. Mais français? Ça va mieux!*'

'*Vous parlez français?*' I am astonished. In the remote north of Denmark, I suddenly meet someone who speaks French. How strange.

'*Mais oui!*' He's grinning now. '*Nous allons à Skagen. Voulez vous venir avec nous?*'

He's offering me a lift. I nearly jump for joy. I beam up at him and accept at once. My French is only passable. I've only ever spoken it with my mother. How I complained when she insisted I learned it. 'What use will French ever be to me?' I used to groan. 'We can't afford to travel to Lincoln, let alone France.' Now I have my answer.

The two men are letting down the tailboard at the back of the cart so that I can climb in. The older man reaches down for my bag, the younger man reaches down and grasps my hand. He pulls me up. I scramble into the cart, catching my skirt and landing on the wooden bench with a bump. At once the cart lurches forward again, tilting slightly with the slope of the beach.

The older man holds out his hand to me. He's expecting to shake hands:

'Hr Ancher,' he introduces himself. I wonder whether Hr means mister. It doesn't sound like a name. He has

63

smooth well-kept hands. The young man's are hard and callused.

'Peter Hansen,' he says. He has an open handsome face, sun-bleached fair hair, and eyes like the sea.

'I'm Marianne,' I tell them, and then to my surprise, I spot something, lying under the front seat of the cart.

'Oh! My trunk!' I can see my name on it. It's so good to see it again.

'Ah! It's yours?' asks Hr Ancher in French. 'The woman at the inn asked us to bring it.'

Everything is going right now, and my spirits soar. I'm curious though, about how this man comes to speak French.

'*Comment parlez vous français?*' I ask.

'*Je suis artiste,*' he tells me. '*J'étudiais en Paris.*'

'You're an artist?' I lean forward, fascinated, a hundred questions rising up in me. 'And you live in Skagen?'

He nods.

'*Et vous?*' I turn to Peter, but he blushes and looks to his companion.

I can see I've said the wrong thing. I feel bad. Ancher explains that Peter fishes with his father for a living and doesn't speak French.

I give Peter a shy smile. He's the one I would most like to speak to, but he's shut out of the conversation. I know the feeling all too well.

'We don't get many English visitors,' Ancher says, looking at me expectantly. 'Especially at this time of the year.'

He is very kind and charming, but I'm not going to tell him the reason for my journey.

'What do you paint?' I ask, determined to deflect attention from myself. He takes the change of subject without a blink.

'Many things,' he tells me. 'The beach, the sun going down, my wife and my daughter. Most often I paint the local people. Many artists come to Skagen in the summer for the light,' he explains. 'I'm just on my way back from accompanying several friends to the train.' He speaks fast and fluent French, and I struggle to follow it. 'You are not an artist?' he asks.

This time I really wonder whether I've misunderstood.

'No, of course not!'

I can't believe he would even ask. I can draw, of course, but can a woman be an artist? I can't imagine it.

The cart suddenly lurches down into one of the streams that slice through the beach. We all hold on as the cart slithers and bumps through the water. The sand is obviously very soft and the horses strain. Finally we stop altogether. Our turn to be stuck.

The driver slaps the reins and shouts, but the horses can't move on. He kicks off his clogs and jumps down into the stream to lead them, but that doesn't work either. Ancher begins to remove his shoes and stockings and roll up his trousers, and Peter kicks off his clogs. I bend down to unlace my boots, but Peter stops me with an uplifted hand, shaking his head at me.

I hestitate, confused.

He jumps down into the stream and then lifts up his arms and beckons me. With a shock, I realize he intends to carry me.

'I can walk!' I protest, shaking my head.

'*Il vous porte,*' says Ancher with a grin.

My heart is beating very fast. I don't want to be carried. Or do I? Peter is waiting, smiling at me. My heart beats faster still. I sit down on the edge of the cart, at the back, where the flap is down. Peter puts one arm around my waist and slips the other under my knees, and scoops me up. For a moment, I panic. I fear he'll drop me, and put my arms around his neck, holding on. He hasn't started walking yet. He's still smiling at me, but his face is so close now. I can see how long his lashes are and how smooth and unblemished his skin is. I meet his eyes fleetingly and feel myself blushing.

He begins to walk, splashing energetically through the stream, carrying me as though I weigh nothing. I realize he's not going to drop me and relax slightly. I can smell the clean linen of his shirt, and the sun on his skin. Just for a second I close my eyes. I feel a bit dizzy.

Then it's over.

I'm standing on the far bank, and Peter is wading back to help push the cart. It seems to be an everyday event in this part of the world, getting stuck. They treat the problem with the same good humour that the peat-cart men did . . . was it only yesterday? I've lost track of time.

While they free the cart, I attempt to smooth my dress and my impossibly windblown hair. It's coming unpinned, and is stiff with salt. I dread to think what kind of appearance I must present. My skin is taut and dry from exposure to the wind. My lips are chapped and sore. I wish I could tidy myself more.

Soon we're under way again.

I can feel Peter's eyes on me as the cart bumps along. After a while I look back at him to show I've noticed. To my surprise, he still doesn't look away. Instead he smiles warmly, his eyes lighting up as he does so. It's an open gaze, curious and friendly. I try to smile back, but colour floods my face and I look away.

Not much further north we come to a wreck so huge that it blocks most of the beach. To my astonishment, I see they've cut an archway in it. The whole cart drives in through the missing section of the iron hull.

'Why are there so many wrecks here?' I ask Hr Ancher. I don't know the French word for wrecks, so I say something like 'broken ships'. He seems to catch my meaning.

'This is a dangerous stretch of coastline,' he explains. 'Strong winds and hidden sandbars.' Ancher points and gestures with his hands, making a pantomime out of the explanation. I notice Peter grinning as he watches.

I look inland, at the towering dunes that edge the beach, cutting off any view of the land.

'And how far does the sand go?' I ask, pointing inland. I've been wondering about this, having seen nothing but dunes rolling into the distance.

'Here? All the way to the other coast,' Ancher tells me. 'The sand blows and shifts with every storm. And there are patches of soft sand everywhere. Whole coaches drawn by four horses have been swallowed up by them. That's why they can't build a road or a railway. Do you see the white building there?' He points inland and I see a white tower with a red roof.

'It was a church. The sand buried it. That's just the top of the tower you can see there above the sand.'

I wonder if I've understood him correctly.

'*Une église entière?* Did they not try to dig it out?' I can't remember the word to dig, so I mime it. I'm awestruck at the idea of a whole church buried under sand.

'Many times,' Ancher nods. 'But the sand keeps coming. They've built a new church in Skagen now. They painted the tower of this one white to warn the ships. A landmark.'

I look down the beach. From here I can see the remains of two wrecked ships.

'It doesn't seem to work.' I can't keep the dryness out of my voice.

My visions of my father living in a neat farmhouse fade. This isn't farming land. But then I knew my father's family fished, and that they owned their own boat. Perhaps Skagen is a flourishing fishing community, with a harbour like Esbjerg or Frederikshavn.

The next building we see is a windmill. Its thatch is as grey as the sky, and its sails are still. There are boats pulled up onto the beach here and there, and I can see a number of men, and women too, wading, hauling on fishing nets. Some are wearing oilskins, others are clad in waterlogged woollen sweaters. The nets are secured around their waists with ropes, held in place with strips of wood. There's a rowing boat further out, and the men are shouting what sound like instructions to one another. I've never seen fishing from the beach before, and watch with interest. It looks hard work.

68

One of the fishermen hails the cart, and Ancher calls to the driver to stop. The fisherman walks unhurriedly to the cart. He's wearing tall boots and oilskins even though it's a warm day. I watch him curiously, noting the lined and weathered face, his stiff, upright bearing. His huge beard is fair but streaked with grey. The man looks stern, intimidating. He doesn't smile as he greets Ancher, neither does he offer his hand. When he speaks, his voice is deep and booming. The voice of a man accustomed to command. He reminds me of the preacher in Grimsby who treated me so scornfully. I feel fearful of this man and turn away a little, pulling my sunbonnet forward to hide my face.

Peter catches my eye and smiles. I smile back shyly and he begins to speak. Of course, I don't understand a word he says. He starts pointing to the people who are fishing, and talks some more. I just keep smiling at him, embarrassed, each time he pauses. What am I supposed to say in return? I say nothing.

At length, Ancher and the fisherman finish their conversation and the cart lurches forward once more.

'*Dav*, Peter!' I hear the fisherman greet Peter belatedly. I keep my face averted so he can't see me. He makes me nervous.

Ancher watches him as we move on. 'That man is one of our important townspeople. He's our . . . ' Ancher mentions a word I don't understand. I must look puzzled, because he tries to explain. It sounds as if the fisherman also holds some official post, but I still don't really follow. But I understand when Ancher says, 'He's a stern man,

69

that one. And strict. He's more judgemental than the parson himself if anyone has done wrong.'

Yes, that's how he looked to me, I think to myself.

The cart turns inland and ploughs across the soft sand of the beach and up onto a sandy track on the inland side of the dunes. The horses are wading in sand up over their hooves. There are houses now, either side of us, straggling along the coast. For the most part, they are tarred wooden shacks thatched with dune grass; some have the craziest shapes. Some are obviously upside-down boats built into dwellings or sheds. I can make a guess, now, where the wood from the wrecked ships went to.

Suddenly the air no longer smells of the sea. I pull my cloak up over my face and choke down my nausea. The town smells like a combination of the privy back home and the inside of a fishing boat. Only ten times worse.

A sudden gust of wind blows across us, bringing a squall of rain. It takes the smell away momentarily.

Outside almost every house there are fishing nets and fish hanging out to dry. Mostly plaice, by the look of them. There are also midden heaps, piled with rotting refuse and fish scraps.

That's what stinks.

Children in rags run barefoot in the dunes and around the houses. Outside some houses, old people are mending nets. They stop to watch as we pass. Some wave and call out greetings.

This is no prosperous town. It's barren and windswept. These people are poor. Miserably poor.

I look ahead, for the taller houses, the harbour. Nothing.

What is this place I have come to?

'*Ça n'est pas Skagen?*' I ask bewildered.

Ancher lifts his brows in surprise.

'*Mais oui, bien sûr!*' he exclaims. 'This part is called Vesterby. In a few moments we'll get to Østerby.'

Østerby, when we reach it, has one or two pretty stone houses painted yellow with red-tiled roofs. But here, too, there are mainly black-tarred wooden shacks. We pull up outside the one large, red-brick building in the place. It looks very new and fine, especially compared to the buildings around it. The men both jump down, and Peter turns to lift me down too. He treats me as though I were a lady.

I am reeling with shock at my surroundings, but I manage to thank him: '*Tak!*'

Our eyes meet and he smiles again, but Ancher is speaking to me:

'Where do you need to go?'

I look around me. And that's when I realize.

Having finally arrived, I have no idea what to do next.

ELEVEN

Skagen, September 1885

I'm silent a moment. Panic wells up in me.

'I . . . I am not quite sure,' I say. I look at the large modern red-brick building behind Ancher. *Brøndums Hotel* is written on the sign. It looks new. It also looks as though even one night would cost more than the few coins I have left.

At this moment I long to find my father more than I ever have done. In this place, he is the one person who can make everything all right. I'm so close now. But I don't want to blurt out my reason for coming here.

'I have a letter to deliver,' I tell Ancher. 'Then . . . I suppose I need to find somewhere to stay.' I lift my chin defiantly. 'Somewhere . . . cheap.'

'Who is the message for?' he asks.

'Lars Christensen.' I almost whisper the name. The moment has finally come when I may find him. I'm breathless with anxiety.

'Lars Christensen?' asks Ancher looking surprised. 'Are you sure the name is Lars?'

'Yes, quite sure,' I say, feeling far less confident than I sound.

'I think you'd better come inside for a few moments,' he says. 'We'll ask Fru Brøndum. She knows everyone here.'

He pays the driver, and then goes into the inn. Peter is hovering near me, waiting to say goodbye. I shake his hand, and make myself meet his eyes for an instant.

Ancher rings a bell and after a moment a woman emerges from what looks like the kitchens, carefully wiping her hands on a towel. She's neat and tidy with a strong stern face, which relaxes into a smile when she sees Ancher. She smiles at him. She obviously knows him. They speak Danish together, and I hear my father's name spoken. The sound of his name, spoken by Danes, makes everything feel real. I'm going to meet him at last.

The woman wrinkles her brow. She shakes her head as she speaks. I'm desperate to know what she is saying. I look from one to the other in doubt and confusion. Time seems to slow to a crawl. There's a silence. I become aware of a ticking of a large clock on the wall to my right.

'He would be about . . . thirty-five years old?' Ancher asks at last.

About two or three years older than my mother was.

'Yes, does she know him?'

'Could there be some mistake with the name?' His face is serious.

'No.' I shake my head firmly. 'Why?'

My mouth is dry, and my hands are damp. He must be here. He must.

'There was a Lars Christensen here in Skagen. He went to sea when he was seventeen, after an argument with his father.'

'Did he not come back?' I ask anxiously. 'Is he living somewhere else?'

There's a pause. They both look at me. My face grows hot from a mixture of anxiety and embarrassment. At last Ancher speaks:

'If it's the same man, he was drowned a year later. On a ship coming back to Denmark. It was wrecked. There's no one else of that name here.'

I think he's stopped speaking, or my ears have stopped working. The small sounds around me intensify and then blur. I try to speak. I want to pretend to shrug it off, tell them it doesn't matter. I don't want them to see how important this is to me. But it seems my voice isn't working either.

They are staring at me, the two of them, from miles away, down a long dark tunnel. The hallway is starting to spin. At first it moves slowly, and then faster and faster, and I'm falling, falling, and it's such a long way down.

The sun is shining across me. Dust motes are swirling in the ray of sunlight. I'm lying on a blue sofa in a room I've never seen before. A beautiful room with blue walls, hung with paintings. There's a vase of flowers beside me. I'm confused. Have I been asleep? I can't think how I come to be here.

I struggle into a sitting position. Hands push me back down, someone is speaking to me, but I can't understand them. A cool cloth is laid on my brow. It feels good. My head is spinning sickeningly.

I lie still a moment, my eyes closed. It's coming back to me now.

My father is dead. They told me that my father is dead. That means I've come all this way for nothing. I've travelled for days and days and spent all of my mother's savings.

That explains why he never came back. Why my mother never heard from him. He was drowned on his way home. I was fatherless before I was born. We should have guessed.

What shall I do now? I'm an orphan.

I open my eyes again. There's a lady in a fine yellow dress and a servant standing by me. Both their faces show kindness and concern. I'm not used to being a centre of attention. I turn my face into the back of the sofa, tears of disappointment and humiliation stinging my eyes and closing my throat.

I wish they would go away.

'Marianne?'

There it is again. That strange way of saying my name.

The lady in the yellow dress is speaking. She has a silver anchor on a chain around her neck. I stare at it, mesmerized. She takes my hand, and hers is soft and warm. I become aware that I'm as cold as ice, and I shiver.

'You fainted,' she tells me in French. 'Are you all right now?'

'Yes, I think so. I'm so sorry . . .'

This time as I sit up no one stops me. The maid stands near me holding the cool flannel. I attempt to smile at her. She puts a tiny glass to my lips and tilts it. I take a sip but then cough and splutter. It's fiery and bitter.

'No, please, could I have some water?'

76

'*Vand*,' I hear and someone gives me a glass. I gulp it down. I've had nothing to drink since early this morning.

I want to go now. I want to escape from these kind people.

'Please don't fuss!' I say, and then I flush with embarrassment in case I'm being rude and ungrateful. 'I mean . . . I don't want to cause you so much trouble.'

I sit holding my head in my hands. Someone has taken my boots off. My stockings have holes in and are bloodstained from my blisters. I feel a rush of shame that these people have seen them, and tuck them back into my muddy skirt. I'm dirty and unkempt to be sitting in such a fine room. I might mark their sofa.

'My name is Anna Ancher,' says the lady. 'You've already met my husband Michael. Is there anything we can do to help you? Do you have friends or family here?'

I shake my head and take a deep breath, trying to steady myself. I had no plans beyond finding my father. I'm embarrassed by this fine lady taking care of me. I need to accept her help however.

'I need a place to stay,' I tell her. 'And to find work.' I flush and speak low. 'I have almost no money left.'

'This Lars Christensen,' she asks, 'was he . . . ?'

'No!' I interrupt too quickly. I realize I don't know what she was going to say. I continue anyway: 'I was just asked to bring him a letter. I didn't know him.'

'No, of course not. I understand he died many years ago.'

I bite my lip, hoping they won't make the connection. It seems so blindingly obvious to me, I can't believe they don't guess at once.

'He has family here,' she continues. 'Wouldn't you like to speak to them? Give them the letter?'

Michael Ancher steps forward.

'Marianne?' he says. 'You've already met Lars Christensen's brother. We stopped on the beach to speak to him. Do you remember?'

I remember all right. I feel a sickening, sinking sensation in my stomach. That man. The one they said was strict and judgemental. He was my uncle. God help me.

'He's a stern man, but a just one. Much respected. Can he help you? I can go and fetch him if you like,' Ancher offers, his voice gentle and kind.

'No!' I cry vehemently. I control myself with an effort and repeat more calmly, 'No, really. Please.'

I imagine myself standing before that man. Giving him my mother's precious letter. Trying to explain my circumstances to him. I imagine his look of disgust. No. I can't do it.

'If Lars Christensen is dead, then the letter is of no interest to anyone else. Truly, it is not important.' I feel hot and ashamed as I speak. These people are so kind. But I would rather get up now and walk all the way back down the beach to Ålbæk than face that fierce-eyed fisherman. He would despise me. And quite possibly not even believe me.

If only I had not run out of money. As I remember this, despair numbs me.

The two women are speaking to one another in their own language. Then Anna Ancher turns to me again.

78

'You say you're looking for work. What do you do?' she asks.

'I sew,' I tell her. 'And embroider. But I'll do anything. I want to earn my keep.'

'There's a cheaper inn where you could stay. Or . . . ' She hesitates.

I know I can't afford more than one night at an inn, no matter how modest, so I'm desperate to hear the alternative.

'Or . . . ?' I ask.

'There's a family who need help. The woman has had a baby. Now she's sick, and can't manage.'

Hope is rising in me. Questions bubble up, but before I can ask any of them, the lady lifts a warning finger.

'They are very poor. And they can't pay you. But you can stay there a while, I think.'

It's a lifeline. I don't hesitate.

'If they'll have me, I should be more than happy to help in any way I can,' I reply at once.

TWELVE

The smell of the midden heaps is so bad that I walk with my cloak drawn across my face, hurrying to keep up with the girl who is taking me to my new home.

She's called Hannah, and she works at the hotel. She looks about my age. I understand she's a neighbour of the woman who needs my help. She speaks only Danish, so we can't understand one other, but she talks anyway, and smiles at me frequently as we walk. She looks friendly.

Hannah leads me along countless small paths among the dunes to the southern part of the town. I feel completely lost. We stop at the craziest, most tumbledown shack of the lot. I have a general impression of a building gone to seed. It is tarred black like the others, but not freshly done. The thatch on the roof looks as though it's coming apart.

A little girl in rags is sitting on the doorstep. She has grubby bare feet, tangled brown hair, and blank, incurious eyes. Her nose is running, green and slimy, right down to her upper lip. Why doesn't her mother give her a good wash? Then I think perhaps that will be my job. I shudder slightly.

My companion speaks to her, and then steps past her over the threshold. I follow her in onto sandy cobbles. There's a small kitchen area ahead of us, open to the thatch above. It's very basic, with no floor, just sand. Dirty pans and crockery lie strewn on the surfaces. There's a strong fish smell. I feel nausea rising in me. I swallow hard, trying not to breathe too deeply. Above the kitchen, there's an open half-loft full of fishing nets and tools.

We step up to the right onto a wooden floor and go into the main room of the house. It's as small as our room in Grimsby. The windows are dirt encrusted.

There are two double beds built into the end wall. In one lies a woman, seemingly asleep. There's a smell of sickness in the room. I remember it from when my mother was ill, and it brings a rush of memories with it.

On my left there is a stove with a cradle pushed under it. A table and chairs stand against the opposite wall. There's not much else, and I wonder where I will sleep. Hannah is trying to rouse the woman in the bed.

'Lene!' she is calling, shaking her by the shoulder. After a minute or two, the woman sits up and stares around her. Her gaze is unfocused, even more blank than her daughter's. She doesn't seem to listen as Hannah talks to her. She's telling her my name.

I don't notice the baby next to Lene until it wakes up and starts bawling. Its mother ignores it completely, so Hannah picks it up. A look of disgust comes over her face, and she at once lays the screaming bundle down on the floor and begins to unwrap it. I recoil as I see it's soiled itself, and has obviously been in that state for some time. There is a thick yellow-brown crust on its skin and clothes. I stand by stupidly as Hannah undresses the baby. From time to time, she speaks to me in Danish. She seems to be explaining how to do this. Am I supposed to change it? I've never even held one in my life. I look indignantly at the mother, but she's lying on her back, gazing blankly at the ceiling as though the baby is nothing to do with her.

'*Vand*,' says Hannah, and points outside. I put down my bag and go outdoors. There is an open well at some distance from the house. It's right next to the midden heap, and I must pick my way through rubbish, fish innards, and human waste to draw the water.

It's revolting. Don't they have a privy?

I look around, but I can't see one.

I lower the bucket on its rope and half fill it with water, and then take it back into the house so that the baby can be washed. Once it's clean, its raw, red bottom bound up in a fresh napkin, Hannah pushes and pulls the mother into a sitting position, and helps her put her baby to the breast. I look away, embarrassed. Abruptly, the wails and shrieks give way to sucking and grunting noises.

Is this where I have to live? Did I come all this way to be surrounded by such squalor and hopelessness? Better by far I had stayed in Grimsby.

No. I pull myself together, and take a breath of the stinking air.

This is just for now. Until I can find work or leave Skagen altogether. Meanwhile, no one here knows anything about me. It's a chance for a new start.

THIRTEEN

I wake up at first light itching all over. When I try to roll over I get an elbow in my back.

Then I remember.

I've been sleeping in a pull-out bed with three girls. It's like sleeping in a drawer. The bedding is smelly and as I begin to scratch, I realize I'm covered in bites. Bed bugs. I look at the little girl next to me, asleep and sucking her thumb. She's incredibly dirty and her hair is crawling with lice. Even in the grey light of dawn, I can see them moving.

As quietly as I can, I get up, slip on my dress and pick up my shawl. No one stirs. Lene and her husband Søren are sleeping in one double bed, both snoring, the two eldest sons in another. The baby's asleep in his crib.

I open the door almost noiselessly and creep out barefoot into the dunes. The sand is damp from last night's rain, and sticks to the soles of my feet. I decide to explore and quickly find myself down on the beach. I thought I'd never want to see it again, but it's beautiful in the early morning light. Where the sun is rising over the sea, the sky is flushed with pink and orange, but the beach is bathed in a light blue, so pale it is almost turquoise. Away from the houses, the air is as fresh as can be.

There are groups of fishermen working hard in the sea already. They wave to me as I go by. My host, Søren Jakobsen, isn't among them, of course. He came in drunk and quarrelsome late last night, after I'd gone to bed.

I walk for a while, thinking about my situation. I can't bear to go on living in that dirty house with a mad woman, a drunk, and a horde of louse-ridden brats. Our rooms in Grimsby were poor, but never squalid. We kept them spotlessly clean. But what alternatives do I have? With less than one krone in my pocket, not many.

Especially now that my father . . .

My throat constricts when I remember that he's dead. I'll never meet him now. I clench my fists and grit my teeth to stop myself from crying. I don't want to go back with red swollen eyes.

I've come all this way for nothing.

I left Grimsby to escape loneliness and poverty. And I've ended up in an isolated huddle of tumbledown shacks where almost everyone is poor. It stinks, and they don't even have privies. Everyone just goes out to the nearest sand dune.

Now I have no money left either. In Grimsby that sum of money would have been a buffer against poverty. Now I am as good as destitute. Dependent on other people's goodwill. How naive and stupid I've been.

Should I go to that man they say is my uncle and make myself known to him? It is possible he might help me. I shudder at the thought. I can't face the shame of it. I would prefer to make my own way, no matter how hard it is.

If I at least had money I could leave here. Although . . . where would I go? There is nowhere in the whole world where I belong. No one anywhere needs me or wants me.

I stop walking and just stand, despair weighing down my limbs. The enormity of what I've done crashes in on me. For a moment I feel completely without hope. I don't belong anywhere.

But there's always hope. While I have the strength to draw breath, there must be hope. I have to find it, no matter how well it is hidden. I push myself to resume walking and to think. There must be some good things about being here. At first I can't think of anything at all.

I try harder.

At the most basic: I have a roof over my head; I won't starve.

I look around me, and I can see that it is beautiful here on the beach. I was so focused on the journey the last few days that I scarcely noticed the beauty of the coastline as I travelled.

My father grew up here. That gives me a connection to this place that I wouldn't have anywhere else. And nobody knows me here. They don't know or care who my father was. It's my secret, and I'll keep it that way.

Those are lots of reasons to be thankful. And then there's Peter. I would like to meet him again. As I think this, I realize that, despite everything, he has been at the back of my mind since yesterday. His blue-grey eyes and the feel of his arms around me as he carried me across the stream. I was strongly drawn to him.

I feel breathless and stop walking for a moment, my eyes closed, remembering. Then I give myself a shake and move on.

Until I can learn some Danish and find some work, I have no choice but to remain here. So I need to find a way to make my situation better at once. The only thing I can think of that I can change here and now is the state of the house where I'm staying. I need to earn my keep in any case.

As soon as I've had that thought, I begin to feel better. Now I'm clear about what I can do, I turn around and begin to walk back.

I've emptied out all the stale bedding from my bed and gathered fresh dune grass and heather to stuff the covers with. I've drawn and heated water from the well and washed all the covers.

I caught the youngest girl, Lise, and washed her too. She's only about four, but she fought and scratched me while I washed her. I felt like slapping her, but I didn't. I just held on and I scrubbed her face and hair and neck with a cake of soap. I finished by emptying a bucket of water over her and telling her to wash her own body. She understood me, though at first she pretended not to. Then I combed the tangles and the crawlers out of her hair. She stamped her foot and screamed while I combed, but I still didn't let her go.

The two older girls obviously guessed what was coming because they disappeared. I'll get them tonight.

Meanwhile I drew more water and scrubbed the wooden floor of the main room and washed the windows until my arms ached. The floor will take another couple of goes to get all the dirt off, but it's a start. All the time the mother lay staring, unseeing, at the wall. When the baby awoke and started to cry, I had to shake her and pull her into a sitting position so that she could feed him. I am already becoming used to the sight of her breasts, swollen with milk.

At last I had time to think about myself. I hung up a blanket to make the kitchen private. Standing on the sand floor, I washed my own hair, scrubbing at the roots with the soap. It always takes a long time to wash and brush my hair; it reaches almost to my waist. Then I scrubbed the dirt from the journey off my whole body. Unfortunately my clean dresses were all packed into my trunk, which hadn't been sent from the hotel yet, so I had to put my old one back on.

Feeling wonderfully fresh and clean nevertheless, I sit down to catch my breath on the doorstep, allowing the warm late afternoon sun to dry my hair. I've worked hard today, and I feel tired. But also very satisfied with what I've achieved.

I'm still sitting on the doorstep when two lads come into view carrying something heavy between them. I squint into the sun, and then I can see it's my trunk they are bringing. I jump to my feet and go to greet them. One boy is barefoot and dressed in ragged homespun clothes. The other is smartly dressed in trousers and a white shirt. He has new leather shoes on, and wears spectacles. I guess he's a year or so younger than me.

He looks at me curiously.

'You are Marianne?' he asks in English.

'Yes!' I cry in surprise. 'Do you speak English?'

'Yes, a little.' They put down the trunk in the doorway and he smiles awkwardly and offers to shake hands. His hands are very rough and dry.

'I'm Mikkel,' he says, 'and this is Jan.' He indicates his companion. I shake his hand too, unsure whether that is the right thing to do.

'Where do you want this?' Mikkel asks, pointing at the trunk.

I've already decided during my day's cleaning that it will need to go up into the half-loft above the living room. There's no room in the house itself. We all push and pull it up the ladder, getting hot and out of breath. They laugh as we struggle, and I feel a little less shy. Once the trunk is in place, we climb down and I ladle some cool well water into cups for us. We all find our way out into the sunshine to enjoy our drink.

'Should I . . . ?' I get my purse out of my pocket hesitantly, not knowing whether to offer to pay them.

Mikkel saves me from my embarrassment.

'Jan would be glad of a few øre,' he tells me. I offer the boy one of my four remaining coins and he takes it gladly and runs off, calling to his friends who have been watching from some way off. Mikkel stands around awkwardly, shifting from one foot to the other. I'm worried he might go too, so I start to talk to him.

'Where did you learn to speak English?' I ask.

'I was studying wery hard at school, so the teacher give me extra lessons,' he tells me. 'Now I know more than he do, but it's not enough.'

'I could help you learn English!' I offer eagerly. 'If you'll teach me Danish in return?'

He looks very directly at me, a measuring look. I blush at the boldness of what I've just said.

'That would be wery fine,' Mikkel says, and we shake hands on our bargain, both secretly delighted, I think. I'm getting used to this Danish habit of shaking hands all the time. At first I found it very strange.

I wonder if I should start my new duties straight away, by pointing out that it's 'very', not 'wery', but decide it's too soon.

'You want to come for a walk?' Mikkel asks. 'I can show you around.'

I've worked enough for one day and the temptation of a companion who speaks English is irresistible. I hesitate just for a moment, wondering about walking alone with a boy, even one who's younger than me. I decide I don't care, and feel a slightly reckless excitement in my decision.

'I'll just get changed.' I go inside and climb the ladder to unlock my trunk. Quickly, I pull out my clean dress. As I do so, a small hard package falls out onto the boards. I'd forgotten my mother's pearls. I lift them to the light that's filtering through the gaps in the roof.

They are so smooth and white. Something beautiful left over from my mother's life before she had me. I'm not penniless after all. Feeling stronger, I fasten them around my neck. As I pull my clean dress on, I arrange it so the pearls are hidden. Leaving my hair loose, I climb back down to Mikkel.

We weave our way between the houses, wading through the soft sand. Mikkel points some of them out and tells me a few words about the families.

'That's Brøndum's Hotel and grocer's, where you went yesterday,' he tells me. 'It burn down a few years ago, and they had to rebuild it. I can remember the fire. And that's Hr Ancher's house.' He points to a low, stone-built cottage, painted yellow with roses growing all around it. It's very pretty, and quite different to the wooden houses around. 'He and his wife are both painters. They sent me to see you today. They thought you might be lonely.'

'That was kind,' I remark. So that's why Ancher asked whether I was an artist. His own wife paints.

'And see over there? That's my house.'

I can see another of the yellow stone houses, a low wooden fence around it. But Mikkel's house has no roses, and looks grand rather than pretty. There's a cow picketed in front, nosing among the poor grass for something to eat. Mikkel steers a path away from his house and leads me down to the beach.

'It looks nice, your house,' I say. In truth, I didn't see much of it, but I want to be polite.

'Yes, much better than Jakobsen's,' is all Mikkel says.

'What is wrong with her?' I ask. 'Lene Jakobsen, I mean.'

Mikkel shrugs.

'I don't know. My mother say she get like that after every baby,' he tells me.

'Poor woman,' I say. My sympathy is stirred, but not enough to want to stay in her bug-ridden house a day longer than I have to. 'And by the way, it should be "my mother *says*".'

I look at him to see how he likes being corrected, but he takes it very calmly, repeating the right verb.

'Where are we going now?' I ask as we head north. We are past the last of the houses now.

'I want to show you *Grenen*, the top of Denmark,' he tells me, and at once I clap my hands in delight.

'I should love to see it!' I cry joyfully.

Mikkel smiles at me. It's the first time; he seems to be very serious. He has a nice smile.

We walk down onto the beach. There are pebbles here as well as sand. We pass an old wooden construction that looks a bit like a catapult.

'That's the oldest lighthouse,' Mikkel explains. 'And over there is the newest: it's called the *grå fyr*, the grey lighthouse.'

I look up at the tall brick building towering above us. 'It's not grey,' I object. 'It's brick.' Mikkel shrugs.

'It looks grey from a distance.'

We walk until there is beach on both sides of us and the seas grow more and more choppy. Then we are on a narrow spit of sand, which finally vanishes into the water ahead. We stop, sea on three sides of us, watching the waves come from both directions, smacking into one another from time to time, sending spray flying up into the air and blowing with the wind. It's better by far than I had imagined. I can't help applauding the waves and laughing.

Mikkel is watching me.

'Now you must take off your shoes,' he tells me.

'Whatever for?' I ask. I don't want him to see my blisters.

'Because it's your first wisit, so you must stand, one foot in each sea,' he explains.

'*Visit*,' I remind him. I start taking off my boots, feeling rather foolish. As soon as they are off, Mikkel grabs my hand and runs with me out into the shallow waves.

'Stand here!' he instructs, tugging me to the right.

Holding my skirt out of the water with my free hand, I space out my feet to what I imagine must be one in each sea.

'Like this?'

This feels like a moment I shall remember all my life.

'Good! Now you can say you have arrived in Skagen.'

He's still holding my hand, but I don't mind. We laugh again, and suddenly Skagen doesn't seem so bad.

'You must never swim just here,' Mikkel tells me, his face serious again. 'It's wery, no, I mean *very* dangerous. The sea.'

'The currents in the water?' I ask. 'Are they very strong?' He nods.

'They can take you out. Into the sea.' Mikkel waves

his hand out at the vast expanse of water around us. 'The *nordstrand*, the north beach, is also less safe than the east coast,' he tells me. I shiver slightly. There's no danger at all that I would come and swim here, or anywhere else, but I don't mention that.

'I won't,' I promise, and instinctively turn back towards the sand. 'But now tell me what the seas are called in Danish,' I ask.

Mikkel points at the North Sea first.

'*Vesterhavet,*' he says slowly. Then he points the other way. '*Kattegat*. And straight ahead is the *Skagerrak*.'

He keeps telling me Danish words as we pick up our shoes (*sko*) and walk barefoot back down the beach (*strand*). I repeat them and then forget them, but it's fun. Some of the words are very hard to say. Discovering this, Mikkel persuades me to try and say '*rød grød med fløde på*', which means something to do with fruit and cream. It's all in the throat and the front of the mouth with impossible vowels. I can't do it at all, and Mikkel laughs until he cries. I can feel myself stiffen and grow hot and angry. I don't like being laughed at.

'Don't be cross,' he says, removing his spectacles and wiping his streaming eyes. 'We always ask foreign visitors to try it. When you can do it, you are speaking Danish properly.'

I determine at once that I'll learn to say it very soon.

Further down the beach we pass a number of groups of fishermen, hauling in their nets. The light is failing now, fading to a luminous blue glow around us. It's almost the end of my first day.

One man detaches himself from the group and wades out of the sea towards us. He's wearing long boots and a huge knitted jumper. I don't recognize him until he's quite close. Then I realize it's Peter, and my heart leaps. I'm so pleased to see him, and I fear I show it too plainly.

'*Godaften*,' he says, shaking Mikkel's hand and then mine. His hand is cold from working in the water. He speaks to Mikkel in Danish, and soon Mikkel turns to me:

'He says he hopes you slept well and enjoyed your first day in Skagen.'

I can answer that for myself.

'*Ja tak!*' I say, and if it isn't entirely truthful, at least it's polite. Peter gives me a broad smile. He shakes my hand again and returns to his work.

After I've said goodbye to Mikkel as well, and I'm walking back in the gathering dusk, I can feel my spirits rise. I have a new friend already. Perhaps two.

FOURTEEN

October 1885

I hush the crying baby in one arm while Lise tugs at my free hand.

'*Mal et billede!*' she whines.

Draw a picture. I've learned that phrase and many others in the last two weeks. It's hard work learning a language. And it feels like such a waste of time when I don't intend to stay here. But for now, I'm trapped by my poverty.

Lise's holding her slate out insistently. She's clean and tidy and I've mended her clothes. She looks so different now. Best of all, that dead look has gone from her eyes. I wish I could say the same for her mother.

Lise trails around after me all day long, chattering to me in Danish:

'*Kom, Marianne!*' Come here, Marianne! '*Prøv se, Marianne!*' Look, Marianne!

She gets in the way, wants to help with the cooking and cleaning and never gives me a moment's peace. But I've learned a lot of Danish from her chatter. Her older sisters go to school and her brothers go fishing with their father when he's sober, so Lise must have been lonely before I came.

I decided to try and help Lise's mother today. I led

her outside and washed her face, hands, and hair. Then I managed to dress her in some clean clothes and comb her fiery red hair to get the crawlers out. Lise watched with great interest, but didn't offer to help.

Lene submitted passively, but I got no response from her at all. She's still sitting in the chair I put her in, staring blankly out of the window.

'*Marianne, mal et billede!*' begs Lise again.

With a sigh, I put the baby down in his cradle. He's just fallen asleep, and it's a relief to be free of his weight in my arms. I ought to be drawing a picture for Mrs Forbes, but there's no point when I can't afford to post it. So Lise and I sit down at the table together. I take the slate and begin to draw.

'*Kat! Kat!*' she cries delightedly before I've got very far.

I wipe out the unfinished cat and begin a new picture. I think a moment. I want to draw something new, but I'm running out of ideas.

Then I begin to draw, more slowly this time, taking care. Lise watches, irritatingly close, hanging on the back of my chair, breathing on my neck. I repress the impulse to ask her to move a bit further away. It doesn't take long before she guesses:

'*Et skib!*' A ship. I smile.

'*Ja, rigtig,*' I tell her. That's right.

I don't stop this time though. I continue, adding sails and rigging and a figurehead at the prow. I become completely absorbed in my ship. Lise grows bored and wanders outside in search of playmates.

After ten minutes or so a shadow darkens the door. I

jump, hoping it's not Lene's husband. I prefer to see as little as possible of him and his evil temper. But it's Mikkel, and I jump joyfully to my feet, holding out my hand to him. He puts a bag that was strapped to his shoulders down by the door, shakes my hand and then goes politely to Lene and greets her. She looks at him, but her eyes don't really focus, and then she turns back to the window.

Mikkel looks around in surprise. I've seen him several times since I came, but he hasn't been inside the house since that first day.

'This looks different.'

I see his eyes rest briefly on the vase of wild flowers I put on the table this morning. It's true. I've scrubbed the house and washed the bedding and curtains until my hands are raw and chapped. I'm sure I would make poor work of any fine embroidery with them at the moment.

'It looks much better,' he says. I feel proud for a moment, remembering the dark and dingy hovel I came to. The family doesn't seem to even notice, but the neighbours, especially Hannah, have commented on the change. I feel I have earned the right to be here and eat their food. Fish, fish, and more fish.

I wish someone could talk Søren into repairing the house instead of drinking every day after fishing. I can't cure the leaky roof or the broken door.

'I see she's no better though,' Mikkel says in a lower voice, nodding towards Lene. 'She washed herself? No, of course not. You did it.'

'Yes. Though she does respond to the baby crying sometimes now.'

'That's good. Do you have time for a walk?' he asks. It's what I've been hoping he'll say, and in answer I unhook my shawl from the back of the living room door. The weather has grown colder now.

Mikkel is looking at Lise's slate.

'Is this yours?' His tone is admiring.

'Do you like it?' I ask, surprised. No one but my mother and Lise ever looked at my drawings before. It didn't occur to me they might be good.

'Yes! It's . . . very good. It's *kunst*. Art. Where did you learn drawing?'

'From my mother. She said . . . ' I hesitate, embarrassed. What she actually said was, 'Every lady should be able to draw', but I can't very well repeat that, poor as I am. 'She said drawing was important,' I say instead. 'Shall we go?'

Mikkel takes another look at the picture and then shoulders his bag again. As we leave the house, we head in a completely different direction to usual.

'*Hvor skal vi hen?*' Where are we going? I ask him, and immediately blush. It's a phrase he taught me the second time we met, and I practise it every time, but I still feel self-conscious speaking his language to him.

'*Nordstranden*,' Mikkel tells me, and I must look blank because he laughs and translates for me: the west coast.

'But *nordstranden* sounds like north beach,' I object, confused.

'Yes, that's right, you are learning Danish fast,' says Mikkel with a smile.

'But why is it called that if it's on the west coast? It makes no sense.'

'It does if you look at a map. The beach up here faces north,' Mikkel explains. 'And by the way, I have a picnic,' he adds with a backward nod at his bag.

I haven't yet been across to the other coast, apart from the top of Denmark, but I assume it's not much different.

'Is it far?' I ask.

He laughs and shakes his head.

'Much fishing is done over there,' he tells me.

We follow a track across the dunes, which turns into windswept heath land. The purple blossoms of the heather, beginning to brown in places now, are a start-ling contrast to the deep blue of the autumn sky.

We pass a woman in a grey woollen dress pushing a heavy, flat wheelbarrow full of fish back towards Skagen. I recognize her as one of our neighbours, and we greet each other briefly as we pass.

'That looks hard work,' I observe to Mikkel as the woman pushes the barrow through the soft sand.

'It is.'

'So how is it that you don't fish with your father?' I ask. I've been wondering about this since I first met him. The other lads his age all seem to be out working, while Mikkel wanders the heath with collecting jars and binoculars.

Instead of answering, he grabs my sleeve and pulls me down into the heather beside him.

'Look!' he whispers.

At first I don't know what he wants to show me, but

then I see some water ahead of us with huge white birds swimming in it.

'*Sangsvane*, song swans. They've come down from Iceland,' he tells me. 'Soon they'll move further south. They stop here for the water. They have this year's babies with them.'

I look at Mikkel rather than at the birds. He's completely absorbed.

'You like birds?' I ask.

'Birds, flowers, all of it,' he tells me. 'The nature. It make my father very angry.'

Mikkel stands up again, and pulls me to my feet. The swans take fright. With a huge splashing and flapping of their powerful wings, they rise into the air and fly over our heads. Each wing-beat whooshes in the air above us.

Mikkel watches them until they're out of sight. Then he looks at me. After a moment he holds out his hands.

'You've seen my hands?'

They are raw and red today, the skin flaking in patches.

I run my fingertips along the dry skin of one hand for a moment, to show my sympathy, but Mikkel snatches it back. He turns away and walks on.

'I can't work with the other men,' he says over his shoulder. 'I can't work in the water with the nets. It tear my skin and start infections.' His voice sounds tight and angry and his English isn't as good as usual, but it isn't the right time to correct it.

'I can row a little, but not strong enough to be any use. I sometimes can't breathe too. I used to try and work but my father got angry at me. All the time, angry.' Mikkel

102

pauses, and clears his throat. I realize he's fighting tears. I wish I'd never asked the question. 'I'm lucky, my father don't really need me. He has a boat, and make a lot of money. Anyway, I don't want to fish.'

He stops walking, looks at me directly again, and tells me:

'I'm going to go to the university one day. In *København*. Copenhagen. I'm going to be a scientist.'

There's a faraway look in his eyes.

But then he sighs, and his eyes snap back into focus.

'It's just a dream. That's for rich people. Fishermen's sons aren't going to the university.'

Mikkel looks so sad as he says this that I want to comfort him. Feeling very daring, I take his hand and give it a gentle squeeze. Then I let it go again, embarrassed.

Mikkel seems to shake himself, and we walk on.

'So what is your dream?' he asks me.

'My dream?' I'm at a loss for what to say.

'Yes. You must have one. Why did you come to Skagen?'

It's the first time I've been asked. Everyone has simply seemed to accept that I'm here, blown in like a seed on the wind. At first I didn't have the language to tell them anything, and now that I do, they've lost interest.

I scrabble frantically in my mind for something to tell him. Something that won't make him turn away from me. He's the first friend my own age I ever had. He's just told me a deep secret. So it is hard now to tell him nothing in return. Even worse to lie to him.

'It was a mistake really. My mother died in July,' I tell him. 'She sent me here, because I had no one in

103

England. She knew someone here she thought might take me in.'

'But they didn't?' Mikkel asks. 'Who was it?' He sends me a curious sideways glance as we walk.

'No, it turned out they died, a long time ago.'

I hope he isn't going to ask me how my mother knew them or ask again who it is, but his mind has moved on:

'What about your father? Couldn't he look after you? Or other family?'

'My father died before I was born,' I tell him truthfully. 'And I never met any of my grandparents.' It's the first time I've said it out loud. It feels more real now I've spoken the words. The loneliness that it implies surrounds me, presses in on me.

'That is very sad . . . ' He pauses. 'But still. You must have a dream,' Mikkel urges.

I can hear he feels I've cheated him. I'm not really telling him anything important. That's what friends do, isn't it? They tell each other secret, important things.

But Mikkel has a proper family and a fine home. They go to church every Sunday and I gather his father is someone important in the town, besides his work as a fisherman. A magistrate or some such thing. I can't bring myself to confide in him. To tell him I'm illegitimate. He might despise me. Worse, he might tell others. I couldn't bear the children of Skagen throwing stones at me. Or dried fish perhaps.

Then I think of something I can tell him. Something true.

'I've always dreamed of having friends,' I tell him. I'm

out of breath by now because we're scrambling up a steep sand dune. 'My life in England was . . . very isolated. And, apart from my mother and an old lady, you're my first friend.'

There's just time for Mikkel to smile at me. I see he's surprised, but pleased, and then we reach the top of the sand dune. The view of the west coast bursts upon me, and wipes the conversation from my mind.

This coast couldn't be more completely different from the east. It is grander by far. I've grown used to a narrow strip of soft, pale sand, full of hardy plants, and a friendly sea with small rippling waves. But here the sand is a smooth, rich gold, with patches of pebbles; a vast flat expanse fading into the distance in both directions. It looks untouched. As if no one has ever set foot here.

Beyond the sand, the blue-green sea heaves and roars, and sends big breakers curling and crashing onto the sand. It's huge, open, and fierce. A mixture of awe and delight sends a shiver through me, making my fingers and toes tingle, and the hair stand up on the back of my neck.

I become aware that Mikkel is standing beside me, waiting for my reaction.

'It's beautiful . . . ' I'm drinking in the size and scale of the beach, soaking up the blues, greens, and golds that are almost dazzling in the autumn sunshine.

'It's big, like the coast near Grimsby,' I tell him. My mother took me to the beach, occasionally. 'This is wilder somehow. More colourful. Is the tide in at the moment?'

'Tide? There's not really any tide here,' Mikkel tells me, surprising me. 'Is there in England?'

'Yes, the sea goes out a long way. So far you can hardly see it.'

'Shall we run down?' asks Mikkel, pointing down the steep slope at our feet. As soon as I agree, he grabs my hand and pulls me over the edge. We half run, half slide, bringing an avalanche of sand down with us. After a few steps, I let go of Mikkel's hand and throw myself down. I roll the rest of the way down, losing any sense of what is up and down, sky and beach merging into a tumbling rush of colours, sand spraying around me. I sit up at the foot of the dune. I'm exhilarated and giddy. Drunk on space and light and beauty.

Mikkel slides down more carefully.

'You're a crazy girl,' he says, shaking his head, but he's smiling.

I've got sand all over my clothes and in my hair, but I don't care. I feel like running along the beach shouting. I only brush the worst of it off and then we race across the beach all the way to the sea. We meander along the water's edge, speaking mainly English, but sometimes I try out Danish words or phrases I've learned.

'*Det er flot,*' I say experimentally. It's beautiful.

'*Ja, det er det,*' Mikkel agrees.

'So many of the sounds in Danish are so hard.'

'You'll get used to them. You're doing very well,' Mikkel praises me.

After a while we're both hungry. We sit in the dunes to eat the food Mikkel has brought. As he unpacks it and I see what it is, my mouth starts to water. Soft white bread, with cheese. Crisp, juicy apples. Fresh milk to drink. I eat the bread hungrily and savour the creamy taste of the milk.

Mikkel watches, surprised, as I begin on my second piece of bread.

'Don't they feed you at Jakobsen's?' he asks.

'No,' I say with my mouth full. Once I've managed to swallow, I tell him, 'I feed them. The woman who lives nearby, Hannah's mother, has shown me what to cook, but . . .'

'But . . . ?' Mikkel prompts.

'Do *you* like fish pie with cods' heads sticking out of it? Watching you while you eat?' The words, held back all these days, tumble out of me. I'm being ungrateful, but I can't stop myself.

'It's very good,' says Mikkel solemnly, but his eyes quiz me from behind his spectacles.

'Then what about baked seagull? Surely you don't eat that?' I demand, wrinkling my face in disgust.

'It's my favourite,' Mikkel assures me. I must look appalled, because he bursts out laughing.

'You don't like our Skagen food?'

'No, I don't. Just fish, fish, fish all the time. Dried fish, salted fish, fish heads and fishy seagulls. And just for a treat that bitter bread. I know why it's so bitter now. It's made with sour dough instead of yeast. The smell makes me feel sick.'

I stop, realizing I'm close to tears. The food is nearly the worst thing about being here. As bad as not speaking the language, as bad as the lice. Though not as dreadful as Søren coming home drunk at night and hitting Lene.

'*Så, så*,' says Mikkel soothingly, gripping my shoulder for a moment. 'They are poor, the Jakobsens. They don't have a cow like we do. We're too far north to grow *hvede* . . . wheat? Most families here only get it when there's a . . . What do you call it? A ship break?'

'A wreck.' *Skibsbrud* is one of the words I've learned already.

'Yes. Then the *strandfoged*, he's the man who is in charge of the wrecks, holds a big auction.'

'People can't just take things from the wrecks then?' I ask.

'Oh no. They do sometimes, of course, but they are punished if they are caught.' Mikkel stares out to sea, a frown on his face. 'My father says we should all be rich here. There is so much fish in the sea. But we got no harbour. So we can't have big boats. And no train or road, so we can't sell the fish we catch.'

As we've been talking, two small boats have come into view. Some of the men on board are pulling on the oars, heading for the beach. Others are hauling at nets.

'Shall we see who it is?' suggests Mikkel, beginning to pack up the remains of our feast.

'I'll let you take the rest home,' he adds with a grin. 'You can have it for supper. Perhaps the little one— Lise—would like some too.'

We're quite close to the boats before Mikkel slows down and hesitates.

'Oh no, it's *far*—my father,' he mutters under his

breath. But it's too late to turn back. A tall man with a severe face, intimidating behind his huge beard, has spotted Mikkel.

'That's your father?' I recognize him at once and realize I should have made the connection before. It's my father's brother. I have so far successfully avoided him during the weeks since I arrived. But if he is Mikkel's father . . . that makes Mikkel my cousin. My friend is my cousin, I think, and a twinge of excitement mingles with the fear I feel as the man approaches us.

Mikkel's father is splashing towards us through the waves, the water running off his thigh-length boots and oilskin jacket. When he speaks to Mikkel, it sounds more like a reprimand than a greeting, from the tone of his voice.

Mikkel is suddenly a different person: younger. He stands red-faced and drooping before the tall sturdy man. His father is the epitome of health and strength, a vivid contrast with his studious, delicate-skinned son.

I'm glad I didn't go to him for help, I think, watching Christensen verbally flaying his son. There is no hint of kindness or humour about him, and he takes no account at all of my presence.

Finally Mikkel speaks:

'*Far, det er Marianne,*' he says and I realize he's introducing me. I wonder whether I have to shake hands or simply curtsy to this terrifying man, but then his father looks at me for the first time, and I forget all about greeting him.

He freezes, and I watch, puzzled, as the colour slowly

drains from his face. He's rigid, motionless, and his eyes don't waver from my face.

'*Far?*' asks Mikkel. It takes a moment for his father to respond. As though there's a delay between Mikkel speaking and the sound reaching him. His father clutches at his chest, takes a deep, shuddering breath, and turns abruptly away. He doesn't speak. With a final backward glance at me, he stomps off back towards his boat.

I stand still, staring at him, until I feel Mikkel take my hand and tug me away.

FIFTEEN

November 1885

The wind is shrieking around the house, whistling through every crack. It gives me no rest. The noise is in my head until I think I'll go mad with it. The wind brings sand in with it, trickling through the gaps between the planks. Every day I sweep it up, every day more comes in. The last two days Søren and his sons had to climb out of a window in order to dig us out, so much sand had blown against the door in the night. I'm no longer surprised by the thought of a church buried in this sand.

It is pitch dark in the house tonight. I lie shivering under the blankets, and for once I don't mind Lise cuddling up beside me, her head against my shoulder, her hand tucked into mine. At least I'm sure she's louse-free these days.

I hear a cry in the night. At first I take no notice. It is faint and quickly carried away in the wind. But then I hear it again, closer. More voices take up the cry. I can hear the word they're all calling:

'*Skibsbrud!*' Shipwreck!

I sit up in my bed, my heart beating fast. Out there in the howling wind and huge waves, people are in danger on the sea.

Lise stirs, but puts her thumb in her mouth and goes back to sleep.

There's a hammering at the door.

'Søren!' calls a voice.

Søren gives a loud, grunting snore and rolls over in bed. He has his head in his hands and he's muttering curses under his breath.

The knock at the door comes again, louder, more insistent.

'Søren! *Skibsbrud!*'

The house seems to come to life all at once. I sit still while Søren swings himself out of bed, snatching at his clothes as he stumbles towards the door. Jakob and Morten, his sons, jump out of bed at the same time. There's a confused babble of voices, and the door bangs open, letting in a blast of cold night air. The baby wakes and begins to wail.

Once the men have left the house, I get up myself. I tuck our blanket around Lise, and lift the crying baby out of his crib. He's wet and I change him quickly before tucking him up with his mother. His cries fall silent as soon as he finds her milk. Lise and her sisters sleep on, undisturbed.

Lighting a tallow candle from the banked-up fire in the kitchen, I pull on clothes and wrap myself in my shawl. I'm wide-awake now, and sit down on a chair by the window, tucking my feet up off the cold floor. I imagine the stranded ship, pounded by the sea, her crew terrified and helpless. I feel restless, wishing there was something I could do.

112

A few moments later there's another knock at the door.

'Marianne,' someone calls.

It's my neighbour, Hannah, standing out there in the wind.

'Bring a couple of blankets and come with me,' she urges me in Danish. I've learned enough by now that I can understand most everyday things.

'Where are we going?' I ask her.

'To watch—and help if we can,' she replies briefly.

Despite the wind and the cold, I don't hesitate for a moment. Eagerly, I pull several blankets from the bed and follow Hannah out into the darkness. The wind is fierce and the sand is stinging like the night I was on the beach. Hannah is heading towards the west coast, bent forward against the westerly wind, her shawl wrapped around her head and shoulders.

We have little breath for talking as we walk. We head further north than the time I came here with Mikkel. As soon as we come out onto the beach we're hit by the full blast of the wind, but it's coming off the sea, so there's no sand in it now. The moon breaks through a patch of cloud, revealing a terrible sight.

The sea is a furious black monster. Huge waves curl and thunder onto the beach. Some distance out, a wooden sailing ship is lying, listing over to one side. The waves are breaking against her and right over her. Her sails are down, torn and flapping uselessly. For a moment I can make out tiny black figures clinging to the sides, and then the moon darkens and only the outline of the ship remains.

I gasp and Hannah puts an arm around my shoulder.

'It's caught between the sandbanks,' she says. 'The most dangerous place of all. We must pray the lifeboats will be here soon.'

'Lifeboats?' I'm only confused for a moment. Of course they must have lifeboats here.

'They use the biggest fishing boats,' Hannah explains. 'There's one kept just up the beach from here and another at Højen.'

'Højen?' I ask.

'It's the part of Skagen that's on this coast,' Hannah explains.

We are not the only people on the beach. Men, women, and children are standing around us, eyes riveted on the ship in distress out there in the waves. More people are arriving all the time, like silent shadows. One shadow approaches me in the dark:

'Marianne,' he says, and offers his hand. It's so dark that I recognize him by his voice only. It's Peter. I wonder how he knew me. As I put my hand into his, he clasps both hands around mine for a few moments.

'*Du fryser*,' he tells me. You're cold. 'It's good you've brought blankets.' His voice is approving. 'They will need them.'

He nods to the ship. I look out to sea again, in time to see a huge wave break over the prow. I can hear cries of distress even over the thunder of the surf. 'Meanwhile, make sure you stay warm.' Peter takes the blankets from my arms and shakes them out. They flap wildly, but he holds them fast, and wraps them around my shoulders. I'm glad it's dark, so he can't see my flush of pleasure. I can see his eyes shining in the moonlight as he looks at me, but his face is in shadow, and I can't make out his expression.

'How long until the lifeboat arrives?' Hannah asks him.

'It's here now,' he tells her.

Abruptly, Peter leaves my side. I turn around.

'Look!' I say to Hannah in astonishment.

Four . . . no . . . six strong horses are emerging from a gap in the dunes behind us. They snort and strain in their harness, pulling a huge wooden rowing boat that has been lashed to a wooden frame with wheels. Men in oil-skins and sou'westers are helping to lead the horses, shouting their encouragement to them. Others are push-ing from behind. I see Peter take a place at the side of the boat and throw his weight into pushing it the final stretch through the soft dunes and down onto the firm beach. The horses are whinnying and shying with fear at the sight and sound of the waves.

'Those are Christensen's horses,' Hannah tells me. 'He's a brave lifeboat man. No storm is too fierce for him. But Kruse is the captain of the Skagen lifeboat. He and his crew have saved many lives. They will tonight, too, you wait and see.'

Christensen again. I feel an impulse to turn away and leave. I master it. He won't see me in the dark.

'Come on,' says Hannah. 'Let's follow. But take care not to get in the way.'

The moon is out again now, illuminating the scene. There's one man obviously in charge of directing the

115

operation. 'That's Hr Kruse,' Hannah explains. 'And the man leading the horses is Hr Christensen.'

I screw up my eyes in the darkness and see that it's Mikkel's father.

'I've met him already,' I say, and move to stand slightly behind Hannah.

'And you don't like him?' she asks.

'No. I don't. He terrifies me,' I admit.

'I know what you mean,' Hannah agrees. 'He's a harsh man. Strict with others and strict with himself too. But I've never heard harm of him.'

Hannah's eyes are on the lifeboat as she speaks. They are selecting the crew, choosing the strongest men.

I can make out Peter in the darkness, jostling to be chosen, but the crew of ten is complete now. He falls back, and Mikkel's father himself takes the final place. I haven't seen Mikkel tonight. I wonder if he is out there in the darkness somewhere, watching as I am. I like to think of him as my cousin, though I don't dare tell him that we are related. It would involve explanations I don't wish to give.

They launch the boat with some difficulty. No sooner is she in the water than the Højen boat is pulled up the beach to help. I look out to sea, eager for a glimpse of the boat. I spot her after a few minutes, by the lantern held aloft at her prow by the man on look-out. There's another man at the stern, steering and calling instructions. The other eight are pulling strongly on the oars.

'She's made scarcely any progress. Why?' I ask Hannah,

pointing to the boat. I have to shout to be heard above the waves this close to the water.

'She can't stay on course,' Hannah shouts back. 'Look at how the wind and waves push her aside.'

She's right. I can see her being swept this way and that in the swell.

'The sandbanks make the waves break all the way out,' Hannah explains. 'The boat has to get through them all.'

It's tiring shouting to each other, and we fall silent. We stand for what feels like hours, sometimes with our arms around each other for warmth. Sometimes we walk up and down to relieve our aching legs. But always we watch the lifeboats.

Suddenly Hannah cries, startling me, 'Look! The lifeboats are turning back!'

'Turning back?' I cry in horror. 'But they didn't get to the ship.'

It seems the people on board the ship have realized it too. We can hear them screaming and crying over the roaring of the sea. It's a sound to move the hardest of hearts.

Those who were left behind on the beach crowd around the boats as they are pulled in, plying the crew with *snaps*, the strong local drink, and warm clothing.

'They're exhausted,' Hannah calls to me.

'So what happens now?' I ask.

'They choose a fresh crew.'

What would it be like to be stranded out there in that raging sea, watching the lifeboats turning back?

'They must be so afraid out there. I know I would be,' I tell Hannah.

She nods, her face serious.

First the Højen boat is filled again. There seems to be no shortage of volunteers. I can see Søren's eldest son, Jakob, but they don't take him. He's too young. There is no sign of Søren himself.

Now they are selecting the new crew for the Skagen boat. The last man they take is smaller and less broad than the others.

'Is that Peter?' I ask Hannah appalled.

She goes closer to the boat, and then returns.

'Yes,' is all she says, but she takes my hand.

I'm proud and terrified all at once. He's too young to go out there into that danger. But he's strong. That's why they've taken him. I've seen him row his father's boat.

They begin to push the boat out into the surf, only to be driven back by a wave that knocks several men off their feet. On the second attempt they launch her successfully, the crew jumping over the sides to take their places, the other men falling back to watch. She's afloat now, the men pulling powerfully on their oars.

The boat is lifted up and back on the crest of a wave, the breaker curling around her. I hold my breath, wondering if she'll be overturned, but then she plunges down the far side of the wave. We can see her stern for a moment and then she disappears from view, until the next wave lifts her.

I clutch the blankets tight around me and shiver with fear. I'm truly a part of the crowd on the beach now; we

118

all have a friend or a relative out there. I care passionately for the safety of the boat, as they do. I glance around me in the darkness. Everyone's eyes are on the boats. Some people are muttering prayers. I'm tensed, fists clenched, scarcely breathing.

After a while it becomes clear that both boats are making better progress than before. Perhaps the crews are stronger, or the storm is easing. One boat reaches the stricken ship. I can hear people around me shouting that they've got the lines across. A cheer goes up around us.

People on board are climbing the rigging to secure the line high up on the main mast. The lifeboats are heading in towards the beach again to bring the other end to the shore.

Peter's boat is almost in when it happens.

A huge wave roars in to the shore. We watch, helpless, as it catches the lifeboat crosswise, flipping her over. The men tip out, like pennies from a purse, tumbling into the surf.

I hear myself scream, as if from miles away. The sound is echoed all around me as others cry out too.

'Peter!' I shout. I want to run down to the sea and plunge into the waves to find him. Hannah stops me, putting both her arms around me, holding me tight. For a moment I struggle, and then I give up. It would be madness. I can't even swim.

One by one, the men swim ashore.

'I can't see Peter,' I say desperately to Hannah.

'No, he's not in yet,' she agrees, still holding me.

It's hard to count the men as they come ashore: there are others wading out in the waves, helping the swimmers. They are still looking, waiting. They grab the empty boat as she's swept towards the beach.

There's a sudden bang and a flash of gunpowder that makes us both jump. I can just make out a rope snaking into the waves. 'They're firing the lines,' Hannah explains. 'Ropes for the men in the water to catch hold of.' Another bang, and another rope shoots out into the water.

My heart is hammering in my chest and my mouth is dry with fear.

One man is pulled out of the water, limp and lifeless. Two men carry him ashore and quickly a group forms around him working to revive him. It's not Peter. I still can't see him.

I watch as they try to help the drowned man breathe again. They are pumping the water from his lungs, blowing air into him, but it doesn't seem to be helping. His family is gathered round. As he remains motionless on the beach, despite everyone's best efforts, the women begin to cry, quietly at first and then louder. A despairing wail that lifts above the sound of the wind. The men stand at a distance, their faces set and sombre.

'Is he dead?' I ask Hannah.

She just nods.

I stare at the body horrified. How would I feel if Peter's lifeless body were brought to the beach? As though a part of me had died. What a moment to realize that I love him, when he's lost out there in that monstrous sea. I scan the waves distractedly for some sign of him.

Despite the tragedy, the rescue continues.

Mikkel's father seems to be everywhere, Lars Kruse too, shouting orders and instructions, their energy driving the other men.

A shout goes up from the water's edge, and several men snatch one more person from the waves. As they heave him out of the water, we all see the rope around his waist.

'The line!' I hear people shout. 'He has the line to the ship!'

It's Peter's waist the ropes are secured to.

'He's safe, Marianne, he's safe,' Hannah cries.

I feel myself go limp with relief. I'm shaking so that I can hardly stand. My face is wet and I realize I'm crying. At last Hannah lets me go. I stumble towards Peter, pushing past others to reach him. He's standing supported by another man, coughing and gasping for breath.

'You're safe,' I say stupidly, putting a hand on the wet oilskin of his sleeve. 'I'm so glad you're safe.' He turns to me, looking surprised. He's still breathing heavily, sea water streaming down his face and clothes. Then he smiles and covers my hand with his. It's wet and cold. He's about to speak when an older woman rushes up, scolding and fussing. She wraps a blanket around Peter and hurries him away. We are parted, but as he is led away, Peter pauses and looks back at me once more.

'That's his mother,' Hannah tells me. I hadn't noticed her appear beside me. I watch them walk away until the darkness swallows them.

The men on the beach have driven posts into the sand while the lifeboats did their work. Now they secure the line from the ship to them, creating a kind of pulley, which they use to drag people over the sea from the ship. One by one they arrive, swinging in a sort of basket suspended from the rope, soaking wet from the waves that have drenched them, and shivering with cold.

'At last we have work to do,' Hannah tells me. 'Come and help get them out of their wet clothes.'

We both help, handing out the blankets we have brought, tying the discarded clothes in bundles to be dried. The crew is Norwegian, and they have passengers on board, including women and children. They are offered food, hot ale, and *snaps* and in pairs and small groups they are led back to people's houses in Skagen, to whoever has room to take them in.

A mother and her daughter are hauled to the beach together along the line. They are clinging to each other. As soon as they reach the beach, the mother collapses. Several women help revive her, wrapping her in a blanket, and chafing her hands.

Her daughter stands, shivering and alone, watching her mother fearfully. Her eyes are wide with shock. She can't be more than nine or ten years old. I wrap my last blanket around her, shivering myself now in the storm. I touch the girl's hand and it's like ice. Instinctively I put my arms around her, holding the blanket close, shielding her from the worst of the wind with my body. She's rigid at first, then she suddenly goes limp. Putting her head on my shoulder she begins to cry. Great sobs shake her whole body, making her gasp for breath.

'It's all right now, you're both safe,' I say, stroking her wet hair.

She understands neither English nor Danish, but gradually her sobs quieten, until only her shuddering breathing betrays her distress.

We stand together as her mother recovers, watching other people being brought safely from the boat. When a woman I know by sight comes to take the girl and her mother to her house, it is hard to let her go.

'You're going to go with this lady now,' I try to explain. 'To get warm, and have some food.'

But the girl clings to me, her chilled hands clutching mine, until her mother herself comes to draw her away.

I look for Hannah in the crowd, and feel comforted when, as soon as she sees me, she takes my hand. Dawn is breaking slowly behind us, lighting up the shape of the ship, lying at a crazy angle out in the swell.

Without warning we hear a great crack, and a long-drawn-out sound of splintering wood. We watch, horrified, as the mast to which the line is secured slowly topples into the sea. The rope goes slack at once, plunging the person who was halfway along it down into the waves.

We can hear terrified screams from the ship. It is not only the mast that has snapped. Strained beyond

123

endurance by the pounding of the waves, the whole ship is breaking up. I can see waves crashing right over her now. People are being swept off the decks into the sea. I feel sick with horror.

'After all that hard work, people are still going to drown out there, aren't they?' I cry. 'I can't bear it.' I can feel tears running down my face.

'Yes,' says Hannah sadly. I realize that for her, this scene isn't new. She's seen it before. Perhaps many times.

Fresh crews are running to man the lifeboats again, ready to try and pick up survivors. I see Christensen himself climbing into the boat to go out again. His voice is hoarse now as he calls for others to go with him.

A third, much smaller boat is being launched. I see it is Søren and his fishing crew.

'Look, Søren is helping at last,' I say, pleased about that at least. 'His boat looks rather small to pick up survivors, though.'

The light is growing, despite the storm clouds, and we can see the lifeboats pause from time to time to pull people out of the water.

I hear an angry exclamation from Hannah. I follow the direction she is looking in and see a shameful sight. A survivor is clinging to the side of the third boat, trying to climb in. Instead of helping him, we both see clearly how Søren uses his oar to push the man away from the boat and back into the sea.

'What are they doing?' I yell, looking at Hannah. 'Why are they going out there if not to save the people?' My stomach twists at the sight of the desperate man.

'It's not people they want to save,' Hannah tells me bitterly. 'It's clothes, food, wine, and any valuables they can steal.' She looks around us. 'I wish the commissioner for wrecks had seen that,' she says. 'They'd be in such trouble.' Most people's eyes seem to be on the lifeboats. One or two others have seen what we saw though. I can hear some angry mutters around us. I wonder how Søren and his friends will dare come back.

'What a family I live with.' Little better than wreckers, I want to say, but I don't know the words for it in Danish. They may be poor, but there will surely be time to loot the ship once its crew and passengers are safe.

One lifeboat returns. They have a survivor, a young man who shivers and shakes as they help him out of the boat. They also have three bodies, which they lay respectfully out on the sand. They are limp, their hair bedraggled and their faces drained of colour.

'Poor things,' says Hannah pityingly. 'They were healthy young men a few hours ago.'

I shudder and turn away.

'The bodies that are washed up after a few days are much worse,' Hannah tells me grimly.

I'm exhausted and cold. My legs and back are aching from so many hours standing. I'm just wondering about going home, when we notice a movement out to sea. The ship is shifting, and slowly, slowly, she sinks beneath the waves until only her stern and her unbroken masts are showing.

I scan the sea for a glimpse of Søren's boat.

'Look!' I say, grasping Hannah's shoulder and pointing.

The small boat vanishes for a few seconds and then reappears. Capsized. Others have noticed it now too. But this time no one hurries to push the lifeboat out.

'Let them take their chance,' growls one man nearby and I hear others agreeing. Everyone is turning away now, packing up. There is little hope of finding anyone else alive.

Hannah and I are just leaving the beach some time later, when another body is washed up, limp and lifeless.

It's Søren. We approach fearfully. His lips are blue, his hair like wet seaweed. Worst of all are his eyes, open and sightless.

'Ugh!' I recoil.

I feel no sympathy for this man I have shared a house with for nearly three months. He did no one any good while he was alive. He drank not only the money he earned, but most of what his two sons earned too. But the sight of him dead on the sand is shocking all the same.

Two men are preparing to carry the body back to his widow. I notice they are less respectful of him than of the drowned Norwegians. I don't blame them. We walk beside them all the way back to the house.

'I wonder what Lene's reaction will be?' I say. She's had nothing but harsh words and heavy knocks from him while I've been here, but they must have loved one another once.

I part with Hannah near the Jakobsens' house, and follow the body in.

To my surprise, Lene is distraught. She sobs, apparently

heartbroken, holding her dead husband's lifeless hand in both of hers.

Lise comes to me for comfort, climbing into my lap and twining her arms about me.

'Why is he dead, Marianne?' she whispers.

I don't know how to answer.

The other girls stand shocked and silent, watching their mother grieve.

Jakob returns safely, but we all wait anxiously for news of Morten who was in the boat with his father. He doesn't return until much later. He comes creeping in under cover of darkness, hugging a sack of wheat guiltily in his arms. He and his brother quickly prise up a loose floorboard in the living room. There's a fair-sized hole dug in the sand underneath. They drop the sack into it. I imagine the hiding place has been put to use before.

Morten has tales to tell of his part in the looting of the ship. I listen, half interested, half disgusted. He's lost a father and gained a sack of wheat. I wonder to see him so unmoved by the exchange.

SIXTEEN

December 1885

It's completely still on the beach.

I stand awed before the vast expanse of sea, which is frozen into silence. There's not even a breath of wind this morning. The sun is rising over the ice, streaking the sky with blues and oranges.

The boats lie idle on the sand, upside down. Snow has drifted about them; their ropes are thick with frost. Ice crystals in the sand catch the first rays of sun and sparkle like diamonds all around me.

This beauty has brought great hardship with it. The frozen sea yields no food. The poorer townsfolk are surviving solely on dried and salted fish, and in our house, even that is running low. There's no fresh fish to trade for grain or fuel, and the Jakobsens had nothing stored ready for the winter. I'm so hungry my stomach hurts.

The sack of wheat that Lene's son Morten stole from the wreck last month has been the saving of us. The bread has kept the worst of the hunger at bay so far.

It's Christmas Eve today. I've escaped the house for an hour to be alone and to think about my mother. It will be my first Christmas without her. I miss her quiet cheerfulness, and the exchange of small gifts that we always made for each other. I usually push my sadness away, but today it overwhelms me with its intensity. Despite my friends, there are days when I'm so lonely.

But this afternoon I'm invited to Hannah's. In Denmark they celebrate Christmas today. It will be a spell of joy and relief away from my life in the Jakobsens' house.

Reluctantly, I turn away from the splendour of the sunrise and drag my feet back to a house which is empty of Christmas spirit. I have chores to do.

'*Hvor var du*?' Where've you been? demands Lene as soon as I re-enter the house. 'You're always disappearing when you're wanted.'

She has come out of her apathy since her husband died, and revealed a temper nearly as foul as his. I find her intolerable.

I don't answer her question, but take off my shawl, put on my apron and begin to cook one of our two meals of the day. There's no longer enough food for three meals.

I slice the dried plaice, which I've soaked, and throw the pieces into the pan, pushing them around angrily. I don't mind working hard, but I'm not their slave to work tirelessly for no thanks. I call to the children to set the table. I had felt guilty about leaving them on Christmas Eve, but I don't care any more.

I scrape the fish onto plates, and try to stop myself from banging them onto the table as I would like to do. They wolf their meagre portions before I've even had a chance to take off my apron and join them.

'*Jeg er stadig sulten!*' I'm still hungry! Lise cries as soon as she finishes hers. 'I want some bread!'

'Shut your mouth, Lise,' Lene snaps, slapping her roughly.

Lise begins to cry. Her eldest sister puts her arm around her in an attempt to comfort her.

'We're saving the bread for supper,' I say gently. 'We're all hungry, Lise, you'll have to be brave.' Guiltily, I think of the pearls hidden under my dress. My conscience tells me I should sell them to buy food, but I can't bear to. They were my mother's. If things get much worse, I will, I promise myself.

To comfort her, and because I'm going out later, I give Lise half my own portion. I give the rest to Jakob. Then I look around at the family. Their shadowed eyes are over-large in their peaked white faces. I wonder if I look the same.

I put on my best dress to go to Hannah's. The daylight is already fading again, though it can only be three o'clock. I'm dizzy from lack of food, and my feet feel heavy.

The younger Jakobsen children have been out begging from the wealthier families and have brought home potatoes, some fruit, and little round biscuits in twists of paper. At first I'm a little shocked, but they assure me it's a tradition on Christmas Eve. Lise asks me to close my eyes and then pushes a biscuit into my mouth. It's sweet and spicy. I give her a quick hug before I go, and she plants a sticky kiss on my cheek.

Hannah pulls the door open and hugs me before I have a chance to knock.

'Marianne! Come and see our decorations!' she cries at once.

'You've made it so pretty!' I exclaim. The tiny house is bright and clean. There is an apple studded with cloves on the table. I smell the warm exotic scent at once. Red paper hearts are pinned to the walls. The table is set simply but prettily, with china and napkins. The soft candlelight completes the atmosphere.

Hannah beams with delight.

'The cloves came from the wreck,' she tells me. 'Mother bought them at the auction.'

Hannah's mother shakes my hand.

'Welcome, Marianne! Come and warm yourself by the stove.'

'I have a small gift for you first,' I say a little nervously, laying two tiny parcels on the table. It has been a puzzle to know what to give them, as I still have absolutely no money. In the end I chose my two best handkerchiefs and embroidered them with the prettiest threads from my sewing box.

The parcels are wrapped in the tissue paper that lined my trunk. I watch anxiously while Hannah and her mother unwrap them. To my relief they both seem pleased. On Hannah's I've embroidered an intricate 'H' in one corner and tiny pink flowers in the others. For her mother, a blue 'C' (her name is Charlotte) and blue flowers.

'Marianne, they're beautiful,' breathes Hannah.

'That was too generous,' her mother tells me, giving me a kiss on the cheek. 'It must have taken you hours.'

132

'Oh no,' I assure her. 'I learned to sew as soon as I could hold a needle.'

They lay the handkerchiefs on their bed, and Hannah's mother puts on her apron and begins to fry fish.

'We only have dried fish for our Christmas meal, I'm afraid,' Hannah tells me apologetically. 'And we need to eat much earlier than usual, as mother has to go back to the hotel to help prepare the Christmas meal there. They have lots of guests.'

'That's no problem at all, I promise.' I am glad the supper will be early. Having not eaten yet today, I'm starting to feel faint.

'But just wait until you see what we have for dessert,' Hannah adds. She hugs herself in excitement, her eyes gleaming.

'Dessert?' I ask, surprised.

I can't remember the last time I had any kind of dessert.

'You look as if you could do with some,' Hannah's mother tells me, coming back into the room. 'Are you going very short of food at Jakobsens'?'

I hesitate, unwilling to lie outright, but not keen to admit the truth either.

'We're managing,' I tell her.

'Well, there'll be no fresh fish while the sea stays frozen,' says Hannah's mother seriously. 'Have you thought of earning money with your sewing?'

'Yes, I have,' I reply. 'But I don't know how to go about it.'

'I may be able to help you. But I won't make any promises until I'm more sure.'

'That would be very kind,' I tell her, feeling hope bubbling up inside me again. I feel quite different all of a sudden. Lighter, more energetic.

Hannah must have been teasing me when she said there was only dried fish for supper. There are also potatoes and carrots with melted butter. It's the best meal I've had in months. I eat hungrily. Then Hannah proudly helps her mother lay two serving dishes of dessert on the table.

'It's *ris à l'amande*,' she explains.

I don't realize for a moment that Hannah's using a French name. Then I understand. Rice with almonds. It looks as though there's a generous amount of cream stirred into it as well. The second dish has fruit in a sauce.

'Does this have a French name too?' I ask.

'No, that's *kirsebærsovs*,' she laughs. Cherry sauce. 'They've made a huge portion for Christmas at the hotel. They gave mother some to bring home,' Hannah explains, handing round bowls and spoons. 'It's what they're eating later tonight, so we are as grand as they are!'

I taste a spoonful of my portion. The rice is rich and creamy, and the pieces of almond crunch deliciously. The cherries burst on the tongue, adding sweetness.

Hannah and her mother are watching me expectantly, waiting for my reaction.

'It tastes so good,' I assure them. 'I love it.'

I eat very, very slowly, tasting every spoonful, making it last as long as possible. I store up the memory of the taste. When we've eaten every last bit, we clear away, and Hannah's mother brews some rosehip tea from the

134

rosehips they picked in the autumn. Then she wraps herself in her shawl.

'*Nu må I hygge jer!*' she says just before she closes the door behind her.

It's a phrase I can't translate into English. Mikkel told me it means something like 'have a nice time' and 'be cosy' all rolled into one. They say it a lot here, and it stands for companionship and hospitality in my mind, making me feel warm and content when I hear it.

Hannah and I sit by the stove in the candlelight and wrap our hands around our mugs. I wonder how Peter is spending Christmas. I imagine him sitting by the fire with his family. I feel a fierce longing to see him. I wonder how long it will be until I do.

Hannah begins to tell me about the Christmas church service tomorrow.

'Why don't you come, Marianne?' she asks. 'You never come to church.'

'The Jakobsen family don't go.' It's a poor excuse, and we both know it. Hannah pounces on it:

'Come with mother and me then: we'd love to have your company.'

I hesitate. I don't go to church because of the shame of my birth. Because my mother never went to church after I was born. I haven't forgotten the coldness of the minister in Grimsby who buried her. All because I have no father.

'What happened to *your* father, Hannah? You never speak about him.' The question pops out before I realize I was going to ask it. It's been in my mind before.

135

She reminds me of myself somehow. So close to her mother.

'My father?' Hannah gives a slightly embarrassed laugh. 'I never knew him. He was a sailor. Shipwrecked off the coast just like the Norwegians who were here at the beginning of the winter. Except he was Swedish.'

I still don't fully understand, and it must show in my face.

'He was here for a few months and then got a passage back to Sweden. Before he knew that my mother was expecting me.'

Understanding crashes in on me, and I can't believe I was so stupid. Hannah is like me. Exactly like me. She's illegitimate too.

It takes a few moments for this new idea to sink in. I feel a flush in my face. I'm ashamed that I made Hannah tell me this. I struggle to know what to say next:

'So he . . . you . . . you're . . . '

'Illegitimate. Yes.'

'And no one minds?' I'm reeling with shock.

'Well,' Hannah hesitates a moment. 'Some people disapproved of my mother, of course. But her parents took care of her, and later the Brøndum family gave her seasonal work at the hotel. So we've always been able to manage. And *I'm* not responsible for my birth, of course.'

She says this last sentence so calmly, in such a quiet, matter-of-fact way that it takes my breath away. I think of how open and confident Hannah is. Everyone welcomes her wherever she goes. I compare her life to my

136

former life. Even now I carry that secret shame within me, afraid that someone will discover it, and the new life I have built will crumble at a touch.

Hannah didn't even really mind telling me. I would rather die than tell anyone the truth about my birth. Hannah can't possibly realize the significance her story has for me. What a connection there is between us.

'*You* don't mind do you, Marianne?' she asks and I think I hear a touch of anxiety in her voice.

'Me? How could I?' I hesitate slightly. 'I never knew my father either,' I begin in a rush. Hannah looks up, her attention caught. I hesitate again, wondering if I dare say it. 'He died before I was born,' I explain lamely. I know I should tell her the truth. It's dishonest not to. A part of me longs to, but I can't. I've learned the lesson of caution too well over the years.

'I'm sorry,' says Hannah seriously. A moment later she's smiling at me again. Mischievously.

'So, will you come to church tomorrow?'

Church. She and her mother even go to church.

A part of me thinks: if they can, I can. I watch the flickering candle flames for a few moments while I think.

'All right,' I agree. 'I'll come with you.'

'Good,' Hannah says, looking pleased. 'I wanted to have my best friend with me tomorrow.'

Best friend.

I can hardly believe she said it. Despite my failure to trust her with my secret, I can feel a warm glow spreading through me. I smile, and she smiles back.

* * *

The walk down along Søndergade to the St Laurentii church is a long one, and it's especially slow in this weather. The powdery snow has been trampled into ice. Either side of the road it lies loose, ready to drift again at the first hint of a wind. The sun is low in the pale winter sky, its beams glinting off the snow.

Christmas morning. I had expected to feel unhappy today but I'm not. I'm with friends, and I'm also looking eagerly around for Peter, hoping to catch a glimpse of him, perhaps even shake his hand.

Hannah walks beside me, her arm linked in mine so we can steady one another if we slip on the ice. Her mother walks and talks with her neighbours just behind us. We are quite a crowd. I can hardly believe I'm going to church like this with everyone else. I feel nervous, as though the minister will take one look at me and I'll stand revealed, my soul stained with sin, for him to see.

Mikkel catches us up. He slaps me cheerfully on the back.

'Marianne! You're coming to church at last! That's good.'

He walks beside us, and I notice that Hannah has gone very quiet. I wonder if she doesn't like him. Or perhaps, despite what she said to me yesterday, she's worried that he won't approve of her. Mikkel's father, after all, is known for his rigid morals. He of all people must disapprove of her illegitimate birth.

138

But Mikkel is talking to her in a perfectly friendly way. Then I see her cast her eyes down and blush slightly at something he says and a suspicion flashes into my mind. Of course. She does like him.

I hope he won't break her heart. I'm sure he's still set on leaving Skagen.

It's bitterly cold inside the church. Breath rises in frosty clouds as people greet one another. They all know each other. I'm surprised how many people I myself know. Acquaintances and neighbours nod and smile at me and I return their greetings. Many greet me by name. I can see the Anchers with their little daughter at the front of the church. In the pew next to them sit the Brøndum family, with their stern, strong faces. At last I see Peter. He's with his parents in their family pew. His mother and father both give me a friendly nod. My eyes meet Peter's across the aisle and he smiles warmly.

I realize that I'm part of this group of people. I'm known to all of them. And strangest of all, I'm welcome. It has happened so gradually that I've hardly been aware of it. Hannah and I take seats at the back of the church in the public pews.

Mikkel's family arrives, his parents and his younger brother and sisters whom I've never met. My relatives. Christensen looks as forbidding as ever. His wife looks as though she chews lemons.

The church is full now, with some of the men standing at the back. The minister begins the service. He hasn't been in Skagen long, Hannah has told me. His name is foreign: de Place. He's wearing a long black cassock. The huge white ruff around his neck looks like a wedding cake with a head on top. It makes me want to giggle, but I don't. We sing a hymn, and this is followed by prayers. Then the minister announces the lesson, and I see Mikkel's father, Christensen, get up from among the congregation to read it. He walks slowly to the lectern at the front of the church, each step measured and deliberate, his carriage upright and rigid. Once he's found his place in the Bible, he begins the reading, though it's clear he barely needs to look at the page: he knows it by heart.

At about the fifth or sixth word Christensen's eyes seek me out and hold me. His eyes glare angrily as he barks out the words of the lesson. It's old-fashioned Danish and I can't really understand it. I can't concentrate. The fierce, unwavering gaze overwhelms me. I look away, upset, but when I look back he still has his eyes fixed on me.

Christensen knows.

I remember his strange reaction to me on the beach that time when I was with Mikkel and I'm suddenly afraid. He must know about my birth. But how could he?

I cast my mind back. The Anchers knew I was looking for his brother. Did they tell him? Small town gossip. Stupid of me not to think of it before.

Still, even if they told Christensen what they know, he can't be sure. He must just be guessing. My father died on the way back from England, before he had a chance to tell anyone here anything. I shiver with fear. Unless . . . my father might have written a letter to his family. I shake my head. No, that doesn't make sense either. What

140

would he have told them? He did not even know my mother was with child.

Perhaps Mikkel's father just disapproves of my friendship with his son. Or perhaps he looks at everyone like that.

Christensen finishes the reading and sits back down. I remain troubled by his behaviour. All through the long, incomprehensible sermon, my mind dwells on Christensen. Eventually I shake myself and tell myself I might have imagined the whole thing.

On the way out of the church the minister shakes me by the hand.

'Welcome to our church, Marianne,' he says. I feel myself flush with pleasure that the minister knows me by name. A number of acquaintances stop and shake hands, exchanging greetings. Hannah introduces me to some of her friends. We stand in the cold for some time, our breath misting the air as we speak. Hannah becomes involved in a conversation in which I soon lose track and I drift away from her a little. Then Mikkel approaches me.

'Marianne, I'd like you to meet my parents. Father, mother, this is my friend Marianne.'

I can't believe Mikkel's trying to introduce me again, after what happened last time. But before I know it, I'm shaking Christensen's hand. The shock of it makes my heart miss a beat. He doesn't smile and releases my hand as quickly as is compatible with good manners. Mikkel's mother is scarcely more friendly.

'You are from England, I believe?' she asks haughtily in Danish.

'Yes, that's right.' I repress the impulse to curtsey to her.

'And do you stay long in Skagen?' she asks.

'I hardly know,' I falter, embarrassed. I'm aware of Christensen looking on in silence. I struggle to compose myself and be more natural.

'Your son Mikkel speaks very good English,' I tell her, summoning what I hope is a friendly smile. 'He's been a great help to me.'

She smiles coldly, and then nods goodbye, summoning Mikkel to her side.

As they walk away, Christensen leans towards me. I tense, not knowing what to expect.

'Stay away from my son,' he hisses. He doesn't look at me as he whispers this. I jump as though I've been stung. Did I hear him right? He's already marching away, catching up with his family. I glance around me, but there's no one near enough to have overheard. I'm rigid with shock. I have a sudden urge to be by myself, and leave without a word to Hannah. As I hurry down the path outside the church, I run into Peter.

'Marianne?' he asks. He grasps my hand and holds it fast. 'Is something wrong?' Peter sounds so concerned, so gentle, that I feel tears coming to my eyes.

'*Jeg skal . . . være alene.*' I need to be alone, I try to explain. Peter looks at me a moment longer, and then releases me.

I turn and make for the beach as quickly as I can on the slippery pathway, so that I can be alone. Alone to think.

My thoughts are bleak indeed. All my pleasure in

Christmas morning is spoiled. I feel an acute misery settling on me. I speculate pointlessly on what Christensen might know. The courageous thing to do would be to go and see him. To confront him with who I am. But even as I think this, I know I do not dare. The man terrifies me.

Am I going to obey Christensen? I decide that would be ridiculous. What can he do to me? The worst he can do is to tell people about my birth, assuming he knows my secret. That would be bad. Very bad. But it would also shame him by association.

No, I'm going to stay here and do as I please. I'm not going to creep away and hide like mother and I did in England. I've had enough of that. I shall be friends with whom I choose. I remember what Hannah said last night: I am not responsible for my birth. The words give me strength. I have done nothing to be ashamed of.

The sun sparkles on the ice crystals in the sand and the beach glows faintly blue, reflecting the sky. Gradually my surroundings soothe me, walking steadies my ragged breathing. I'm calmer, but my resolve remains.

I turn around and head back towards the town. In the distance, I see Hannah coming towards me.

'Marianne!' I hear her call, and she's waving to me. 'Are you all right?'

I smile and wave back. My friend, I think, and I'm comforted.

SEVENTEEN

January 1886

I t's the first day of the New Year, and I'm stuck
indoors, with only Lise and her mother for company.
The temperatures have dropped lower still. My
fingers are numb with cold, and I have to stop sewing
frequently to rub my hands together in an attempt to
get the blood to flow.

Just as I sigh and begin to think about putting the fish
in to soak for supper, there is a firm knock at the door.
With a quickness born of boredom, I run to open it,
hoping to see Mikkel, or perhaps Hannah.

I'm confused rather than disappointed. Peter is standing there.

He has never come to call before. What can it mean?

'*Dav*, Marianne,' he says, as he briefly shakes my hand
in greeting.

'*Dav*, Peter,' I respond. 'Would you like to come in?'

'Thank you, but no,' he declines.

I'm almost thankful. To have to sit and make conversation with him under Lene's gaze would be a sore
trial.

'My mother has sent me to fetch you,' he tells me.

My confusion grows.

'Your mother?'

'Yes. She'd like to meet you, if you are willing. She's heard you are looking for sewing work.'

Suddenly everything is clear.

'Did Hannah's mother speak to her?' I ask.

'Yes, I think so,' says Peter. 'She'll explain when she sees you. Can you come with me now, or should I call back another time?'

'*Ja, ja selvfølgelig,*' I stammer. Yes, indeed. 'I can come now.'

I fetch my shawl; wrap it around my head and shoulders as the local women do, and lace up my boots. Calling briefly to Lene that I'm going out, I close the door on her grumbling. She is sour about having to prepare the evening meal herself.

The snow crunches underfoot as we walk. The air is so icy it hurts to breathe it in.

'It's very cold,' I remark. I don't know what else to say.

'Yes, and likely to remain so for some time,' Peter tells me. 'Once the sea freezes, the cold spell can sometimes last the winter.'

My heart sinks at the thought of months of hunger.

'Have you walked on the sea yet?' Peter asks.

'Walked on it? No. Is it safe?' I ask, surprised.

'Yes, near the edge it's safe. Why don't we go down to the beach now?'

I hesitate a moment.

'Isn't it too cold?'

Peter is warmly dressed in a heavy overcoat, a fur hat with earflaps, a scarf and gloves. I have only my winter shawl. He looks at me for a moment.

146

'There's no wind today,' he says. 'So we should get warm walking. You'd better borrow my gloves and scarf at least.'

He wraps his scarf around me and pulls off his fur gloves and hands them to me, still warm from his own hands. They are huge on me and I have trouble getting them to stay on. We both laugh and suddenly I'm not so shy any more.

To my surprise there are lots of people on the sea, walking and even skating. Peter helps me scramble over the uneven ice at the edge of the sea and then draws my hand through his arm as we begin to walk out.

'To make sure you don't slip,' he explains. But the ice isn't as slippery as I expected, because it isn't completely smooth. There's also a covering of snow on top that crunches and squeaks underfoot. We walk a short way out to sea, and then turn and head northwards along the coast. At first I feel nervous that the ice might give way under my feet at any moment, but Peter laughs this fear away.

'The ice is very thick here on this coast where the sea is so shallow,' he assures me. He stamps down hard on the ice to show me it's as solid as the ground. 'You would have to go further out to be in any danger.'

A skater swoops past us, spraying snow up behind him.

'Do you skate?' I ask Peter.

'Yes, I do. When the sea is frozen, little work can be done. There's time to have fun. And you?'

'Oh, no. I never tried. There seem to be a lot of things everyone does here that I never tried,' I add.

Peter smiles down at me. 'You'll learn our ways in time. You are going to stay here, aren't you? You seem to be settling in well. You've learned a lot of Danish in a short time.'

'Yes. I mean no. Well . . . I haven't really decided. I wasn't planning to stay, but you're right, I am settling in,' I tell him. I fall silent, confused, thinking I've probably said the wrong thing.

I do think about leaving sometimes, but I still don't know where I'd go. I seem to be drifting, without any definite purpose. But almost to my surprise I'm happy here. I have friends.

I'm just getting used to the idea of walking on the sea, when Peter turns and leads me back to the beach again.

'We're level with our house now,' he tells me.

With Peter's help, I scramble back over the piles of ice that have blown onto the beach at the edge of the sea. Each time he turns to help me, he smiles at me, and holds my hands a little longer than strictly necessary. At first I blush, my heart beating fast. But then I find myself smiling happily back up at him.

When we can find no more excuses to linger on the ice, we walk through the sand dunes to his house. As we approach it, I can see a lamp lighted in the window, though the curtains are not yet drawn. I feel very nervous at the thought of meeting his family. I've only ever seen them at a distance.

We go through the front door into a hallway. The house seems very fine compared to the houses I've been in up to now. I wipe my boots nervously on the mat.

Peter takes my shawl. I return his scarf and gloves to him with a smile.

'They kept me very warm,' I tell him. 'Thank you.'

In the living room, a woman is sitting at the table with an embroidery frame, needle, and silks in her hands. When she sees us, she puts them down at once and comes to greet us, hand held out in welcome.

'*Så du er Marianne!*' So you are Marianne! 'I've been looking forward to meeting you,' she tells me with a friendly smile. I can see at once that she's Peter's mother. She has the same colouring, the same depth and indefinable colour in her eyes. Here in the house they appear grey, but I can imagine they would be blue or even green outdoors, as Peter's are.

'I'm Annette Hansen,' she tells me, drawing me to the table. '*Sæt dig.*' Sit down. I do so and at once notice the tablecloth. It's beautifully embroidered with a scattering of wild flowers. Sewn with exquisite, tiny stitches, it awakens my admiration at once. Peter's mother notices, and smiles.

'Charlotte tells me you are looking for work, sewing and embroidering. She showed me the handkerchiefs that you embroidered for her and Hannah for Christmas. Can you work like this too?' Annette asks, indicating the cloth.

I hesitate, unsure of my own abilities.

'Not exactly like this. I learned a different style in England . . . I'm not sure I can do anything as beautiful as this. But I would love to learn.'

Annette smiles, and pours me a cup of coffee into a fine china cup, stirring in a generous amount of cream and sugar. It tastes quite delicious. She offers me a dish of elegant little home-baked biscuits. I accept one and it melts on my tongue, leaving a fragrant buttery, vanilla flavour behind.

There are only two places set for coffee. Peter has withdrawn to the next room already. His mother sees me looking for him.

'Peter knows better than to sit listening to women's chat,' she says. 'He is the best son a mother could wish for,' she continues, dropping her voice confidentially. 'As soon as he heard I wished to speak to you, nothing was too much trouble. I was going to call on you at Jakobsens', everyone knows where the English girl is staying. But Peter insisted on going to fetch you.'

I flush with pleasure hearing this. I wonder if he's listening.

'Peter felt we would be more comfortable here,' continued Annette. 'How are you getting on staying at Jakobsens'? It is not what anyone would wish for, staying with that family.'

'I'm very grateful that they took me in,' I say, unwilling to criticize the family.

'It is no doubt more comfortable for you all without Jakobsen?' Annette says bluntly. I look at her amazed. 'You'll have to get used to my plain speaking,' she says. 'I can't be doing with the notion of only speaking well of the dead. The man was a drunken wastrel, and his dying doesn't alter it.'

I decide it's safest to say nothing.

'No doubt you'll wish to move on,' Annette continues

briskly. 'And I may be able to help you on your way with a little work, if you are able to sew as well as I think you do.'

I'm overwhelmed by her chatty manner, and her outspokenness. I can't help liking her for it. I've never met anyone like this before. It's as though she can read my thoughts. Not all of them though, I hope fervently.

'You have work for me?' I feel a great excitement at the prospect of earning my own money once more.

'I have more work than I can manage by myself now, but it is seasonal,' Annette explains. 'We have a small shop on the main street, Søndergade, where we sell the items I make to the summer visitors. Handkerchiefs, tablecloths, aprons and suchlike. There seem to be more visitors coming every year, and last summer I sold out before the season was over. I shouldn't like that to happen again this year.'

She pauses to refill my cup and to sip her own coffee.

'Would you like to help me? The only drawback is that I can only pay you a very little now. But I'll provide you with materials, and you'll be paid more when the items sell.'

'Yes, yes, of course . . . but . . . ' I falter a moment, and then ask in a rush, 'But why me? Is there no one else here in Skagen who embroiders?'

Annette laughs and her laughter is merry, like bells.

'Yes, but I require a very high standard. Do you know what we hear about the English?' she asks. 'They are too modest, too shy. I can see it's true.'

I'm not sure what I think of this. I sip my coffee again to cover up my confusion.

Peter comes back into the room. He draws the curtains and lights some candles.

'Don't tease Marianne, mother,' he says quietly.

I was right. He has been listening.

He catches my eye and smiles. My heart turns over. There's a happy glow spreading through me. Sitting here in this warm, candlelit room, with the prospect of work before me, and of coming and going in this house, I feel a thrill of delight. I look around me, drinking in the prettiness and daintiness of everything. The house itself is not so very different to where I live. But it's cared for. The walls are hung with shelves of china, instead of stinking fishing nets. The furniture is all freshly painted, with small white painted daisies adorning it. There's a picture of King Christian on the wall. I've become used to everything being functional, damaged, and shabby. The room feels spacious too, and I realize it's because there are no beds in here: they have separate bedrooms.

'Marianne?' Annette recalls my attention gently. 'Do you accept? Would you like to bring some of your work here tomorrow for me to look at?'

'*Ja. Ja, tak!*' Yes, thank you. I accept warmly, ashamed at my slowness. 'I was looking at your room. It's so pretty.' I can see at once I've said the right thing. She looks pleased.

'Good. That's settled then. Can you find your own way here, do you think? If Peter takes you home now?'

152

'Yes, of course,' I assure her, delighted at the thought of coming here again tomorrow. Annette twists the rest of the biscuits in a small piece of paper and presses them into my hand as I leave. 'For the Jakobsen children,' she says. I thank her and tuck them into my pocket.

Peter smiles as his mother tells him everything is settled. I shake her by the hand and take my leave. Peter wraps my shawl around me, and as we step out into the dark, he draws my hand through the crook of his arm again. I feel proud and happy to be walking through the town with Peter like this.

The short winter day is already over. The snow gleams in the darkness, lighting our way, and the sky is full of glittering stars.

'It gets dark so early here,' I remark.

'In the winter it does. But then in the summer it's light almost all the time.'

I take a deep breath of the clean pure air, and the cold is invigorating. The thought of summer is unimaginable at this moment.

When we reach Jakobsens', my heart sinks a little at the thought of going back into that noise and squalor. We stop, standing close to one another in the dark.

'I expect I'll see you tomorrow when you come to see my mother,' Peter says. 'There's no fishing to be done in this weather.' He hesitates a moment, and then draws a small package from his pocket. 'I have a small gift for you,' he says. 'It's nothing much,' he adds hurriedly. 'I was going to give it to you on Christmas Day, but you seemed upset.' He holds it out to me. My hands are clumsy with the cold as I unwrap it. There's a length of very fine ribbon and a paper twist of liquorice sweets from Brøndum's store.

'The ribbon's blue, to match your eyes,' he tells me softly.

'Thank you. Thank you so much.' I'm surprised and touched by his thoughtfulness. I offer my hand. Peter takes it, but instead of shaking it, he just holds it in both his.

'You're welcome,' he says, but he doesn't let go. I stand still, hardly daring to breathe. His hands are warm, despite the cold air. Our breath steams into the icy night, swirling and mingling. Peter moves a little closer, and my heart begins to hammer painfully in my chest.

But Lise opens the door behind me and puts her head out.

'Marianne!' she cries joyfully, wrapping her arms around my legs, which is as high as she can reach.

The spell is broken. Peter releases my hand, wishes me goodnight, and disappears into the darkness.

EIGHTEEN

March 1886

I had hoped it might be Peter when I heard the knock on the door this afternoon. But I should have known better. Since the thaw came at the end of January he's been out fishing every day. He's rarely home now when I go to Annette's. I only see him on Sundays, when he often walks me home from church. But having been trapped in the house for a week by heavy rain and flooding, I was pleased to have any visitor. The sight of Mikkel at the door was a welcome one.

The floodwater's up to my knees now and it's bitterly cold. My feet are so numb that I can no longer feel whether it's sand or grass underfoot.

'We're nearly there,' Mikkel encourages me. 'The boat is just round here.'

It's all very well for him. He's borrowed his father's thigh-length fishing boots.

'Will it get any deeper?' I ask, struggling to keep my dress dry. I'm also carrying a parcel of finished embroidery for Annette.

'Just a little. Why don't you let me carry your parcel for you?'

Reluctantly I hand it over, and hitch my skirt right up above my knees. It's been raining non-stop for the last week. Not merely raining, either. Pouring out of the sky as though it will never stop, finding every leak in our ill-thatched roof, and splashing into the wooden pails I've set to catch the drips. I even have to get up in the night to empty them. Today is almost the first pause we've had, and the sky is threatening even now.

'There's the boat,' says Mikkel pointing.

But I'm looking at the flooded town, which I haven't seen until now.

'All the paths have been turned into waterways,' I exclaim. 'Does this happen often?'

It seems to me everyone is taking it very calmly. They are merely getting out their small boats and rowing where they usually walk.

'We often have a week or so under water each year,' Mikkel tells me.

Getting into a small boat is much harder than I expected. As soon as I try and put any weight on the side, it tips wildly towards me.

Mikkel is laughing, and it's catching.

'Wait!' he orders, and wades around the boat in order to hold down the far side.

'You can climb in now—but remember: it's a boat, not a tree!'

As if I've ever climbed a tree.

I try to get in elegantly, but end up in a mad scramble, getting my skirt wet after all and stubbing my toes.

'Ouch!' I hold my bruised, numb toes in one hand

and cling to the side with the other, waiting for the rocking to stop.

Mikkel hands me my precious parcel and unties the rope. He then hops neatly in.

'How do you do that so easily?' I ask, jealous.

'I've had lots of practice, of course,' Mikkel answers with a shrug. Boats are a part of his life.

'I shall obviously have to try this a few more times,' I remark ruefully.

Sitting facing me, Mikkel pushes the oars into the water, fitting them into the rowlocks. With a few deft pulls, he steers us out into deeper water and towards the main street. I watch him rowing and decide it looks quite easy. He's pulling strongly on the oars now.

'I'm glad you came,' I say. 'I was so bored. Yesterday I even ran out of sewing to do. It's kind of you to take me to Annette's.'

'You're welcome. I thought you might be getting tired of Lene's company by now.'

We grin at each other, and then come round a half submerged sand dune into the main street.

'Oh!' I cry in surprise. 'So that's why so many of these houses have little bridges in front of them.'

I had simply accepted the bridges as an architectural feature of Skagen, but now I can see that each house is built slightly raised, and the bridges link the submerged road with the houses. Many of the bridges have small craft tied to them, and a number of people are rowing up or down the street, or pushing their boats along with a long pole.

'Our very own Venice!' Mikkel tells me, and there's a note of pride in his voice I've rarely heard there before.

'*God dag, Mikkel,*' calls a man I don't know from another small craft.

Mikkel merely nods to him and seems a little out of breath.

'Would you like me to take a turn?' I ask.

He pauses and looks at me. There's a smile lurking in his eyes.

'Have you ever rowed?'

'Well, no. But I've watched. And you can teach me how. I'm much stronger than when I first came here.'

It's true and Mikkel knows it, but the smile in his eyes has deepened.

'Maybe on the way back,' Mikkel says, and there's a teasing note in his voice. 'You wouldn't like to get your sewing wet before you've delivered it.'

I bite my lip and look away. I won't give him the angry reaction he's hoping for. No one ever teased me before I met Mikkel, and it hasn't been easy to learn how to respond. I try to think of something to say to regain my dignity, but nothing comes to mind.

We are passing Mikkel's house now. It's built on higher ground, and the floodwater hasn't quite reached it.

'Did your father build the house?' I ask.

Today, Mikkel is more communicative than usual.

'No, my grandfather built it. My father's father. But my mother is from a well-to-do farming family south of here. So when they were married, my father extended the house.'

'And is your grandfather still alive?'

'No, he died before I was born. In fact I think it was his death that brought my father back to Skagen.'

'Back? From where?'

I'm curious about my uncle, and even more curious to hear something about my father.

'Father doesn't talk about it,' is Mikkel's reply, as he pulls hard on the oars again to get out of the way of another boat.

'Never? But surely you must know something of where he went? I mean, why did he leave Skagen? I didn't think many people did.'

Mikkel rests his oars a moment, and looks straight at me. He's glowing with the exercise and his eyes are very bright.

'You're asking a lot of questions.'

'I'm interested. You don't talk much about your family.'

'You don't talk about yours at all,' he retorts.

I sit back and look down at my feet. 'Sorry,' I say.

'It's all right,' he sighs. 'My father had arguments with his father, I think. They didn't get on. So he and his brother ran away together. They worked on various boats, and saw a bit of the world.' Mikkel pauses, and then bursts into speech again. 'So he can't really tell me I must spend all my life here, can he? I mean, he didn't. He went away.'

I want to shake the information out of Mikkel. He just mentioned my father and now he's off on a different tack.

I've known Mikkel for half a year and I can see he

159

doesn't fit in here. He knows everyone, and is well liked, but nevertheless, he's an outsider. His interests and his intellect divide him from those around him. He loves the place; the heath land, the wildlife, the coast, but there's no suitable companionship here for him. I suppose he seeks my friendship because I, too, am different.

'Are you sure it wouldn't be worth speaking to him again?' I ask.

Mikkel shakes his head impatiently.

'He'll never listen. He doesn't understand.'

I nod sympathetically. We've talked about this before.

'Perhaps he even went to Copenhagen himself,' I suggest, and I feel like a louse, trying to extract information from my friend in this way.

Mikkel is staring out at the water, his eyes unfocused, allowing the boat to drift. He doesn't answer me.

'So what happened to his brother?' I ask.

Mikkel looks at me blankly.

'You said your father went away with his brother.'

'Oh. He drowned. Crossing back from England, I think,' Mikkel says vaguely. It's obviously not a subject that interests him much.

'Was your father with him in England?'

'No idea. He's never mentioned going to England. Why are you so interested in my family history all of a sudden?'

We're as close to Peter's house as we can get now, and Mikkel is busy shipping his oars and climbing out.

Because you're my cousin, but I can't tell you, I think silently. But I just smile and say, 'Because you're my

160

friend, that's why.' And as I climb out into the icy water, I pause and give his shoulder a friendly squeeze.

Mikkel grins, pleased, and puts his free arm around my shoulders and gives me a quick hug in return.

Together we turn towards the house, and I see both Annette and Peter standing at the door. I'm slightly embarrassed when I realize they've been watching us. Annette smiles and calls out:

'Come in, come in and warm yourselves!' She throws the door wide open.

Peter, on the other hand, stands stiff and unsmiling. His handshake is formal and cold. The shock goes right through me, leaving my hands tingling unpleasantly. What can be wrong? I'm so bad at reading and understanding people's behaviour. I haven't had enough practice.

We've come in through the outer workroom today, so Annette leads us past the nets hanging partly mended and the salting vat, three quarters full of fish. There are chickens clucking softly in a pen in one corner. I hesitate before following Annette through into the kitchen but Peter has gone back to mending his nets and doesn't even glance at me again. Reluctantly, I leave him.

The kettle is singing over a bright fire. It's a welcome and cheerful sight. A contrast to the greyness of the weather outside the house.

'You'll want some coffee to warm you up. Go through and take a seat by the stove.'

Mikkel and I both go through into the living room and sit as close to the stove as we can get. It radiates

161

heat, and I can hear the cheerful crackle of the flames inside.

My toes are thawing, tingling painfully in the warmth, when Annette comes in with coffee for us. I can feel my cheeks beginning to glow.

'I brought the aprons and handkerchiefs back,' I tell Annette. 'They've been ready for two days but I didn't know how to get here to give them to you and fetch more work. Mikkel very kindly offered to bring me in his boat.'

Annette smiles approvingly at Mikkel. 'If I had known you'd have these done so quickly, I'd have sent Peter by with some more.'

How I wish she had known.

She's unpacking the work I've done. As always, I'm nervous, holding my breath as she examines them.

'Beautifully done, Marianne. You can be proud of yourself.'

I let my breath go in a sigh of relief.

'Thank you.' A flush of pleasure adds to the colour in my cheeks.

'Yes, very nice indeed,' repeats Annette. 'And do you have a little time, Mikkel, to wait while I show Marianne what I'd like her to do next?'

'Of course,' says Mikkel politely.

Annette fetches more work for me, spreading it out on the dining table. I get up to look.

Mikkel wanders out. I can hear him talking. I'm straining to hear if it's Peter he's talking to, and what they are saying, but I can't make it out.

'Now, Marianne. I'm giving you a tablecloth to do next, and I'd like you to put some of your blue flowers in each of the four corners. You do those so beautifully. And something in the middle. Do you have any ideas? I thought perhaps a wreath of flowers?'

I force myself to focus on what she's saying to me.

'A wreath would be pretty,' I respond absently. My mind is with Peter.

Usually I enjoy my time with Annette, but today I'm longing to escape. I want to see Peter again before I leave, hoping to read something more friendly in his face.

There's a knock at the front door and Annette hurries to answer it. When I hear her ushering friends in, I slip out to the workroom to find Peter and Mikkel. They don't see me at first. Peter is scowling at Mikkel. As I walk in, I hear him say, 'Why don't you just take your sweetheart and go, and stop bothering me with idle chatter.' It sounds so unlike him. I pause in the doorway, astonished.

'I told you, she's not my sweetheart, we're friends,' says Mikkel, sounding taken aback.

'So that's why you were hugging her right under my nose, is it?' demands Peter.

I can't believe it, he's jealous. *Jealous*. He's dropped the nets and is glaring at poor Mikkel. Mikkel sees me. His fair face is flushed red.

'Marianne, Peter seems to think . . . '

I, too, am embarrassed by the situation. 'It's true,' I stammer. 'We're just friends.' Peter looks sceptical. I walk over to him and put my hand on his arm, forcing myself to look directly at him. 'It's true,' I assure him. As we look at each other, I see the anger and jealousy fade from his face. His eyes soften, making me feel breathless. I hear Mikkel shift uncomfortably behind me, but he is spared by Annette bustling into the room, my parcel of work in her arms, and some coins in her hand.

'Ah, there you are, Marianne,' she says. 'Here's your next work and your payment.'

Peter grins a little shamefacedly at me as we shake hands to leave. I also hear him muttering a brief word of apology to Mikkel.

'*Farvel*, Peter,' I say. Goodbye. And then I step outside and wade back to the boat.

As Mikkel takes the oars and turns the boat to row away, I look back. Peter is at the door with his mother, and lifts his hand in a farewell gesture. I wave back and smile.

'Can I have a turn rowing?' I ask Mikkel as soon as we are out of sight of the house.

'I wish you'd said before we started,' complains Mikkel. 'Now we'll have to change places. Can you wait until we are out into the main street? There'll be more people on hand to help when you overturn us.'

This time I completely take his bait:

'What do you mean, overturn us?' I cry indignantly. 'What makes you—'

And then I stop myself abruptly. Mikkel is grinning broadly at me. Annoyed with myself, I dip my hand into the water, scoop up a handful, and throw it at him.

It catches him in the face, leaving droplets of water

on his spectacles. He takes up the challenge at once. Unfortunately for me, he has the oars. A great wave of water drenches me, leaving me gasping.

'Please, don't: it's much too cold!'

Then we're both laughing. The awkwardness following the misunderstanding at the Hansens' has been overcome.

'All right, you can row. As long as you promise not to use the oars to splash me.'

'That's hardly fair,' I point out indignantly.

'Promise, or you don't have a turn,' Mikkel insists.

'Very well then, I promise.' I'm keen to try rowing.

It is harder to change places in a small boat than I had thought.

'Keep your weight as low as possible. Whatever you do, don't stand up,' Mikkel instructs.

I do try, but the boat rocks wildly as we get in one another's way trying to swap seats. I end up banging my knee and stubbing my toes again. Unladylike words rise to my tongue, but I bite them back.

'Take the oars,' says Mikkel, holding them out towards me.

I grasp them.

'But they are so heavy!' I can't help exclaiming, as I struggle to hold the unwieldy shafts.

'What did you expect?'

Mikkel's chuckling. He enjoys teaching me things he can do well. It gives him a sense of superiority. He needs that. His dreadful father despises him so much.

'You need to make sure they are tilted right, with the blade vertical, before you try to pull with them,' Mikkel explains. 'Lean forward, push the oars back, lower them into the water. That's right. Now pull on them.'

One oar digs deep and gets stuck, the other flies up out of the water, spraying us both. The boat spins wildly and I almost fall off my seat.

'No, not like that,' Mikkel laughs. He leans towards me. Putting his hands on mine, he guides my next few strokes until I get a feel for how it should be.

After a few minutes, Mikkel lets me try alone again. This time I do better, but I'm amazed at how much strength it takes. My strokes are ragged and uneven, and my arms quickly begin to ache. I'm weak after the two long months we had without enough food. I know I've lost weight, because my dress hangs loose on me still.

Mikkel is a patient teacher, and I persevere. We make our way slowly back through the town, turning only the occasional circle. Mikkel takes the oars again the last stretch. I wouldn't admit it to him, but my arms, my shoulders, and back are aching unbearably and my palms are sore.

'Would you like to practise some more tomorrow?' Mikkel asks.

I hesitate a moment, thinking of Peter. But I'm not going to miss the chance to learn to row.

'Yes, please. I should like that very much. Perhaps we could go down as far as the post. I have a letter to send to England now I finally have some money.'

'Yes, of course,' promises Mikkel. 'You did well today,' he admits. 'I was surprised. Boats must be in your blood.'

'Yes, I think they must be,' I agree quietly.

NINETEEN

April 1886

I awake at first light, which is early now that we're in April. The days are lengthening. I have to get up to prepare breakfast for Morten and Jakob before they go fishing. Their team is working on the west coast at the moment. I ease myself out of bed, trying not to disturb Lise or her sisters. But this morning she must be sleeping lightly, because she wakes at once.

'Try and go back to sleep,' I whisper.

I shake the boys awake and then go out to the kitchen. Lifting the turf I laid over the embers last night, I painstakingly feed and gently blow on the glow until I have a small fire. It's a good morning when the fire lights easily.

'*Må jeg hjælpe?*' asks Lise. Can I help? She's already out of bed.

'Shhh!' I hush her. 'Don't wake your mother and sisters yet. You can break up the bread,' I tell her, passing her a stale rye loaf. I pour water into the pan from the jug, and put it in front of her. She pulls the bread into chunks with her small fingers and drops it into the water, while I slice the dried fish for the midday meal and put it in water to soak. It is wonderful to have enough food in the house again after the months of hunger we endured.

'Don't throw the bread in, Lise,' I remind her as the water splashes right out of the pan.

When she's finished, I add some ale and put the pan over the fire to bubble gently. It makes a thick, sour gruel, which we eat some mornings for our breakfast. When money is very short we have to make do with dried or salted fish only. The gruel is more filling.

It's a relief not to be standing ankle deep in water in the kitchen any more. There have been many days over the last few weeks when I had to do just that. Now the water levels have dropped and the sand floor is merely damp. The advantage of the high water was that I learned to row. I'm proud of my rowing skills.

Morten and Jakob stumble out into the tiny kitchen, fully dressed, rubbing their eyes and yawning. They eat their breakfast standing up, shovelling the hot food into their mouths as quickly as possible, because dawn is turning the sky grey in the east. They set out barefoot for the west coast. Like most of the poor families in Skagen, they can't afford boots or waterproofs, but work up to their chests in seawater all year round, dressed only in thick, hand-knitted woollens. Often the fishing is done at night. It's a wonder to me they keep healthy.

'Come and help me put away our bed, Lise,' I urge, as soon as I hear the baby crying and the other children stirring.

'*God morgen*, Lene,' I say as I see she's awake. But Lene chooses to ignore me today.

After breakfast, once the older girls have gone to school, I spend a couple of hours mending everyone's clothes. I look longingly at my embroidery, but that will have to wait until the chores are done.

At noon I fry fish and wrap them for the boys to eat.

'I want to come with you,' Lise begs me. 'I don't want to be left behind with mother.'

I hope she didn't overhear that.

'It's too far to the west coast, Lise,' I tell her. She hunches an angry shoulder and stalks off behind the house.

Taking the wheelbarrow from the shed to bring the boys' share of the catch back in, I head for the west coast. In fine weather, it's one of the pleasantest parts of the day. There's also always the hope I'll see Peter out fishing, but today I don't.

I find the fishing team on the beach sharing out the morning's catch.

'*Frokost!*' Lunch, I say to Morten and Jakob as I hand over the food.

'*Tak*,' Morten replies, as he loads the barrow with their share of fish.

Pushing it back home is hard physical work, but I've got stronger through the spring.

On the return journey I spot a figure with binoculars lying in last year's dead brown heather. It can only be Mikkel.

Glad of the excuse to rest, I abandon my wheelbarrow and pick my way through the heather towards him, wary of adders.

'*Hej*, Mikkel!' I greet him.

He rolls over to look at me, a finger on his lips and I

169

approach as quietly as possible until I am crouching beside him.

'Can you see the larks? They are full of joy that the spring has come at last!' Mikkel whispers, his face shining with pleasure.

I smile at him.

'I'm very well thank you, how are you?' I respond.

Mikkel looks puzzled.

'I didn't ask how you were, did I?'

'No, but as you haven't seen me for over a week, it would have been polite,' I remark.

Mikkel merely grins and turns back to the larks.

I can hear them singing before I see them. Mikkel is right. It's a clear song, ringing with joy.

He points out the tiny brown lark to me as it spirals up into the sky. It is hard to believe such a big song can come from such a small bird.

'Would you like a turn with the binoculars?' Mikkel asks. 'Here. You focus them by turning this,' he explains. I notice his hands are raw and cracked, and have been bleeding.

'Your poor hands!' I exclaim.

He whips them out of sight, and I understand he doesn't want to talk about it.

I turn away and look through the binoculars. It takes me a few moments to find the lark. I catch my breath, as I realize I can see every detail of its markings; it looks so close I could touch it.

Mikkel is sketching it as I watch. His drawing isn't bad.

'Can I have a go?' I ask longingly.

Taking a last, long look, I hand over the binoculars and sketch the bird. It feels good to have a pencil in my hand again. As I try to capture the essence of its shape and markings, I become completely absorbed, forgetting where I am.

'Superb, Marianne!' breathes Mikkel. The scent of the heather and the sound of the lark's song return as his words reach me. 'I wish I could draw like that.'

'I'll try and teach you,' I promise, handing back the sketchbook regretfully.

I get up, brushing bits of dried heather from my skirt.

'I haven't seen much of you,' I say, trying not to make it sound like a complaint. 'Have you been busy?'

Mikkel's face darkens.

'My father decided it was time to have another go at making a fisherman of me.' He gets up too, and the pleasure that lit his face while he was watching the lark is gone.

'And has he succeeded?' I ask cautiously.

'Hardly. I was shouted at for not rowing strongly enough. And when I was helping with the nets . . . ' Mikkel falls silent, scowling at a memory.

'Tell me?' I encourage him.

'The nets tear my hands and the salt water burns them. I was trying my best to ignore it, I really was. Pulling hard on the nets. Not hard enough for my father though. He kept taunting me. Comparing me to Christen, my younger brother. Reminding me that he's two years younger than me, but already doing the work of a grown man.'

Mikkel pauses again, audibly grinding his teeth.

'So I pulled even harder. And slipped. I was standing up to my waist in water at the time, so I went right under. I swallowed seawater. My father practically hauled me out of the water by my hair. And he forced *snaps* down my throat. He knows I hate the stuff. It made me choke and I was sick. Over him, of course. He sent me home in disgrace and that was that.'

'I'm so sorry! You should have told me before,' I say, but I can see in his face why he didn't. He's ashamed of his failure. 'I'd hoped to speak to you on Sunday after church,' I add.

Mikkel looks embarrassed.

'Believe it or not, my father has ordered me to spend less time with you in future. He doesn't think you are . . . well, he doesn't want me to see you as much.' Mikkel's words are filled with a cold anger.

'Not fit company for his son?' I ask bitterly. It's my turn to blush. It's a shock, but hardly a surprise. He ordered me to stay away from Mikkel and I ignored him. This is the next logical step. I can feel anger towards Mikkel's father building up in me again. We walk the last few steps towards my wheelbarrow in uncomfortable silence. We don't look at one another.

'I'm sorry. I shouldn't have told you that,' Mikkel says at last.

I pick up the handles of the wheelbarrow and give it a vicious shove, imagining Mikkel's father's face beneath the wheel.

'You'd have to explain somehow. Did he tell you why?'

'No, he wouldn't say,' Mikkel replies, shaking his head.

'Are you going to obey him?'

Mikkel hesitates.

'You are! Why? Does he beat you or something?' I ask.

Mikkel nods ruefully. 'Not often. I usually take care not to give him reason. He's always been very strict with all of us. He has quite a reputation.'

'So I've heard. Does that mean we can't be friends any more?' Even I can hear the forlorn note in my voice.

'Of course we can still be friends. He hasn't forbidden me to see you entirely. I just thought, on Sunday, when he was watching, it was better to avoid angering him. Can I push that barrow for you for a while?'

'If it won't hurt your hands too much.'

He shakes his head, and I let him take it. I am confused and hurt and it's making me feel sick. I've put up with so much hardship here, and it's my friendships with Hannah, Peter, and Mikkel that have kept me going. I couldn't bear to lose him.

Mikkel is not the only person out on the heath today. Sitting in a sheltered hollow, we see a lady sitting at an easel, painting. A little girl, two or three years old, is playing with some shells at her feet. I recognize Anna Ancher and her daughter Helga at once.

Curiosity overcomes my shyness, and I approach her to look more closely at her painting. The Anchers are a class apart, living quietly through winter until the artists from Norway, Sweden, Copenhagen, and even Paris, gather in Skagen for the summer months. The Anchers are well liked. I myself found out how kind they were when I first arrived in Skagen.

Anna Ancher looks up as we approach.

'Ah!' she says, and smiles. 'Marianne, isn't it? And Mikkel.'

I'm surprised that she remembers my name and instinctively drop a polite curtsey. Then I feel stupid, because that's an English habit, and not really the Danish way of doing things.

Anna continues painting as she asks me, 'How have you settled in here, Marianne?'

'Very well, thank you. I even have work now, for Fru Hansen.'

'And you've learned to speak Danish very prettily too, I hear. Well done.' She flashes me a quick smile, but I hardly notice. My eyes are devouring the painting of Helga and the way she is delicately touching the colours onto the canvas. What amazes me most is the way she's captured the sunlight falling onto her daughter. It looks so real. I wonder how she's done it.

'It's beautiful,' I tell her impulsively. Then I crouch down to speak to the little girl to hide my shyness.

'How do you like to have a picture painted of yourself?' I ask her.

She looks at me with the curious, open gaze of childhood.

'Oh, mother is always painting me,' she says indifferently.

Anna laughs.

Mikkel has flipped open his sketchbook, and is showing

174

her my drawing of the lark. Anna Ancher looks at it, and then looks eagerly at me.

'That's good,' she says warmly. 'Can you paint?'

'No,' I reply quietly. 'I've never tried.'

'Do you draw a lot?' she asks. 'I'd be interested in seeing your pictures.'

'I do, but mostly on a slate,' I tell her. 'So I'm afraid there's nothing to show.'

Anna nods, looking disappointed, and turns back to mixing more blue and white on her palette and adding it to the sky. We walk on, and Mikkel pushes the barrow for me again.

When I'm home and Mikkel has taken his leave, I sigh, wrap a large apron around myself, and begin to behead and gut the fish. It's a smelly, messy job and I loathe it. I know my hands will stink of fish for the rest of the day, no matter how thoroughly I wash them.

I tie the cleaned plaice up on the big wooden drying frame outside the house, and toss the heads and entrails onto the midden heap. A couple of gulls come to squabble over the scraps.

I'm in the middle of hanging up the washing the following morning when a ragged boy appears. He's barefoot, and has a flat parcel tucked under his arm.

'*Hedder du Marianne?*' he asks. Are you Marianne?

'*Ja, det er mig,*' I agree, and he holds out the parcel to me. Hastily wiping my wet hands on my apron, I take it, but I wonder if there's been a mistake.

'From Fru Ancher,' the boy enlightens me. 'She gave me ten øre for bringing it to you!' And with a delighted grin at the thought of such riches, he leaves.

I carry the parcel carefully indoors, and lay it reverently on the table. It's wrapped in brown paper and neatly tied with string. Lise is jumping up and down excitedly.

'Oh, Marianne, what is it?'

Lene looks sourly on, and Lise dances around me. With trembling fingers, I carefully untie the knots and unwrap the paper.

Inside is a beautiful sketchpad. We all gasp in surprise. The sheets of paper are creamy and smooth. I run my fingertips over them in a daze. Wrapped separately inside the parcel are several pencils.

'She's so kind,' I murmur. There's a little note, hand-written in Danish. I stare at it, without being able to make sense of it for several moments. It simply says, *Til Marianne, med hilsner fra Anna Ancher*. To Marianne, with best wishes.

Lise is already tugging at my hand, wanting my attention: 'Can I have the wrapping paper, Marianne?' she's demanding.

I'm speechless, and can only nod.

TWENTY

May 1886

I see Hannah walking quickly towards the house while I'm washing Lise's hair. My own hair is still drying.

'What can Hannah be doing here at this time?' I remark conversationally to Lise, starting to rub her hair dry with a towel. 'She should be working at the hotel.'

'Ow! You're hurting me,' Lise complains.

'Go inside now, Lise, and ask your mother to comb your hair,' I order her, handing her the towel.

My attention is on Hannah. As soon as she sees me looking at her, she breaks into a run, slipping a little in the soft sand.

'Marianne!' she calls out.

'Is something wrong?' I ask as soon as she reaches me. But Hannah is smiling and her eyes are shining.

'They want you to come, and you can share a room with me. It'll be such fun—say yes!'

I give her a friendly shake.

'Tell me slower, Hannah!' I ask. Danish can still confuse me when it's spoken fast.

Hannah takes a deep breath and lets it go, beaming at me.

'Hr Krøyer arrived in the night, when no one realized he was coming.'

'Who's Hr Krøyer?'

'He's a friend of Michael Ancher, a famous artist. He nearly always comes here in the summer to paint. Usually we know when he's coming and the whole town goes to greet him with flowers and music and everything. Only last night, he arrived without warning, and no one knew he was here until he walked into the hotel.'

'And what does it have to do with me?'

'He's brought a French gentleman with him. He's an artist too. And his wife is with him. She needs a new maid, and she only speaks French. So we thought . . . we wondered if you'd like to be her maid while she's here. Because you speak French. She's very grand, Marianne. She has silk dresses and jewels and lots of luggage.'

'But I've never been a maid. I wouldn't know what to do.' The world is suddenly spinning faster. Hannah is so excited, and I'm having trouble taking it all in.

'She already knows that, and you'd earn a little less to begin with. But the hotel will pay you for any extra work you do. Oh and, Marianne, you can come and share my room at the hotel with me!'

'Leave here? Really?' I look around at the squalor and ugliness and think of the beauty of the hotel that I glimpsed last summer. It's beginning to sink in now. I could leave this house. I've been longing to get away since I came.

'It sounds too good to be true,' I say.

Lise, who didn't go indoors as I asked her, has understood enough so that she's started to cry.

'Don't go away, Marianne! Please don't leave us,' she begs.

I pick her up and hug her close. I feel guilty that I can go so easily, when I know how much I've meant to Lise. But I have to take this opportunity.

'*Du må ikke græde*, Lise,' I tell her. Don't cry. 'Nothing's certain yet. And if I do go, it won't be far. I promise I'll come back and visit you.'

But Lise is inconsolable.

'Marianne, the French madame wants to meet you right away,' Hannah urges. 'Come on, put on your shoes and come with me.'

I carry Lise indoors to her mother and peel her off me.

'I have to go to Brøndum's Hotel,' I explain to Lene. 'It seems they might give me a job.'

Lene greets the news with an even more stony silence than usual. I'm not even sure if she's heard me.

'You don't need me any more now,' I say, unsure whether I'm trying to reassure her or myself. She looks away.

I quickly change my work clothes for my smart dress and brush and pin up my hair. It's still damp, but I don't think it shows. At least Hannah didn't fetch me in the middle of gutting fish.

'I'm very nervous,' I confide, as Hannah and I wade through the sand of the main street, heading north to Brøndums Hotel. 'What if she doesn't like me?'

179

'Don't worry, Marianne,' says Hannah. 'She'll love you, we all do.'

She stops in the middle of the main street and gives me a big hug.

I feel a rush of affection for her, but she's already walking on, talking again.

'We are going to be so busy. They're expecting lots more visitors. There will be parties and grand dinners and fun.'

A most unwelcome thought strikes me, and I interrupt her in a panic:

'Hannah, I'm not sure I can remember a single word of French! I've filled my head up completely with Danish!'

'Won't it come back to you?' asks Hannah.

'I can only hope so,' I say, thinking frantically.

'*Bonjour, Madame*,' I say experimentally. '*Je suis Marianne. Comment . . . har De det . . .* Oh no, that's Danish. This is no good. Danish words keep getting in the way.'

Hannah points the French lady out to me in the garden and gives me a little push. 'Go and tell her who you are,' she says. 'She's expecting you. Her name is Madame Perroy.'

Madame Perroy is reclining languidly in a deckchair in the shade, her eyes closed. Her embroidery is lying beside her on the grass. I address her tentatively.

'*Madame?*'

The lady opens her eyes. They are dark, with long dark lashes. She's a petite brunette, and my first impression of her is that she's young and pretty. She's wearing a pink dress, cut low to reveal as much of her plump bosom as is decent, or perhaps a little more. Her hair is elaborately dressed, and rings flash on the hand she waves sleepily at me.

'*Ah, vous êtes la bonne?*' You're the maid?

'*Oui, Madame.*'

I drop a curtsey, English style, and the lady nods approvingly.

'*Très bien!*' she exclaims. 'Jean-Pierre!' she calls imperatively and a man detaches himself from a group of guests and walks over to join us. He's not particularly tall and is, like his wife, expensively dressed. I look at his handsome face; dark haired with an elegantly curled moustache, but no beard. He looks completely different to the men of Skagen.

Husband and wife are chattering in French together, much too fast for me to follow. After a few minutes, the gentleman turns to me.

'I am Monsieur Perroy,' he tells me in French. 'My wife will be very happy to employ you as her personal maid.'

He takes me aside.

'We can agree a wage, I think, no?' he asks. He suggests a sum, and it's more than I hoped for. I calculate the sum in my head quickly, wondering how long they will be staying here. My heart misses a beat with excitement.

'Thank you,' I say with a curtsey and a smile. 'I accept.'

'*Très bien,*' he nods in satisfaction, and we return to his wife.

'Marianne, you must come to me *tout de suite*.' At once, Madame insists. 'For I need someone to do my hair for dinner tonight.'

Her hair looks beautifully dressed already to me, and I hesitate a moment. It seems ungrateful to the Jakobsen family to leave in such haste. They gave me food and shelter when I most desperately needed it. But I've worked hard for many months to repay them. I don't want to offend my new employers.

'At once? *Mais bien sûr*,' I say at last, and curtsey again. 'I just need to pack.'

I find Hannah and tell her the good news. She has anticipated it by begging a couple of hours off to help me move.

'But first you must come and see our room,' Hannah tells me, and leads me up several flights of stairs to the hotel attics.

We have a tiny room with a sloping ceiling and a bed to share.

'Everything is so new and clean,' I say, admiringly. 'I've never lived anywhere this nice!' I run my hand along the bed and the wall, hardly able to believe it's all real.

If I stand on tiptoe, there is a view from the small window down across the garden. Hannah hugs me again excitedly.

'I'm so glad it's you I'm to share with! It's the first year I've lived in. Last summer I slept at home still. It's going to be such fun, Marianne, just wait and see. Company and parties; all the grand visitors. And it's still only May! We have the whole summer before us.'

I smile at Hannah, enjoying her delight. I'm still in a bit of a daze. But my heart is beating faster and my hands are trembling. I think it must be excitement.

Hannah and I walk back to the Jakobsens' together. I stop at a store on the main street to purchase a few gifts for the family. A ribbon for Lise to wear in her hair and sugar and butter for the store cupboard.

'Marianne, that must be all your money,' Hannah whispers.

'Most of it, but I'll soon be earning more,' I whisper back. 'I have to show them my gratitude somehow.'

Hannah sniffs. I know she doesn't think I have anything to be grateful for.

It doesn't take long to pack my few possessions. Leaving my trunk to be collected later, I bid farewell to Lene, Lise, and the other children. Lise is very tearful, and hugs me for a long time.

'I promise I'll come back and see you,' I reassure her. 'Look, Lise, I'm going to tie this ribbon into your hair. This is to remember me by. Isn't it pretty?'

I worry for her. I don't trust her mother to look after her as well as I've done.

I pick up the baby for a goodbye kiss. The other children hug me too, and even Lene shakes me by the hand and says a gruff farewell.

I leave as I came, my carpet bag in one hand, accompanied by Hannah. It occurs to me, as I walk, that this job might give me the means to leave Skagen altogether. I don't ask myself if that's still what I want. The answer is too confusing.

TWENTY-ONE

Madame is pouting at herself in the mirror again. She doesn't like the way I've done her hair.

'*Non, non*, Marianne!' she announces at last with an emphatic shake of her head. '*Encore une fois!*' Do it again.

My heart sinks.

For the third time this evening, I take out the pins and brush her long, glossy hair.

I've only ever attempted simple hairstyles before. I've been here a week now, and I'm finding Madame very demanding.

In fact she's a lot like Lise. Only far more spoiled.

She should be equally easy to manage. Once I've learned to do her hair.

My fingers are aching by the time her hair is done. I'm becoming hot and bothered. I don't think I'm cut out to be a maid; I feel like leaving the room and slamming the door behind me. Luckily, this time she's satisfied. Suddenly she's all smiles. I'm her *chère Marianne*. That will last until I do something else wrong, and then she'll be throwing her hairbrush or her shoes at me again. I hope I can last the summer without throwing them back.

185

Madame is powdering her face now, and spraying scent on her bosom. I fasten her sapphire necklace, and she contemplates her reflection in the mirror.

'*Bien!*' she announces at last. 'I will go down now. I will send for you when I'm ready to go to bed.'

'*Oui, Madame.*'

I curtsey in mock humility as she sweeps out of the room, silken skirts rustling. With a sigh, I begin gathering up the discarded gowns that are lying higgledy-piggledy on the bed, and the several pairs of costly leather shoes that were rejected. There's going to be a grand dinner party tonight, and dressing for it was a lengthy process. A large party of artists and other important visitors are coming to dine together at the hotel. I've been helping in the kitchen most of the day and must hurry back there as soon as I've finished tidying Madame's room.

I can't wait to go back down. I've whipped cream and chopped vegetables and fruit. I've helped prepare foods so exotic I'd never seen them before.

Last night the artist Carl Locher arrived from Copenhagen. He came by boat from Copenhagen to Frederikshavn, and his cart was pulled up the beach to Skagen by oxen. The whole town turned out to greet him, lining the main street, waving and cheering as he passed. Outside the hotel he was stopped and presented with a huge wreath of flowers. It was a bit like a royal visit from Queen Victoria herself. Hr Locher's not staying here at Brøndum's. He prefers quieter lodgings. He's coming to the party tonight though.

Tying on a large apron I hurry to take a turn with the washing up. The kitchen is full of steam and delicious cooking smells. Over the clatter of saucepans and crackle of the fire there is the chatter of excited and flustered voices as everyone works to prepare the meal. Fru Brøndum works everyone hard, but no one harder than herself.

'Hurry up with that sauce!' she cries across the kitchen.

'Where are the knives that were polished this morning?' cries another voice in a panic.

I still feel very new and I'm glad to have Hannah. I look over to where she is basting the leg of pork on the spit. Her face is shiny and red and her hair is sticking to her forehead. She sees me looking at her, and we exchange a smile.

Finding an excuse to come across the kitchen, Hannah stops by me and murmurs, 'And how did Madame look? Will she outshine the local beauties?'

'I'm quite sure she thinks so,' I answer, and we both laugh quietly. Her vanity has quickly become known in the hotel. So far I've only confided in Hannah about her terrible temper. But in fairness I have to add: 'She did look very fine though. You can see she's come straight from Paris.'

'I can't wait to see them all in their beautiful dresses,' Hannah says wistfully.

'You'll have plenty of opportunity, waiting on them at table,' I remind her.

I haven't been asked to do that. I'm glad of it. It would make me nervous. And perhaps it would not suit

Madame's vanity to have her personal maid waiting at tables. No one will see me in the kitchen.

But later, after the first course has been set before the guests, Hannah appears beside me again. She tugs me away from the tabletop I'm scrubbing to come and look at the supper guests; I go willingly enough.

Wiping my hands on my apron and removing it, I follow Hannah down a corridor to a side door into the dining room. The door is standing open and we peep through.

The dining room is panelled with dark wood, and there are portraits and paintings of the sea hanging on the walls. I've been in here once or twice before, but it looks different tonight. The tables have all been set together in the middle of the room and brightly lit with candles and oil lamps. The light glitters on the glasses and the silver cutlery, and winks on the ladies' jewels, giving an impression of grandeur and opulence.

I gaze at it all in wonder. This must be how my mother lived until she was my age. I don't think I realized before how hard it must have been for her to lose all that. I try to imagine her sitting at ease among all these fine people, in a beautiful dress herself, but it doesn't quite work. That's not how I knew her.

'It's strange to see all this wealth and luxury alongside such poverty,' I remark to Hannah. 'Do the local people not resent it?'

I look at the bottles of French wines and the elegant dinner dishes and think of how we starved in the winter.

'Of course not!' Hannah exclaims in surprise. 'Why would they?'

'So many of the families here barely have enough food,' I try to explain.

Hannah looks thoughtful.

'The artists didn't make us poor,' she says after a moment. 'On the contrary, many of us have well-paid work in the summer because they come. And Hr Ancher sometimes gives parties for the whole town. They make the summer special. They're making Skagen famous. Other tourists come here because of the paintings. Mother says if it continues we may get a railway and even a harbour here.'

'It would be nice to *be* an artist,' I say musingly. For a split second, I see myself sitting at the table among these people, laughing, lifting my glass.

'What an idea!' Hannah gives a small choke of laughter. 'That's Hr Drachman over there. He's a poet. And look at your Madame.' Hannah giggles.

She's talking to Hr Krøyer, obviously doing her best to please him. But all her smiles, hand waving, and fan fluttering are in vain. He sits unsmiling and brooding.

'She's not getting much response from him, is she?' Hannah whispers. Sure enough, we watch as Madame abandons her attempt to charm Krøyer and turns to her other neighbour. I get a small shock as I see it's Mikkel's father, Hr Christensen. What is he doing here among the artists? I look around the room more closely and see a number of important townspeople at the table.

I want to go back to the kitchen now. I don't want to be seen peeping at the guests like this. But Hannah won't let me go.

'Wait,' she says. 'Have you seen the lady in the white dress? Isn't she beautiful?'

I glance briefly at her, but it's her neighbour I notice. She's sitting next to Monsieur Perroy, my employer, and he's looking straight at us.

I draw back immediately, pulling Hannah with me.

'Come on, Hannah, Monsieur is watching us.'

Back in the kitchen, carefully washing the first of the expensive china plates they are now clearing from the table, I think about Monsieur and his twinkling eyes. I've only met him a few times, but he always seems to have a smile lurking somewhere. I'm not sure whether he's laughing at me or with me. I don't dislike him exactly. It would be hard to: he's very charming. But there's something in the way that he looks at me that disturbs me.

The noise from the dining room grows as the evening goes on and the guests relax and enjoy their wine. Bursts of laughter reach the kitchen at frequent intervals, and one of the girls serving at the table exclaims, between giggles, about having her bottom patted.

When I've finished the next batch of dishes, I am sent down to check the water jug in the privy. It would never do to leave the guests unable to wash their hands.

It's a beautiful, cool night; the wind is hushing through the newly unfurled leaves. There's a scattering of bright stars in the sky. The privy is right at the bottom of the garden, and though it is merely a simple earth

190

closet, it's a wonderful luxury after nine months of living without one altogether. It is clean and well maintained for the guests, and there are even scented soap and towels laid out.

The jug is almost empty, so I exchange it with the one I have brought. I empty the bowl of used water behind the building.

On the way back through the garden, I linger. The early flowers scent the evening air, mingling with the more distant smell of fish. I stop to touch the leaves of the bushes. The breeze on my overheated skin is refreshing. I'm in no hurry to return to washing up in the hot kitchen.

As I pass the door to the studio, I pause. The studio is a small, separate building with a window in the roof, and Michael Ancher and some of the others paint in here, especially on rainy days. I was confused at first about the close connections the Anchers seem to have with the hotel, when they have their own house close by in *Markvej*. But Hannah told me that Anna Ancher is a daughter of the Brøndum family, and that they lived in the house at the end of the garden here when they were first married. They are the only artists to have their home in Skagen.

I can't resist trying the door handle, and it's unlocked. Guiltily, I slip inside to take a look at the paintings. I shouldn't be here.

It's almost dark now, but what light there is falls through the skylight onto the large easel in the centre of the room and the painting on it. I recognize the subject at once. It's the lifeboat being pulled through the sand dunes by the horses. There are fishermen in oilskins and hats helping to push the boat. And in the distance—yes! The stranded sailing ship. I remember the whole scene, though I saw it from a different angle. Michael Ancher has painted the boat from behind, as though he was following it. I myself was already on the beach when the boat arrived.

The painting looks almost finished. It's so huge, and so real that it almost takes my breath away. As I stand gazing at it, there's a soft click behind me. I jump and spin around. Someone has followed me into the studio.

'*Bonsoir*, Marianne!' says a soft voice, and a slight figure steps forward into the light. It's Monsieur Perroy.

'I'm sorry,' I say quickly. I make a move to leave, but he blocks my exit.

'No, stay a moment,' he says in French. 'Most understandable that you were curious. You like the painting?'

He comes to stand close, too close for comfort. His voice is in my ear, intimate, his breath tickling my cheek. I move away a little, trying not to do it too obviously.

'Very much. I was there, and it brings it all to life again.'

'Indeed? Yes, my friend Ancher has a fascination with painting the local people. I predict great success for him. I myself prefer something more refined and pleasing to the eye. Would you like to see my painting?'

The situation is embarrassing, but I'm curious, so I nod. Perroy takes my hand and leads me across the studio to another canvas. His touch gives me a shock. It seems inappropriate. Not like when Mikkel or Hannah

192

take my hand and it's comfortable and friendly. Or when Peter does, and I wish he'd never let go. This is something else. As soon as I can, I snatch it back. Perroy seems not to notice. He lights a candle so that we can see his painting.

I recognize her at once. She's a guest at the hotel. The lady in the white dress he was sitting next to at dinner. I don't know her name, but I've often seen them in conversation together in the garden. I didn't know he was painting her.

She's fair haired, tall, and slender in a pale pink dress that falls in elegant folds to the ground. Very different from his wife. I wonder briefly what Madame thinks of this. Perhaps it could explain her temper.

There's no doubt Perroy is a talented painter. He's certainly captured the elegance of his subject. I admire the folds of the dress and the smoothness of her hair. As I look, I think about how intently Monsieur Perroy must have studied the woman to paint her like this. Her face, her lips, the voluptuous curve of her breasts beneath her dress. I shiver, uncomfortably aware of the artist himself standing close to me in the semi darkness.

'I must go,' I say abruptly, but before I can leave, he grasps my wrist.

'Not so soon, *ma petite*. You haven't told me what you think of my painting.'

I can smell the wine he's been drinking and a whiff of cigar smoke. My heart thumps uncomfortably and I long for the fresh air in the garden, just a few steps away.

'*C'est très beau*,' I tell him truthfully. I hesitate, and

then add boldly: 'But you haven't used the light like the others do.'

Perroy stiffens, and to my relief, lets me go. I back away a step or two.

'You are an artist yourself?' He chuckles softly to himself at the thought.

'Not yet,' I tell him, stung by his tone. I can't believe I said that. I haven't even told Hannah or Mikkel how much I long to paint.

'And what sort of pictures would a maid paint, I wonder?' he asks, mocking me.

He blows out the candle, leaving us in darkness. I turn and run out of the studio, taking deep breaths of the summer air as I cross the garden. I'm annoyed; with myself as much as with him. Anna Ancher didn't laugh at the idea of me painting.

'Marianne, where have you been?' Hannah calls as soon as I reappear in the kitchen. I stand blinking in the light for a moment while my eyes adjust.

'Madame wants you,' Hannah tells me urgently. 'She's waiting in her room. She's torn her dress and wants you to mend it. She flew into a terrible rage when we couldn't find you.' Hannah's voice sounds slightly awed. Madame's temper is obviously no longer a secret.

I turn and hurry up the stairs immediately. She'd better not throw anything at me, I think resentfully.

TWENTY-TWO

June 1886

Hannah's favourite task of the day is ringing the big dinner bell that hangs in the courtyard. But taking drinks to the studio is mine. Balancing the tray of drinks carefully, I step out into the garden. The sunshine is strong, and the weather warm. The chill is gone from the wind and there's a scent of things growing in the soil and of flowers mingling with the ever-present smell of fish.

The door of the studio is open today. Ancher, Krøyer, and Perroy are in their painting smocks, brush in hand. The studio is hot and smells strongly of linseed oil and white spirit. I breathe the scent deeply. I find it exciting.

'Ah, refreshments!' calls Hr Krøyer gladly. 'This is thirsty work.'

I carry the tray to each of the three men in turn, offering them a tall glass of cold beer and a tiny glass of *snaps*.

'*Skål!*' cries Monsieur Perroy, lifting his small glass. Cheers. It's the only word of Danish that he's learned so far to my knowledge.

The town is full of artists now. There are so many that the hotel cannot house them all. They are staying in lodgings and rented houses. And what they all have in common, Swedish, Danish, and Norwegian alike, is that they've studied painting in Paris, and speak at least some French.

They look each other in the eyes as they raise their glasses. It's an unvarying ritual around drinking. Monsieur Perroy also looks at me over his glass, his brown eyes holding mine for a few seconds before I turn away to clear the coffee cups they brought out from lunch with them.

I hear him say *skål* again softly. I know that was meant for me, but I pretend not to notice. As I stack the coffee cups and saucers onto the tray, I sneak a few surreptitious glances at the paintings. Ancher is working on a new painting now, a smaller one, a study of two fishermen, their faces lined and ravaged by exposure to the wind and sun.

I can't see Krøyer's painting from here. I can see Perroy's though, and it seems to me he has made little progress with it. He spends far longer deep in conversation with his model than in actually painting her, and still longer eating and drinking with his fellow artists.

I always make clearing the cups away take as long as possible, so that I can absorb as much as I can of the way they work. The mixing of the colours on the palette, the touch of the brush on the canvas.

I don't have a chance to see much today. The men remove their smocks and rub the oil and pigments off their hands with rags dipped in spirit. Perroy manages to walk past me twice, brushing against me as he does so. I shudder slightly. Finally, they wash their hands in the bowl of the washstand, take their drinks, and go out to join the ladies in the garden.

196

Never mind. It gives me the chance to look quickly at Krøyer's painting. It's a strange picture he's working on. Simply a table in the garden, with a white tablecloth. But I like the way the sunlight seems to gleam on the cloth. I examine it closely, trying to see how he's achieved this. The cloth looks white, but when I look closely I can see he's used many different colours side by side to paint it. I feel a thrill of excitement, and long to try myself. I pick up a brush, to feel what it's like to hold it.

I hear someone returning. Replacing the brush quickly, I pick up the heavy tray instead. I carry it carefully back to the kitchen. They use expensive china here and I would hate to smash any of it.

'So, how are the paintings coming along, Marianne?' asks the kitchen maid as I enter. 'Marianne thinks they'll not paint at all unless she goes to check at least once a day,' she says to the kitchen at large. There's some good-humoured laughter around me, and I realize my wish to learn to paint is not quite as secret as I'd supposed. It's hard to keep much to yourself in this place.

'Hr Ancher's and Hr Krøyer's pictures are progressing well,' I tell them, unsure if they want to know, or whether it was merely an opportunity for some gentle teasing. 'But Monsieur Perroy's scarcely changes.'

'You'd best make haste and send up your bill then, Fru Brøndum, ma'am,' says the maid to the proprietress, who's rolling out dough, her hands covered in flour. 'Or all you'll be getting in payment will be a half-finished painting!'

She roars with laughter at her own joke, and Fru

Brøndum shakes her head reprovingly. I don't join in the general laughter; it touches me a little on the raw. The hotel has paid me their part of my wages, but the Perroys haven't paid me an øre yet.

Hannah is at the door beckoning me: 'Marianne? It's time to get ready. Hurry!'

She's been in a state of restless excitement all day long, fidgeting and unable to concentrate on her work. We've both been invited to a wedding. Peter's eldest sister, Ellen, is getting married and we have been allowed a few hours off work to go. It's going to be a big celebration with lots of guests. I'm nervous as well as excited. I don't know what to expect. I do know that I'm longing to see Peter again, hoping against hope to spend some time with him. Since I've been working at the hotel, we've barely had a chance to exchange a word.

I was surprised to be invited, as I hardly know Peter's sister. But Annette said I was a friend of the family now, and couldn't possibly be left out. I was especially touched by her thoughtfulness in inviting Hannah as well, so that I wouldn't feel lost in such a large gathering.

Neither Hannah nor I can afford new clothes, but I've been busy altering our best dresses and making them a little finer with scraps of lace and ribbons that Annette gave me from her workbox. I've also embroidered flowers onto the bodice of each dress. We're both looking forward to wearing them.

It was Hannah who had the idea of dressing our hair as I've learned to do for Madame. I'm not convinced it's such a good idea, but she won't take no for an answer.

However, once we've washed and dressed and Hannah has fumbled for what feels like hours with my hair, I'm surprised at the difference it makes.

She has plaited small strands of my hair, and then tied it loosely, high on my head. It brings out the fairness of my hair better than my usual tight bun. I feel older and smarter now, almost ready to face a party.

Hannah's hair is a thick glossy brown, with shades of red in it. I brush it until it glows, and then braid it into a single long plait, which I wind around a piece of lace into a bun low on her neck.

'There. Now you look as pretty as one of the paintings,' I tell Hannah, holding up our small mirror so she can see herself. She turns and hugs me, and then we run down the stairs together.

I'm excited too now as we wade through the soft sand of the main street to go to the church. The building is full to overflowing. Many of the guests are known to me. It's a gathering of local townspeople rather than the artist community I've become used to seeing in recent weeks.

'I've never been to a wedding before,' I tell Hannah as we squeeze into a pew near the back of the church. She looks at me in astonishment.

'Never?'

I shake my head.

'No, I've only seen pictures. But Annette let me see the wedding dress she was making for Ellen,' I tell her proudly.

'Is it pretty?' asks Hannah, her eyes shining.

'Wait and see,' I tease her. Ellen is already up at the altar, but we can't see what she's wearing as she's covered by a large wrap. All the women are craning their necks for a first glimpse of the dress. When she removes the wrap, Hannah sighs in delight. The dress is creamy white, falling to the ground in snowy folds. The bodice is tight, showing Ellen's slender figure, and the skirt is full. She has white roses in her hair.

'Wouldn't it be lovely to wear a dress like that?' Hannah whispers.

I imagine myself dressed in white, waiting for Peter at the altar.

'Your face has gone red,' whispers Hannah, nudging me with her elbow. 'Are you thinking of Peter?'

'Shh!' I tell her. 'The service is starting.'

The ceremony is very long, but the minister preaches a joyful sermon. The couple exchange vows and rings. I hold my breath as the bridegroom kisses Ellen. I can see Annette dabbing at her eyes with a handkerchief at the front of the church. Then there is rousing music as the couple walk down between the rows of guests. They look radiantly happy.

We pour out of the church, a large crowd walking back up through the town to the house where Peter and his parents live. The mood is festive and merry already. Hannah quizzes me as we walk: 'So were you thinking of Peter? Is that why you blushed?' I shake my head at her.

'People will hear you,' I whisper, hot with embarrassment.

'There's no one listening. It wouldn't hurt to be a little

more open, you know,' Hannah chides me quietly. 'You're so secretive all the time. Don't you trust me?'

'Of course I do.' I look down at the sand. She's right, I know she is. I feel a little ashamed. 'I can't change myself.'

'Yes you can!' says Hannah, surprised. 'People change all the time.' She slips her hand in mine. 'Here we are. Oh! How pretty they've made it!'

There are long trestle tables and benches laid out in the garden. The tables are beautifully set.

'Where do we sit, Hannah?' I ask.

'There are place names, look!' Hannah tells me. 'And the musicians are already playing the first course onto the table!' A group of men with fiddles are standing in the corner of the garden, playing for all they're worth. The music is lively and happy.

We find our seats side-by-side, some distance from the top table where Peter's family is sitting. It is a good place to watch everything from, and to nod and wave to acquaintances.

Once the vicar has arrived and said a lengthy grace, we are served a clear meat soup. It is very welcome after several hours in church. The main course consists of roast chicken and roast lamb, with new potatoes, rich gravies, and a selection of vegetables. There are also rolls of white wheat bread.

'The food is almost as fine as at the hotel,' I exclaim, awed by the variety. I take some chicken, and some buttered potatoes with carrots.

'Can I pass you the bread?' asks the young man beside me politely.

I thank him shyly, and he asks my name. Hannah leans forward to greet him: '*Hej*, Niels!' she says.

Niels asks us about the guests at the hotel. I can tell Hannah enjoys casually mentioning the names of all the artists and other well-known guests who are staying there.

The noise level increases as the *snaps* is passed around and successive toasts drunk to the bride and groom. Each time a toast is drunk, the entire party rises and lifts their glasses to the happy couple.

There is homemade fruit juice for the younger guests to drink, a rare treat. I choose it rather than the ale, sweetened with syrup, which Hannah seems to be enjoying. The waiter also pours us a *snaps* each. Hannah persuades me to try it. It is clear and has almost no scent, but when I take a tiny sip, it catches at the back of my throat and I choke and cough. The young man next to me slaps me on the back and laughs. My eyes are watering as I gasp for air. I look at Hannah accusingly, unable to speak.

'You knew that would happen,' I croak at last.

'Of course,' Hannah laughs, as I wipe more tears from my eyes. 'But you have to try it sometime!'

'Do you drink it?' I ask.

'I can if I have to,' she tells me.

To my surprise she lifts her glass, and throws it back in one go, like the adults do. Her eyes water only a little from the strong drink.

'Now you finish yours,' she tells me. 'The trick is not to taste it, just swallow.'

I try to do as she says, but I'm only partly successful. I manage to swallow some and feel it burning all the way down my throat. I feel strangely light-headed almost at once, but it soon passes.

'I prefer the juice,' I say.

Throughout the meal, I'm aware of Peter talking to the young woman who is sitting next to him. She's very pretty, with long dark hair with a red rose in it. As I watch, I see Peter raise his glass to her, looking into her eyes. I look away, as a most unreasonable stab of jealousy strikes me. I wish it were me sitting next to him. But perhaps he prefers dark-haired girls. I feel cross and dissatisfied, despite the festive atmosphere.

I catch Mikkel's eye across the garden. He's sitting with his family near our hosts. He raises his glass to me in silent greeting. I give him a small wave in return. I've seen less of him since I've been at the hotel and he's been fishing. I miss him. I give his father an angry stare, but he doesn't look in my direction.

The dessert is being brought around now. There's cake, and also fresh waffles with homemade jams to spread on them.

Once coffee has been drunk, the minister stands up again and leads a thanksgiving prayer. He then takes his leave. No sooner is he out of sight than the musicians strike up again. The tables and benches are hastily cleared to one side and the bride and groom are led forward to the middle of the lawn.

'The bridal waltz,' Hannah explains. 'The newly-married couple always start the dancing.'

They look happy as they circle together in time to the music, smiling to each other. Everyone is clapping, and calling out good wishes. Then, gradually, more and more couples join the dance. The music speeds up; merry tunes that make your feet want to move. Mikkel appears beside us. He shakes us both by the hand, and sits down next to us.

'How's life at Brøndum's?' he asks me.

'I love it,' I tell him enthusiastically. 'There's plenty of work, of course, but always something happening. It's a very friendly place.'

'And Marianne likes to watch the work in the studio,' Hannah teases quietly.

'Yes, that makes sense,' says Mikkel with a smile. 'And how is your sketchbook coming along?'

'It's more than half full.'

'I'd like to see it sometime,' says Mikkel. 'By the way, I've found some stone martens living in an abandoned house in Vesterby. Can you find some time one evening to come and sketch them for me? You can do it so much better than I can.'

'What's a stone marten?'

'It's like a pine marten, only a little smaller. They like living in the roofs of houses. They're beautiful, but very shy.'

'I'll do my best,' I promise.

'And so, who's going to dance with me first?' he asks. 'Marianne?'

He gets up and bows formally to me, laughter in his eyes. I would like to join in the joke, and sweep him a curtsey in return, but instead I become interested in a stain on the tablecloth. I remember Hannah's words. He's my friend and Hannah too, so I can tell them: 'I've never danced. I don't know how.'

There's a look of astonishment on both their faces for a moment, but they don't laugh at me, as I feared they might.

'It's not hard,' Mikkel reassures me. 'Few people here learn the correct steps. You just make it up as you go along. Come on, I'll show you.'

I get up slowly, my heart beating fast. As Mikkel takes my hand, I whisper, 'I can't, not in front of all these people.' I can't bear to think that Peter might see me making a fool of myself.

'They won't be looking at you. Just relax.'

'What about your father?' I ask. 'He won't be happy if he sees you dancing with me,' I say.

'He's right over there, drinking with Hansen and some other friends,' says Mikkel. 'He won't notice. And I don't care if he does.'

He puts his right arm around my waist and takes my left hand in his. I feel shy standing so close to him. I concentrate on the roughness of his hand made so much worse by the work he's doing.

'Relax,' Mikkel says again.

I take a deep breath and try to.

'Now feel the music,' he instructs. I'm used to learning Danish from him, and rowing, surely I can learn to dance. I follow his steps nervously, treading on his feet from time to time. He's as tall as I am, he must have grown during the winter.

I soon realize Mikkel's right: no one's looking at me. The music speeds up and it starts to be fun. So much so, that when the tune ends, I'm sorry to stop. But Hannah has been waiting long enough, and it's her turn to dance.

We find her surrounded by several friends. She's had other invitations to dance, but has been waiting for Mikkel. They all go off, and I sit down and pour myself another drink of juice. It's a warm early summer's evening, not yet dusk.

There's an elderly lady sitting by me who wasn't there before. She's tapping her foot in time with the music, and humming a little. She catches my eye and smiles revealing gaps in her teeth.

'*Jeg elsker et bryllup,*' she announces. I love a wedding. 'But at your age, I was always dancing, never sitting watching.'

'I have been dancing!' I say defensively.

'Ha! I saw you. With Christensen's son, too. Yes, I know all the families here, though I don't live here any longer.'

'*Hvor bor du så?*' Where do you live? I ask.

'When my first husband died, God rest his soul, I married again and moved down to Frederikshavn,' she tells me. 'That was a long time ago. I've buried him too. That's the trouble with living to my age. I was ninety last birthday.'

'Ninety?' I ask, astonished. She looks old, but very robust. 'It's a long journey for a wedding at the age of ninety,' I say admiringly.

'It's not too far. I walked up today, and shall walk back down again in the morning.'

I can't have heard her right. My astonishment must show on my face because she cackles with delighted laughter.

'Thought I was past it did you? No, no.'

I look at her with huge respect. She returns suddenly to my affairs, showing a mind as sharp as any young woman's.

'Take care you don't lose your *kæreste* to that pretty girl,' she says, nodding to where Mikkel and Hannah are dancing together. Hannah dances well, much better than me. She looks very happy.

My *kæreste*. She has that wrong.

'He's not my sweetheart,' I say. 'We're good friends.'

'Humph! There's no such thing as friendship between a handsome young man and a pretty girl. He'd be a good catch, for all he's not as strong as his father.' She lifts her tiny glass to me with a smile. Drinking it down in one, she remarks brightly: 'You may have lost Christensen's son, but there's another, even more handsome young man at your elbow, so you'd better take him and be quick about it!'

I look round quickly, and start with pleasure to find Peter standing behind me.

'I see you've met my great-grandmother,' he says, with a self-conscious smile.

'Ask her to dance then, Peter,' urges the old woman, and cackles with laughter again. She's pouring herself another *snaps*.

'I was just about to,' says Peter.

He's holding out his hand to me, his eyes on mine. I stand up shyly, feeling clumsy and awkward.

'I can't really dance,' I admit. 'I've only tried once.'

It is so much worse admitting this to Peter than to Mikkel.

'I saw you dance with Mikkel,' he says. 'So surely you can dance with me?'

'Of course,' I say quickly. I scan his face for any sign of jealousy, but he's smiling. 'I just wanted to warn you, I'm not very good.'

Peter leads me out among the other couples and puts his arm around me. He's taller than me and I'm on a level with his chin.

'I like the way you've done your hair tonight,' Peter remarks, touching one of the plaits Hannah did for me.

'Thank you,' I reply, pleased. 'You are looking very smart too,' I venture, wanting to return the compliment.

The music is slow and gentle. Peter's arm is warm around my waist. I'm breathless and slightly dizzy. I try to concentrate on not treading on his feet, but soon forget about the steps, and enjoy the closeness.

'You don't come and see my mother as often now,' he says softly. 'We miss you. Life at the hotel must be very busy?'

'It is,' I agree. 'And your mother said she had enough things to sell for this season now. She said not to worry if I couldn't manage much more until the autumn.'

He can't know how much I miss going to his home. Even when he's not there, I feel his presence around me, knowing that he sits in the chairs and drinks from the cups.

'I'm thinking of building my own house,' Peter tells me unexpectedly.

I look up into his eyes for a moment and then away again. He's so close.

'Your own house?' I ask. I don't know how to react. 'Your parents' house is so lovely,' I say lamely.

'Yes, but I hope mine will be a good house too,' he says. 'Smaller than theirs at first, of course.'

Peter tightens his hold on my waist, drawing me still closer to him. I'm right against him now. My heart is jumping. Daringly, I slide my hand further up his arm to his shoulder, feeling the warmth of his body through the fabric of his sleeve. I'm trembling on the inside. I don't want the dance to end.

But all too soon the music stops, and Hannah is beside me.

'I'm really sorry, Marianne.' She casts an apologetic look up at Peter, too.

'We have to go back now. I've just asked the time, and we promised not to be out as late as this.'

I look up at Peter.

'*Synd*,' he says. That's a shame. He presses my hand before releasing me. 'But I'll see you again soon, I hope.'

TWENTY-THREE

June 1886

The evening sunshine gleams on the pearls in my hand. The sheen on them glows. Should I sell them or shouldn't I? I kept them when we were hungry. Is it right to sell them now to buy painting things? I hold them up again and admire the creamy lustre. They are all that's left of my mother's youth. A rush of sadness sweeps over me. I wonder what she would want me to do. She didn't sell them. Still undecided, I slip them into my pocket.

Mikkel is waiting for me outside the hotel.

'I don't have long,' I warn him as soon as I reach him. 'I must be back before Madame needs to go to bed.'

Mikkel nods. 'Let's hope the martens don't keep us waiting then,' he says with a smile.

Swiftly, we walk down Søndergade into Vesterby. Mikkel takes me to an empty house, half tumbled down. We're not far from the Jakobsens' here.

'Be very quiet now,' Mikkel warns me. He eases open the broken door and we creep inside. The walls are buckling and I can see the sky through holes in the thatch. It smells damp and musty. Mikkel sits down on a rickety chair by the window, and points to another for me.

'Now what?' I whisper.

'We wait. To see if the martens appear. It might be too light for them.'

Mikkel sits quite still, his eyes on the window. I'm not good at staying still. I soon feel restless. For something to do, I begin to sketch Mikkel's profile. He soon notices what I'm doing and grins.

'I told you I'm going to Frederikshavn for a couple of days tomorrow, didn't I?' he asks quietly after a while.

'Yes. And I wanted to ask you to do something for me.' I draw the pearls from my pocket, weigh them in my hand one last time, and then hand them to Mikkel. 'Would you be able to sell these for me?'

It's hard to see them go, so I resume sketching to take my mind off them.

Mikkel lifts the pearls to the light and whistles under his breath.

'Where did you get something like this?' he asks.

'They were my mother's. She came from a wealthy family. This necklace is the only thing she had left from that time.'

Mikkel considers the pearls. 'No,' he says at last. 'They're valuable. I shouldn't think anyone in Skagen has anything so fine. Not even your Madame. I don't want to be arrested on suspicion of theft.'

'Would you be?' I ask, surprised.

'I imagine so. Where would a fifteen-year-old boy come by such a thing? Besides, if they were your mother's, you should keep them.'

'I know, I know.' My pencil is still moving busily on

the page. Mikkel catches hold of my hand to stop me drawing. He turns my hand palm up and drops the pearls back into it.

'Keep them safe.'

'I've finally worked myself up to letting them go, and now you're giving them back,' I say in an annoyed whisper.

Mikkel smiles. 'There you are, you see. You've had doubts about it too.'

'I never even saw my mother wear them. I want to buy paints. I want to learn to paint so very much.'

'You sound wistful,' Mikkel says. 'Do you remember the time I asked you if you had a dream, and you didn't really know what I meant? Well, you have one now, don't you?'

'I suppose I have.'

'But not impossible like mine,' Mikkel adds bitterly. 'I'm sure we'll manage to get you paints somehow. Only, don't you need someone to teach you?'

'I don't know. Who would I ask?'

I sigh, and we sit in silence for a while. I start sketching again, but stop when I hear a scratching in the roof.

'The martens!' says Mikkel, his face lighting up. 'We're in luck.' We both look out of the window. At first there's nothing to see. Then a long red-brown shape flows down the wall and hops up onto the broken bench outside our window. At first glance it looks like a cat. But the body is too long, and the head the wrong shape. A second, smaller marten appears. He sits up on his back legs and grows very tall. He has a white patch of fur on his throat and chest. He's staring right at us. I hold my breath, willing him not to take fright. He gazes at us for a long moment and then dives under the bench. I lean forward and see his long body flatten as it slides under the wood. The two martens begin to play, jumping up and down from the bench, chasing one another and wrestling. They even stand up on their hind legs and look as though they're dancing together. We're both smiling as we watch.

I begin to sketch. 'It's hard to draw them,' I whisper to Mikkel. 'They never stay still.'

'They're *legesye*. Playful. Have you seen them before, in England?'

'Never,' I say, continuing to draw. 'Grimsby was industrial. They were building all around, and there was an iron foundry right behind us pumping out smoke from morning till night. No place for wild creatures.'

'You never speak about it,' says Mikkel curiously. 'Why?'

It used to be easy to keep my secrets. That was before I had friends. Now my past is restless inside me, wanting to burst out. If I start talking, one thing will lead to another, and I might tell it all. With an effort I repress it.

'Nothing much to tell,' I shrug. Mikkel is silent. When I glance at him, there's a hurt look in his eyes. It makes me feel bad.

The martens suddenly stop playing, and disappear from sight. We both sit back, disappointed. I continue my sketches.

'What did you draw in England?' Mikkel asks.

'Oh, vases with flowers, fruit, that sort of thing. We

214

didn't go out much, you see. And I used to draw my mother over and over.' I smile sadly at the memory.

'So where are the pictures?' Mikkel is nothing if not persistent.

'I threw most of them away before I left. A lot of them weren't very good. But I kept the ones of my mother. They're in my trunk.'

'Then why did you tell Anna Ancher in the spring that you had nothing to show?'

I wince uncomfortably, and concentrate hard on drawing. I could tell him I forgot about them, but he wouldn't believe me. Impulsively, I decide on the truth.

'I find it hard to look at them. Most of the time I'm busy, and I don't think about my mother. But when I get the pictures out, they make me cry. I miss her so much.'

Mikkel reaches over and squeezes my shoulder briefly. He doesn't say anything. I suddenly feel much better. Hannah is right. I need to overcome my habit of keeping everything secret.

I put a few final touches to the last sketch. Mikkel holds out his hand for the book.

'May I?'

He flicks through. First the stone martens in various poses. He smiles as he looks at them. Then the picture of himself: 'Hey, do I really look like that?' Then he goes further back. There are some of the sand dunes and the sea, ships in the distance. There is one of a wreck, lying forlornly half in the water, waves crashing over it. I'm proud of that one. Right at the beginning there's one of

Jakob mending fishing nets, and another of Lise picking wild flowers.

'These are good. Really good.'

'Thank you. But I'm not satisfied, you see. In Grimsby everything seemed drab and grey. I suppose any big town is like that. But here, everywhere I look, I see beauty and colour and light. I can't show that with a pencil. I see the artists capturing it all so beautifully in oils. I want to try.'

Mikkel nods. I think he understands. 'Can I borrow this for a few days?' he asks unexpectedly.

'Why? I was going to do some more work on you and the martens,' I say hesitantly.

'No need. I'll give it back to you on Sunday, I promise.'

'All right then,' I agree reluctantly. 'And now I really must get back.'

When I lock the pearls away again in my trunk late that night, I'm not sure whether I'm glad or sorry that I still have them. Hannah is in bed, leaning on one elbow, watching me.

'Did you see the martens?' she asks.

'Yes. They were beautiful. Funny too. Have you ever seen them?'

'No, never. How was Mikkel?' There's a slightly strained note in Hannah's voice, and I give her a quick glance, wondering if she's a little jealous.

'He was well. He sends his regards to you. You should tell him you'd like to see the martens: I'm sure he'd take you.' I blow out the candle and climb into bed beside Hannah. I hear her sigh with tiredness as she stretches out.

'He's going away for a few days, isn't he?' asks Hannah in the semi-darkness.

'Yes, will you miss him?' I ask. When Hannah doesn't reply, I ask quietly: 'Do you care for him very much, Hannah?'

There's a moment's silence, and I think she's not going to reply. Then she whispers: 'I love him. More than I can say.' I can see her eyes shining in the darkness.

She rolls over to face me, leaning up on her elbow again. Her face is in shadow now.

'Did you guess?' she asks softly.

'Yes. I've suspected as much since Christmas.'

'But you won't tell him, will you?'

'I wouldn't dream of it.'

'Marianne?' Hannah whispers again.

'Yes?'

'I know you care for Peter. So why won't you admit it?'

I hug myself under the sheets, and let my thoughts dwell on Peter. His eyes, his smile.

'Yes, I love him,' I whisper at last. 'So much so that it scares me.' I shiver. There's something both frightening and delicious about exchanging secrets in the darkness like this.

'I knew it,' says Hannah, triumphantly. She lies back on her pillow, sighing with pleasure.

'You won't tell either, will you?' I ask anxiously.

'No, I promise.'

I snuggle down pleasurably into my sheets. Thoughts of Mikkel and Peter gradually mingle and blur with images of the martens and paintings as sleep overcomes me.

The next afternoon, when I go to clear the glasses from the studio, Monsieur Perroy is there alone. It's most unusual for him to work longer than the others. He's started a new painting. It's of a different woman, his first model having left the hotel. There was a great deal of whispering about the two of them before she left. Madame smashed a vase in her room one afternoon she was in such a rage.

'Ah, Marianne!' Perroy greets me enthusiastically. I suspect he's bored, working alone. There's a half empty bottle of *snaps* beside him. I wonder if he's drunk all of it himself. He lifts his tiny glass in a silent toast, and then tilts his head back and empties it.

'Put the tray down and stay and talk to me!' Perroy orders. I hesitate. I dislike being alone with him.

'They'll be wondering where I am,' I object.

'Pshaw!' he exclaims. 'I employ you, do I not? It is I who pay you!'

'Not yet,' I say boldly. He waves this away impatiently.

'A mere trifle. You will be paid, trust me.' I watch him as he turns back to his canvas, cleans his brush and mixes the colours on the palette: blues, greens, white, and yellow.

'And so, Marianne, do you still wish to paint?' Perroy asks softly, without looking at me.

'Yes,' I reply simply.

'Come here then,' he says. I don't know what he means, so I don't move.

He turns towards me, holding out a clean paintbrush, and beckons.

Step by step I'm drawn closer. As I reach out for the brush, he pulls it out of reach. For a moment I think he's mocking me again, but he says: 'Come closer.'

I take another step and then another. Now I'm between him and the canvas. Perroy puts one hand on my shoulder and turns me to face the picture.

'Why don't you help me paint the sky?' he suggests. 'This huge northern sky.'

I take the brush, and look longingly at the paints and the canvas.

'I'm frightened to spoil it,' I say hesitantly.

'Mistakes can be rubbed out,' he murmurs, holding up a rag. His breath is tickling my ear. 'Try now. What colour is the sky?'

I dip my brush into the blue and touch it to the canvas. The colour sits there, a small raised blob.

'And does that look right?' asks the voice in my ear.

'No, it looks all wrong,' I answer, perplexed.

'And why do you think that is, *ma petite*?' I shiver slightly at his closeness, from a mixture of excitement and fear. I edge away an inch or two.

'I don't know.'

'Is the sky blue?' Monsieur asks. 'Just blue?'

'No, not always.' I think a little. 'You see white clouds, grey clouds, yellow-black thunder clouds. It can be deep summer blue, or pale winter blue. Rain-washed, or sun-baked.' I visualize all the different skies as I describe them. 'Pinks, reds, and oranges at sunrise and sunset,' I continue.

'*Bien*, it's enough,' he stops me. 'You have looked, I grant you. But this is the important thing. Even a blue sky is not simply one colour. When you are painting, you need to mix colours to find shades. You also paint different colours side by side to give depth.'

Monsieur takes hold of my brush hand and dips the brush in the blue and the white and mixes the colours on a clean patch of palette. Then he mixes in an opaque substance. 'This is glaze,' he tells me. 'It makes the colours less flat. So that you feel you are looking into the sky, not at a flat canvas. Now try.'

This time as I paint the colour onto the canvas, I can see there is a richer, more textured look to the blue. He takes my hand at each mixing of the colours and then lets me paint it on myself. The patch of sky grows slowly.

'Good, Marianne,' he murmurs. 'You have real talent for this. A natural instinct. How unexpected.' I glow with pride and long to prove myself further. Perroy's voice becomes brisk again as he instructs me once more: 'Now as you move down towards the green of the garden, you need to put some yellow and green in with the blue.'

'Why?' I ask, puzzled.

'Because otherwise the change of colour is too abrupt. It looks like a child's painting. Look here. In the greenery,

I've put brushstrokes of blue near the sky, do you see? Not mixed, but side by side.'

I look closely, fascinated, and it's a revelation. 'Of course,' I breathe. 'It makes sense.'

I feel as though I've been told a secret. A sense of excitement fills me. As we continue, I become absorbed, forgetting my work, losing my sense of time. The nearness of Perroy adds to the heady thrill of the painting. I don't know how much later it is that I'm roused by the door opening behind us and someone coming in. It takes me a moment to react. As I turn my head to look, I realize Monsieur is standing too close, one hand on my waist, the other hand on mine.

Embarrassed, I move away, letting go of the brush. It clatters to the floor, leaving a smear of green paint on my white apron.

'Marianne?' The kitchen maid is at the door, her eyes wide as she takes in the scene.

'Yes?' I ask brusquely, mortified at what she must be thinking.

'Madame has been ringing for you,' says the maid. 'We couldn't find you. She's angry.'

'I'll come at once,' I reply, but before I can leave, Monsieur catches hold of my hand, rubs a little paint from my finger, and lifts my hand briefly to his lips.

'Thank you for your so valuable help, *mademoiselle*,' he purrs, and his eyes are alight with wicked laughter. 'The same time tomorrow?'

I snatch my hand away and flee from the studio. As I run across the garden, I press my hands to my hot cheeks.

* * *

It's late when I climb wearily into my bed that night, having tucked Madame up in hers. Hannah is still awake.

'I've been waiting for you,' she whispers. 'It's not true that you were kissing Monsieur in the studio earlier, is it?'

'No, certainly not!' I hiss, horrified at how the story has been twisted already.

'What were you doing then?'

'Painting. He let me paint. Just for a minute or two. Well, perhaps longer. I don't remember. Oh, Hannah! He said I have a natural talent for painting!'

'Did you ask him if you could paint?' asks Hannah, astonished.

'No, of course not. He invited me to.'

'So it isn't true that you arranged a meeting with him tomorrow?'

'No, not at all. That is, he did say come again tomorrow. But he was teasing me, or else making mischief.'

There's a silence for a minute, then Hannah whispers: 'You won't go, will you?'

'I shouldn't think so,' I reply, trying to sound off-hand.

'Marianne, promise me you won't. You're my friend. I don't want you to get into trouble.'

'I won't!' I say indignantly. She sounds so worried.

There's another pause.

'Marianne? You told me yesterday you loved Peter. You don't want to lose him, do you? Because if you and that awful Frenchman become lovers . . . '

'Hannah!' I exclaim angrily. 'It's not like that at all. Anyway, he's married.'

'That didn't stop him before,' whispers Hannah. 'With that other woman. Everyone knows about them.'

'I just want to paint,' I assure her. 'I don't even like him.'

'Oh, Marianne, be careful. Don't put yourself in a situation where you are alone with him. Please don't meet him again.'

I scowl at her. My wonderful lesson and the praise Perroy gave me have been spoiled. The whole thing has been made to feel sordid somehow.

Hannah puts her arm around me. Annoyed, I push her away and roll over to face the window. But it's a long time before I fall asleep.

TWENTY-FOUR

23 June 1886

The morning after I had spoken to Hannah about Perroy, I made up my mind to take her advice and stay away from the studio. Inside I was in turmoil. All day, a fear that Hannah could possibly be right battled with the longing to paint.

It was purely the paints that attracted me. The thrill of watching the picture take form beneath my brush. My secret ambition to become an artist myself. Perroy had praised me, I reminded myself. I had talent. It couldn't be wrong to want to learn more.

But was it true that Perroy might try to seduce me? Not in a studio in the hotel garden in the middle of the afternoon. And that in itself would surely protect my reputation. Besides, I reasoned, how would Peter ever know?

I felt my resolve weakening.

Nonetheless, I kept to my decision all day. Until the late afternoon, when I found my feet treading the path to the studio. I was drawn like a moth to a candleflame. And I've gone there every afternoon for the last three weeks. Sometimes Monsieur isn't there. More often he is. The lure of the oils and the canvas is too great for me to withstand.

But today is Sunday. More importantly, it's our Sunday off. I'm still deeply asleep when Hannah shakes me.

'Marianne,' she says. 'Wake up. I want you to come to church with me.'

I groan and roll over. She shakes me again.

'Come on, it will put your thoughts in a higher place.'

I'm wide awake now and sit up crossly in bed.

'Did you just say what I thought you said? There's nothing ungodly about art, Hannah.'

She purses her mouth disapprovingly. 'Perhaps not. But there is plenty that's ungodly about a married Frenchman with a moustache,' she says tartly.

'I don't think about him at all,' I reply. Hannah looks politely incredulous, her eyebrows raised.

'And are you quite sure he doesn't think of you?' she asks seriously.

Now I'm irritated again, and I don't like to be cross with my friend. I swing my legs out of bed and reach for my clothes.

'I'll come to church with you, on the condition that you don't mention him again today.' As always, the hope of seeing Peter is an added incentive to going to church. Hannah knows that, though she doesn't mention him.

We're late and the church is overflowing. There's not a single space left in the pews and many of the congregation are standing at the back of the church.

'It's all the summer visitors,' whispers Hannah. 'We should have come earlier.'

226

I can't see Peter anywhere, and disappointment washes through me.

'I don't feel like standing up,' I whisper back. 'Shall we go?'

Hannah shakes her head.

'Well I'm leaving,' I tell her and walk away. I tell myself I don't care whether she follows me or not, but I'm pleased when she does.

As we leave the church, Mikkel looks around from his family pew near the front of the church and catches my eye. We haven't walked far before he comes running along Søndergade after us, sand spraying up behind him.

'Marianne! Hannah!' he cries, panting. We wait until he catches us up.

'I told Mother I was about to be sick,' he tells us with a grin. 'She practically ordered me out of the church. Shall we bathe?'

'That's a good idea,' says Hannah.

'I'm not sure that bathing will do me as much good as church. Spiritually, that is,' I say piously to Hannah. She laughs, but turns at once to Mikkel.

'You tell her, Mikkel,' she urges. 'Tell her she must stay away from that dreadful Frenchman.'

'I've heard some gossip,' Mikkel admits. 'It sounds as if you did ask someone to teach you to paint after all. I'm not sure it was a wise choice.'

'I didn't ask,' I contradict. 'He offered. Is it all over the town?' I can't get used to this small community where everyone knows everything almost before it's happened.

Mikkel nods. 'I even heard my father discussing it with someone.'

My heart sinks, but I'm also angry. What business is it of theirs?

'I'm doing nothing to be ashamed of,' I say finally. But a slight flush rises to my cheeks all the same.

'Tell her, Mikkel,' Hannah urges. But Mikkel shakes his head.

'Marianne wants to learn to paint. It's important to her. I don't think she should let a bit of idle gossip stand in her way.' He turns to me. 'Just ignore the talk,' he says. 'People will soon get tired of it and find something new to whisper about. But take care around that Frenchman. Keep the studio door open or something.' He grins at me. I feel much better at once. As though a burden has been lifted from me. I beam at him. Hannah looks disappointed though. She expected Mikkel to support her. But Mikkel understands what it is to long to do something and have people stand in the way. He would brave anything to study science.

When we reach the sea, the water is crystal clear, and inviting. The sunlight is shimmering on the seabed. We kick off our shoes and paddle a little. The water is cold on my hot feet. I watch as Hannah and Mikkel strip down to their underwear and plunge into the shallow waves, shrieking with cold and excitement. They are unembarrassed to be wearing so little. The Skagen children bathe completely naked, even the older ones. I was shocked at first, but I'm quite used to it now. It seems natural.

'Come on in, Marianne!' Hannah cries.

'I can't swim,' I plead.

'Then it's about time you learned!' she cries. 'It's not deep unless you go way out. It's very safe. Not like the west coast.'

I'm torn between the appeal of the cool water and my reluctance to undress. It's one thing to approve of nakedness in others, and quite another to try it myself. Eventually the lure of the water wins. I bravely peel my dress and petticoat off my hot skin till I'm wearing only drawers and a shift, then I wade in. I've never been in the sea further than to my ankles before. It's deliciously cool on my sun-heated skin. I stand hugging my arms to my chest, trying to gather the courage to get right in.

'Get right under, come on,' urges Mikkel. Hannah threatens to splash me and I hurriedly crouch down, gasping at the cold.

'It hasn't had time to warm up yet this year,' says Hannah. 'You'll get used to it.'

'Try to float on your back,' says Mikkel. 'We won't let you sink.' I lie back, looking up at the sky, feeling the cold on my back and my head. Suddenly I panic and try to sit up. I go under, swallowing salt water. Hannah pulls me up again, spluttering and choking.

'Try again,' she says.

I try over and over again. I try to float, I try to swim a few strokes, but all I seem to be good at is swallowing the water.

'Enough,' I gasp at last, having been hauled back to a sandbank by Mikkel for about the fifth time. My eyes are stinging from the salt, and I'm starting to feel sick. 'I'll try again another day. You two have a swim.'

They don't argue. I expect they've had enough too. They swim north along the coast, one fair and one dark head, side by side. They're talking as they swim. I wade up onto a sandbank where the water only comes to my ankles, and enjoy the warmth of the sun. I'm still coughing up seawater.

Shading my eyes, I look out at the ships. One sailing ship is close in to the coast, it seems to me. I watch her idly for a few moments. I notice some bright flashes from the mid-deck. They're dazzling. As they continue at regular intervals, I wonder if she's signalling.

I run along the sandbank to Mikkel and Hannah.

'Look at the ship!' I cry. 'Is she in trouble?' They turn to look, and then Mikkel looks inland, scanning the beach.

'She is signalling, but I don't think it's a distress signal,' he says. 'I think they have a passenger to drop off. Look!'

Two fishermen are launching a small rowing boat from the beach. We watch them as they row out towards the ship.

'It must be an important passenger to stop the whole ship,' remarks Hannah. 'Shall we go and watch?'

We wade back towards the beach, and pull on our clothes. My underwear is wet, and my skin sticky with salt, making my dress cling in all the wrong places.

The rowing boat has grounded on the sand now, as close in as they can get her. The two fishermen jump out, and carry their passenger to shore between them. Not a drop of salt water lands on his expensive-looking suit or his smart leather shoes.

'It's Christian Krogh,' whispers Mikkel. 'He's Norwegian: a writer and a painter.'

The boat is hauled onto the beach, and the valises unloaded. Krogh slips the fishermen several coins each. I see their dour faces light up as they cheerfully shoulder the luggage and follow him up to Østerby, presumably to the hotel.

'I don't know about you, but I'm hungry,' says Hannah. 'Shall we go back and see what there is for lunch?'

'That sounds like a good idea,' I agree. I look at Mikkel, and can't help but smile. He looks the picture of health, his face tanned, his hair still wet from the swim. 'You're going to have some trouble persuading your parents you were unwell,' I tease.

He grins. 'I'll think of something,' he promises. 'I don't want to pretend to be too ill, or I won't be allowed out to watch the bonfire later.'

'I can't wait! See you this evening,' Hannah calls to Mikkel merrily. 'I'm so excited about tonight,' she confides as we make our way through the dunes. 'It's my favourite night of the year.'

'Remind me what you call today?' I ask.

'It's *Sankthans*. The midsummer festival. Just wait until later!'

TWENTY-FIVE

The bonfire has been built of old, broken fish boxes and driftwood. It's on the beach just down from the *vippefyr*, the old lighthouse that's no longer in use. To my surprise, there's an effigy of a woman tied to a stake in the middle of it. She's made of old stuffed clothes and has a paper head.

'What's she for?' I ask Hannah.

'She's the witch. We always burn a witch at midsummer. In the old days it would have been a real one,' says Hannah gleefully.

'How grisly.' I shudder. 'You can be quite bloodthirsty at times.'

Hannah laughs.

'It's a bit like burning the Guy on November the Fifth in England,' I add. Hannah looks as though she might be going to ask about this when we see someone hold up a burning torch.

'They're lighting it now,' Hannah says, excitedly. From where we are standing in the crowd, I can see someone thrust a burning branch into the pile of wood. We watch, delighted, as first the smoke curls, and then the flames begin to spread. It's eleven o'clock in the evening, and only just dusk. The sky is glowing a deep blue and the wind has dropped. It's cool now, and we'll be glad of the warmth of the fire when it gets going.

'Look! The witch has caught,' cries Hannah, clapping her hands. The crackle and hiss of the flames mingles with the talk and laughter around us. I watch the flames run up the witch's back and engulf her paper head. I shiver at the thought of what it must have been like to watch a real woman burn alive at the stake.

As the witch burns, voices around me begin singing. More join them, until only I am silent. I've never heard the song before. I look around at the people, their faces reflecting the flames. I see tears gleaming in some people's eyes as they sing. They're singing about how much they love their country. I love it too. I love the open sky and the clear air. I love the warmth of the people I've met. I've found my home. Hannah takes my hand and smiles at me, almost as if she can hear my thoughts.

We edge a little closer to the fire as the song ends. As it burns lower, a group of men play their fiddles, and couples start to dance in the sand. The artists have donated barrels of mead to be drunk tonight, so many of the adults soon grow merry. Hannah and I stand watching the fire burn.

'Look, Hannah,' I say. 'Hr Krøyer is sketching the scene!'

'He's not the only one,' says Hannah, and she points out two more shadowy figures, sketchbook in hand, drawing. 'They've been drawing since we arrived. Do you wish you'd brought your sketchbook too?'

'I should have done.' I look around at the fire-lit scene and imagine drawing it. Like so much else, the colours would be important. My mind turns to Perroy's palette, as I wonder which paints I'd select. When Mikkel joins us and begins to speak to Hannah, I wander across to look over the artists' shoulders. It's the same scene each time, but viewed quite differently from different angles and by different eyes.

'Marianne?' The voice behind me makes me jump. I feel a rush of delight and I know who it is before I turn around.

'*God aften*, Peter,' I say. I offer him my hand, and he shakes it but doesn't smile.

'Can we talk?' he asks.

'Of course,' I say. My heart beats a little faster as he leads me apart from the crowd, down to the water's edge. The waves are not much more than gentle ripples tonight, lapping almost silently on the shore. The moon has laid a silvery path across the sea. The sounds of the midsummer merriment fade slowly behind us as we walk. I steal a couple of curious sideways glances at Peter, wondering what it is he wants to speak to me privately about. His face is grave.

'I don't know quite how to say this,' he begins at last. 'But please bear in mind that I'm speaking to you as a friend, with your own interests at heart.'

I nod, but this is a bad start.

'There's been a great deal of talk about you recently, Marianne,' Peter says at last. 'I've heard gossip that has surprised me.'

My heart plummets. It's the last thing I want to hear.

'Gossip?' I ask, cautiously. I feel anger as well as disappointment at his words. I know what he's going to say before he says it.

'About you and that French artist.' Peter spits the words out as though they burn his mouth. 'That you're meeting him in secret. Some even say . . . '

'Say what?' I demand angrily. 'You might as well tell me the worst.'

'That you're lovers.' Peter almost whispers the words. He looks drawn and sad in the darkness.

'Do they?' I reply icily. I want to defend myself and explain. But my pride is in the way and keeps me silent. I'm shaking with hurt and anger. How can Peter believe such stories?

He reaches out and takes my hand. 'Tell me it's not true, Marianne?' he begs.

'Do you need to ask?' My voice is stony. 'This place is just like England,' I snarl suddenly. 'Full of malicious gossip.'

'Malicious?' Peter shakes his head, puzzled. 'No, I don't think so. Your friends are worried for you. You're very young, and that man is an experienced flirt, and worse. He's taking advantage of your innocence.'

I'm slightly mollified. We walk on, my hand still in his, and it's comforting.

'But you believe the stories,' I persist.

'Why would there be such rumours?' Peter asks. 'You've been seen late at night together on the beach.'

'That's a lie,' I cry, angry again, and I snatch my hand away. 'I've done nothing wrong. I've only painted with him in the studio. Who's been saying such things?'

Peter turns to face me. 'So you admit you've been meeting him alone?' he asks.

'To paint! In the middle of the afternoon. Nothing more,' I insist. I'm close to tears. I never realized before how important Peter's good opinion is to me.

Peter is silent for a moment, watching me. 'I believe you,' he says at last. 'But it would be better if you had nothing more to do with him. Will you promise me to make sure you are never alone with him again?'

'Don't ask me to make a promise like that!' I beg, distressed.

'Listen, Marianne,' he says. 'This may be innocence on your part, but it's not on his, I can assure you.' This sounds uncomfortably like what Hannah said. I don't want to hear it, so I turn away. Peter follows. 'Everyone knows about him and that married woman he was painting,' he continues. 'Why do you think she and her husband left Skagen in such a hurry? Everyone knew she was his whore.'

The word, even in Danish, triggers a reckless rage in me. That's the word they used about my mother. And it was a lie.

'He'll ruin your life, Marianne.'

'I'm not such a fool. I won't let him.' I stamp my foot in frustration, but then take a deep breath to try and calm myself again. 'I have to learn to paint,' I explain, and my voice only shakes a very little. 'Perroy says I have talent, Peter. He says I could make a living from painting. Don't you see . . . ?'

'There must be some other way to learn,' Peter argues reasonably.

'No,' I reply flatly. 'Not for me there isn't.'

'Marianne,' says Peter in a different voice. He's changed tack. His voice is coaxing now. He's taken my hand again, drawing me towards him. 'Is learning to paint more important than everything else?'

He's close now, like when we danced together. I can feel the warmth of his arms about me and his breath on my hair. My senses are swimming, my anger forgotten. I think he might be about to kiss me and I want him to so much. Peter puts one hand under my chin, pushing it up, until we are looking into each other's eyes.

'Please promise me you won't see him on your own again, Marianne,' he whispers.

I sense that this is a battle of wills and it's vital that I don't give in. If I do now, I always will. I'll never be able to stand my ground, or explain to him when something is important to me. But he's so close to me, it would be so easy to promise, just to forget everything else.

'Promise me?' he repeats, and he just brushes his lips against mine.

'No,' I say, and it comes out as a gasp. I feel him tense at once.

'No?' he asks incredulously.

'No. I have to learn to paint. It matters to me, Peter. I wish I could explain how it makes me feel. How

238

important it is to me. But I do promise you that there is nothing more than painting between myself and Perroy. And there never will be.' I can hear the pleading note in my own voice. I don't want to choose painting over Peter; I want both. I want him to understand. But he doesn't. He releases me abruptly.

'That's not good enough,' he says, breathing fast. Before I can take in what he's said or think of a reply, he turns and stalks off down the beach, away from the party.

I watch him walk away, and feel I'm being torn in two. Blindly, I turn and walk back towards the bonfire. The heat it's giving off is intense. I'm vaguely aware that I'm shaking.

I search for Hannah or Mikkel. When I see them, they are sitting a little apart from the crowd, hands clasped. Hannah looks so happy. I don't want to disturb them. I try to be pleased for Hannah, but it just makes me feel the yawning emptiness inside me all the more acutely. I can feel sobs building up. I need to get away from here before they escape. I stumble away from the fire.

On the way up the beach, I pass Monsieur himself, standing in the shadow of an upturned boat. He's deep in conversation with someone. I see him receive a roll of something, and put it into the inside pocket of his jacket. My surprise is distant and detached; my own troubles are uppermost in my mind. It's not until the man he's with turns around that I pause. It's Christensen. He sees me staring at them, and clears his throat loudly. Monsieur looks around and spots me at once.

'*Ah, ma petite* Marianne!' he says suavely. 'Surely you're not leaving the party already?'

I feel a wave of pure hatred towards him, and turn and walk away before I say anything I regret.

My pillow is wet through with tears before Hannah comes in. I don't even try to control my sobs which are shaking the bed. Hannah doesn't say a word. She just puts her arms around me and holds me tight.

TWENTY-SIX

July 1886

'It's very good, Marianne. A little more yellow. *Bien!*'
Monsieur's voice is in my ear.

'Please don't stand so close, Monsieur,' I beg.

'Ah, won't you call me Jean-Pierre, *ma cherie*?' He laughs softly and I can feel his breath on the back of my neck. I shiver slightly.

'No, it wouldn't be proper,' I tell him, edging away. He moves even closer and takes my hand in his, guiding my brush to put a little more paint on the canvas just where it is needed.

'Always so cautious, the little English girl,' he mocks gently.

I hate it when he tries to flirt with me. It makes me feel confused and anxious, and I wonder whether everyone who has told me not to come here to paint with him is right and I am wrong.

But then he retreats behind his own easel without being asked again. He never goes too far. I suspect he just likes to tease me. And he is an unexpectedly good painting teacher.

I'm attempting to paint Lise gathering flowers. As she bends over, plucking the blossoms, the sun is shining on her. I'm frustrated because I can't get it to look as I want it to. I don't have the time to spend on it, nor the skills I need. Frowning, I try a different colour combination, and then a little more glaze.

'You look cross today, Marianne. You've looked out of temper for over a week now,' Monsieur Perroy remarks.

I shrug. 'Have I?'

I'm hardly likely to tell him what's wrong. That half the town thinks we are lovers, and that Peter's either so shocked or so jealous that he won't speak to me. Annette, too, passed me in the street with only a distant nod. Some days I feel my heart will break. If only I could explain to them the importance of what I'm learning. How painting transforms my life, and makes me see everything differently. I dream that it will be a way out of my poverty too. Thank goodness Mikkel still supports me. Without his constant encouragement, I might have given in by now.

This hour in the afternoon, when Madame is resting in her room and I take up a paintbrush, is reward enough, I tell myself. I've learned more than I could have imagined in so short a time.

But now my time is up for today. It always goes in the blink of an eye.

'I must go. Madame Perroy will be ringing for me any minute,' I tell her husband. I put down my brush and remove my borrowed smock. I put my painting discreetly against the wall to dry, and go to look at Monsieur's painting. He too has made faster progress by spending more hours in the studio.

But today he hasn't been painting. He's been sketching.

'But, that's me!' I say, astonished. 'You didn't ask if you could draw me.'

'If I had, it would have been a different picture. You would have become self-conscious,' he says without remorse.

I tilt my head to one side, looking at the sketch critically. 'Did I really look as cross as that?' I ask.

He chuckles quietly to himself. 'The last few days, *certainement*. I shall name it *La Bonne Qui Peint*.' The Maid Who Paints.

I snort crossly. 'And what happened to your painting?' I ask.

'I sold it,' he tells me. I'm surprised.

'To whom?'

'An admirer, *bien sûr!*' is all he will tell me. 'And that brings me to something else I wish to speak to you about. Stay a few moments longer. Henriette can wait.'

'She'll be angry,' I object, but he just laughs. It's an unkind laugh.

'She's always angry. I have something to ask you.' He adds a few more touches to his sketch and frowns slightly. 'Henriette and I are leaving in a few days,' he says abruptly.

For a moment I don't comprehend what he's saying. Then it begins to sink in. The implications for me are very great.

'Leaving? Already? I thought . . . ' I don't know what I thought. That they would stay all summer, I suppose. My lodging and wage are dependent on their stay.

Monsieur holds up a hand.

'*Un moment!* My wife asks if you will come with us when we leave.'

'Go with you; where?'

'To Paris, of course. Think of it, Marianne. Beautiful Paris. The centre of artistic excellence. You can continue your painting. We will learn together.'

His voice is low, seductive, and for a moment I'm drawn by the idea. I imagine myself in Paris, painting, perhaps even as a student of art. Then reality breaks into my brief daydream.

'Why?' I ask. 'Why would you want to take me with you?' I think of the cost of the journey, and how much cheaper it would be to engage a new maid when they reach France. Monsieur hesitates before he replies. But the answer, when it comes, is as smooth as ever.

'Because we've both grown fond of you, of course,' he says lightly. I look at him through narrowed eyes, but his face remains bland.

'Can I think about it?' I ask. 'I can't take such a decision in a rush.'

'Of course,' Monsieur Perroy replies. 'But you will have to let me know tonight. I need to arrange the journey.'

'Tonight. Very well.' I nod, and leave the studio. When I reach Madame's room, I find her still asleep, cucumber slices laid over her eyes.

'Madame?' I say quietly, drawing back the curtain. The early evening sunshine pours into the room, waking her. I lay out her blue evening dress with the matching shoes.

'It's too bright!' she complains pettishly.

Strange that Monsieur should have spoken of her being fond of me. I'm quite sure she's not fond of anyone, least of all me. She's affectionate and bad-tempered by turn, but I've sensed no warm feelings in her. Nor in him, now I come to think of it. So why do they want to take me with them?

I pour a bowl of water out for Madame to wash, and fetch a clean towel for her.

She yawns, and casts a glance at the dress I've laid out.

'I'll wear the pink dress tonight, Marianne,' she says languidly. 'With the pink scarf and shoes. And my yellow dress needs washing. Why did you hang it back up?'

Smothering my annoyance, I hang the blue dress up again. It doesn't suit me to be at this woman's beck and call. Do I really want to leave my friends here and go with these people? I know the answer to that. But there's the question of what will become of me here once they go.

Madame Perroy hums to herself as I brush and arrange her hair.

'Madame is happy tonight,' I say. 'Is it the prospect of going home?'

'Ah, so my husband has spoken to you,' she replies. Her reflection in the mirror is watching me. 'Yes, we leave this horrible place on Friday. Do you come with us?' Her dark eyes take on a sharp, almost greedy look.

'I haven't decided yet.'

'*Tiens!* But of course you must come! What is there to stay for? It stinks of fish here, and it's always windy. There are no real shops, it's so dull. *Bien sûr* you will accompany us.' Her eyes don't leave me.

I look at her in the mirror as she speaks. You are thinking of your life, not mine, I think. What do I care for shops, I have no money. I love the wind and the open landscape here. For me it spells freedom. A Parisian garret could so easily be a prison. I say nothing more.

I pace our tiny attic room, waiting for Hannah. I want her advice. It's late when she comes, almost time for me to go and put Madame to bed. I scarcely give her time to come into the room before I begin speaking.

'Hannah, I have something to ask you about.' We sit down on the edge of the bed, and I tell her about the offer. She looks more and more horrified as I speak.

'Friday? Three days' time? Marianne, no!' she says at last. 'You can't go with them. I can't believe you're considering it. They haven't even paid you yet. Do you trust them? What would you do alone in Paris if they decided they didn't need you any more? You'd have nowhere to go.'

'I have nowhere to go here,' I point out ruefully. 'Once they leave, I lose my place here. That's my main consideration.'

'I haven't said anything yet, but mother and I have already agreed to ask you to stay next winter with us,' Hannah says quickly. Her eyes are large and sorrowful as she looks at me. Impulsively I hug her.

'You're so kind,' I whisper. 'But how can I possibly be dependent on your goodwill?'

'You won't be dependent, you'll be able to pay your way with the work you have. Please, at least consider it.'

It's delightful to see Hannah so earnest about keeping

me here. Perhaps I asked her advice because I wanted to be persuaded to stay. My father is dead, there's no reason for me to be tied to Skagen. Except that I no longer want to leave.

'And another thing,' Hannah says after a pause. 'How do you know Monsieur won't get bored with teaching you to paint? Then you'll have left your friends for no reason at all. What if he tries to seduce you once he's got you living in his own house? Do you know what I think? I think you are running away, because of the gossip and because you've had a fight with Peter.'

I think about what she's said and sigh. 'Perhaps you're right. It's been very hard these last weeks.' I feel sure that I've lost Peter for good, but I still can't bear the thought of going right away, of never seeing him again.

Hannah senses me weakening, and slips her hand in mine. 'I thought you liked it here,' she says softly.

'I do, I love it. I love the sea and the sky and the landscape. I love the way of life and, best of all, I love you and Mikkel,' I tell her.

'And Peter,' she adds provocatively. I don't reply. It's too painful to think about him. Our estrangement is an empty ache I carry around inside me.

'Thank you,' I say at last. 'For helping me decide. You are right: I do love it here. Perhaps I hadn't fully realized it before, but Skagen is my home now. It really is.' I pause a minute, thinking how true that is, and wondering why it took the chance to leave to make me understand it.

Then I groan.

'I won't be able to learn any more painting.' My heart plummets sickeningly as I realize this. I've given up so much in order to paint, and now I'm losing that too. I haven't forgotten that I still have my pearls. But even if I buy the things I need for painting, who will teach me?

I hug Hannah and hurry off to Madame's room.

I don't find her at her dressing table as I expected, but sitting in a comfortable chair, reading, with an oil lamp on the small table beside her.

'Ah, Marianne,' she says, as I knock and come into the room. 'I don't need you to put me to bed tonight. I'm not at all sleepy. I'll read for a while. But you look very tired; you should go to bed at once.'

I'm not the least bit tired. I stare at her in surprise, then remember my manners and lower my eyes.

'Wouldn't you be more comfortable reading in bed?' I ask.

'No, just go,' she says. 'Oh, and by the way, my husband wants a word with you. He's downstairs in the sitting room.'

I withdraw, wondering at her. She's never put herself to bed before, nor expressed any interest in how I might be feeling.

Monsieur is ensconced on a sofa, laying a game of patience. It's late now; his companions have evidently gone to bed.

'You've come to tell me that you're coming with us, *n'est ce pas*?' he asks quietly, as soon as I come into the room. I shake my head.

248

'No, Monsieur,' I say firmly. 'I've come to tell you that I'm sorry, but I can't go with you. I don't wish to leave Skagen. I belong here.'

He looks surprised for a moment, but then he laughs softly and shrugs.

'So be it. I shall miss you.'

'Not for long, I don't suppose,' I say, and he laughs again, with genuine amusement this time. 'There's another thing,' I say boldly. 'When will I be paid for the two months I've worked?'

Perroy glances at me briefly, and then looks away. 'I will send for you tomorrow morning and settle with you. Will that be satisfactory?'

I curtsey. '*Merci*.' I turn to leave. I'm almost at the door when he speaks again.

'Marianne? I have a word of warning for you.'

'What kind of a warning?' I ask in surprise.

'Not everyone in this town you love so much wishes you well,' he says quietly. He looks quite serious now. The satirical laughter is absent from his face for once. 'You might like to know that I've come into some money. Enough to pay my hotel bill, my journey, and more.'

'You sold a painting? You told me.' I can't imagine what this has to do with me.

'Not at all. Well, yes, that was the bargain for the world to see. But my painting was not worth so much. No, *ma petite*, I was offered a large sum of money for my painting, and in return, I was to remove you from Skagen. To take you far away. And keep you away.'

There's a singing in my ears. I stare at him in shock and dismay.

'Who would do such a thing?' I hear myself say, but even as I speak, I know who it was. I even saw the transaction taking place. 'It was Christensen,' I say, and my voice sounds very far away. 'Why?'

'I know nothing of why.'

'And that's what you were going to do?' I ask, horrified. He shrugs. 'Of course.'

I feel faint with shock. The floor isn't entirely steady under my feet.

'So why are you telling me?' I ask.

Another shrug and a grimace.

'Maybe I have a soft spot for you after all,' he murmurs. 'Maybe I'm pleased you're too wise to come.'

'And will you give the money back?' I ask, stupidly. My mind seems to be working very slowly. Perroy shakes with silent laughter. His serious look has vanished, and his laughter is mocking me again.

'*Non, ma innocente!* What is he going to do about it? Set the police on my tail for failing to kidnap you? No. The wolf has been fleeced, and I find it *fort amusante!*'

I frown at him. I've never found anything less funny in my life. My own uncle wants to be rid of me. So urgently that he will pay someone to remove me. And who's to say the Perroys would have kept me with them once we were away from here? Anything might have happened to me.

'So was it all a lie, then?' I ask faintly. 'You told me that I'm good at painting. Was it just part of this scheme?'

I can hardly bear to hear the answer. But to my relief, he shakes his head.

'I tell you truly, Marianne, that you are a more gifted painter than I. I do not like to admit it, but it is true. It was a pleasure, teaching you.'

I feel unaccountably tearful suddenly. 'Thank you,' I say finally. 'Thank you for everything. I'll see you in the morning.'

Perroy starts to laugh again. 'I wish I could see Christensen's face when he finds us gone and you still here,' he says. He is still laughing softly to himself as I leave the room and make my way up the stairs to bed.

When I go into Madame's room in the morning, it's empty. The bed hasn't been slept in, and her hairbrushes and perfumes are gone from the dressing table. In three swift strides, I cross the room and pull open the wardrobe. Only two dresses are hanging there. Every other item of clothing is gone. In a panic, I turn and run down to the kitchen to find Fru Brøndum.

'So, Marianne,' says Fru Brøndum, coming back into the office where I've been nervously awaiting her. 'It seems that you're right. As far as I can discover, Monsieur Perroy and his wife left in the early hours of the morning in a cart they hired in Vesterby. They will have boarded the early morning train from Frederikshavn by now. Are you telling me you knew nothing of their plans to leave last night?'

'Friday. They told me Friday. He said he had enough money to pay his bills. I know he had, I saw it.'

'Well, he hasn't paid us for the last month, and he hasn't paid you at all, you tell me. I'd be surprised if he hasn't left other debts in the town besides. But he has left one picture and his painting tools and his wife has left two dresses.'

She pauses and smiles at me. Her rather severe face relaxes and looks kind.

'Now it seems to me that you can least afford the loss. You need something by way of payment. Would you like the dresses? They look good quality and might sell well.'

I catch my breath, knowing what I'd like to ask. I wonder if I dare. It's generous of her to consider me at all.

'If it's agreeable to you,' I venture, 'I should prefer the painting things instead.'

She looks taken aback. 'Well yes, if you like, but I should say they're worth far less.'

'Not to me,' I assure her.

'Very well, that's settled then. Now, as to your position here. We're still busy, so I can offer you lodging and a small wage until the end of July, possibly a little longer. It would be for general duties—kitchen work, cleaning, whatever needs doing. Will that suit you?'

'Thank you,' I say, touched and relieved. 'Thank you very much indeed. You're very kind.'

TWENTY-SEVEN

It's hot and sticky in church today. I can feel the perspiration trickling down my back and my head is aching. Next to me, Hannah is trying to fan herself with her handkerchief. The sermon seems to be taking forever. I glance at Hannah and she grimaces at me.

From where I'm sitting, I can see the back of Peter's head, his fair hair neatly combed. I gaze at him longingly, thinking of the smiles we used to exchange, the walks home after church. I despise myself for my weakness, but I long to be friends again. I ache to feel the touch of his hand on mine, to see his eyes light up in laughter. I can't help wondering if he too is unhappy, or whether he has forgotten me already.

On the way out, we gulp at the air, expecting it to be cooler, but even outdoors it's sultry and humid. I feel a cool hand on my arm and turn around to see Anna Ancher smiling at me. Glad to see a friendly face, I smile back.

'I hear you've been learning to paint,' she says. I feel the familiar mixture of anger and shame rush over me. My face must cloud over, because an amused look crosses her face.

'I'm not interested in gossip,' she says calmly. 'Just in painting. I had my first lessons from a visiting artist too, you know. Karl Madsen taught me and my cousins. A more trustworthy teacher than Perroy turned out to be.

'I've seen your sketchbook, Marianne. I was very interested. I wanted to mention to you that I and two of my friends are planning to start a small school for women to learn painting. So few people will teach women, you see. That makes it almost impossible for them to gain entry to the Academy or any other art school. So if you would like to call round one day soon I'd very much like to talk to you further about this.'

'Thank you, I will,' I answer warmly. 'I'd be delighted to in fact.' I'm so excited it's hard not to shout for joy.

'That's settled then,' says Anna Ancher with a smile. 'I'll look forward to seeing you soon.'

She moves on past us and leaves the church.

'Did you hear?' I breathe to Hannah. We only have time to exchange gleeful looks, before the minister, Andreas de Place, stops us. He's standing just outside the church greeting as many of his parishioners as he can.

'How do you do?' he asks, shaking us by the hand. 'Very hot today, very hot indeed. We sometimes get this weather towards the end of July. There's a thunderstorm on its way, mark my words.'

We barely have time to nod and smile at him before he's talking again: 'Of course, it will be much better for us once the church has been extended. You know about our plans, of course? Yes, indeed, next year we hope. The church is overflowing, especially with all the summer visitors. Most gratifying!'

De Place beams at us as though he's personally to be congratulated on the growing popularity of the town. 'Ah! Hr Christensen, a hot morning, is it not? As I was just observing to these young ladies.'

I turn and see Christensen just behind us. He avoids looking at me, merely stepping past me to greet the minister. Mikkel, standing behind his father, manages to send me a swift apologetic glance. His mother glares at me. I meet her eyes straight on, meeting her dislike with my own. Indignantly, she gathers her skirts and sweeps past me. I smile to myself as they all walk away.

'What's going on?' Hannah asks in a quiet voice. She sounds hurt. 'Why did Mikkel ignore us? We haven't done anything wrong, have we?' I sigh and tuck my hand in her arm.

'No, Hannah. It's because of his father. It's he who doesn't want Mikkel to be friends with me. I don't think you have anything to do with it.'

'What does he have against you?' Hannah sounds bewildered. I haven't told her everything that Perroy told me the night he left. 'Is it those stupid rumours about Monsieur?'

'No, it started before that. Soon after I arrived here. I can't explain it. Perhaps he plans a wealthy marriage for Mikkel and is terrified he'll fall in love with a penniless nobody like me.' I try to speak lightly, but Hannah is very quiet. Perhaps she's thinking that she, too, is almost penniless. Fatherless too. Whereas Christensen owns not only his own house and boat, but also several other properties in the town. And it's common knowledge he married for money.

'Did you think he looked well?' Hannah asks after a while.

'Who? Christensen?'

'No, silly. Mikkel. I thought he looked pale and ill.'

'Living with that father is enough to make anyone ill,' I remark bitterly. 'Would you like to catch up with them and see if we can speak to Mikkel alone?'

'I can't. I promised to hurry straight back after church.' Hannah sounds wistful. It's not our Sunday off, we both have to work.

'I'll go then. If I run, I can be back in a few minutes. No one will miss me.'

'Give him my . . . best wishes,' says Hannah.

I leave the sand street and weave round on small paths behind the dunes and houses until I judge I've overtaken them. Then I cut back through to the street, hiding out of sight behind a shop. I wait, out of breath, for Mikkel to appear. It's only a moment until his parents march past, arm in arm, stiffly upright in their Sunday best. Mikkel's brother and sisters are with them. Mikkel has dropped a few paces behind, moodily kicking up sand as he walks. I step forward and wave to him as he passes. I don't dare call to him in case his parents hear.

He notices me at once and his face lights up. Then he nods to his parents with a frown and walks on past. What now? Do I wait? I decide to give him a few minutes.

256

Sure enough, I soon hear running footsteps in the sand and Mikkel comes tearing around the corner.

'I told them I had to call on my friend Carsten,' he says softly. 'Where's Hannah?'

'She has to work. So do I, but I wanted a word with you. Are you all right? Hannah is worried about you. She says you look ill.'

Even as I say this, I realize it's true. Mikkel's face is pale and drawn, and there's a look of deep unhappiness in his eyes.

'Marianne, I can't be seen with you. Something has made my father absolutely furious. He's forbidden me to ever speak to you again. He's been in such a rage the last few weeks, I don't know why.'

I could tell him why, but I don't. He looks anguished, and I'm sure there's more.

'Tell me everything,' I invite him.

'I'm forbidden to continue my studies with Mogens, the schoolteacher. You know he was still coaching me. I told you what my dream was. It's over. My father burned my books. From now on I'm to concentrate on fishing and helping him in his other businesses. I can't bear it, Marianne.' Mikkel's voice breaks and he turns away, angrily brushing his hand over his eyes. I put my arms around him and hug him. I don't know what else to do.

I'm up to my elbows in brown soap and water for the next few hours, washing floors. The humidity grows and the temperature soars. My anger keeps pace with it. By

257

mid afternoon, I can scarcely breathe, and I don't know whether it's the weather or my own rage. I'm scrubbing at a particularly stubborn piece of dirt when it becomes clear to me what I must do. Something I should have done months ago. I wipe my wet hands on my apron and go and seek Fru Brøndum.

'I'm sorry to ask,' I say, 'but would it be possible to have an hour off work? There's something I urgently need to do. Of course I'll make up the time later.'

Fru Brøndum is covered in flour, baking almond cakes for tea. I've never known anyone who works as hard as she does. She looks surprised, even disapproving for a moment, but then, unexpectedly she nods.

'You're a hard worker, Marianne. I trust you to make up the time,' she says. Rare praise. I'm pleased.

I change as quickly as possible into my best dress, and brush my hair. Then I take my mother's letter to Lars Christensen out of my trunk. I only have a short distance to walk, no time for my courage to fail. It's not until I'm knocking on the door of Mikkel's house that it deserts me. Mikkel's mother answers the door. She stares at me, a look of incredulous outrage on her face.

'I wish to speak to Hr Christensen,' I say, and my voice shakes only a little. She gasps.

'Impertinence!' she exclaims. I wonder what her husband has said to her about me. She begins to close the door, but my anger flares up again, and I put my foot against it and push my way into the house. I'm not as tall as Fru Christensen, but I draw myself up to my full height.

'I insist on speaking to your husband,' I say loudly. 'Is he here?'

'Not for you he isn't!' Fru Christensen tells me haughtily.

As I hoped, the sound of our voices carries, and Christensen himself appears.

'What's going on?' He gives me a withering look, but there is a flash of something else behind the look that makes me pause momentarily. It looked almost like fear.

'I'll thank you not to come making a scene in my home,' Christensen says. His words are cold and biting.

'I want to speak to you. Alone. At once.' I don't know where I'm taking the courage from to speak to him so boldly, but it works. He hesitates only a moment before pulling his watch from his waistcoat pocket and consulting it.

'I can give you five minutes of my time,' he says, and snaps his watch shut. He then leads the way through the sitting room, where Mikkel and his brother and sisters are sitting. Mikkel has a copy of the Bible open in his hands, but he's not reading. He sends me a look of pure horror when he sees me. I shake my head at him very slightly as I follow his father through into another room. It has a bed, but is obviously mainly used as an office. There's a large desk strewn with papers. Christensen sits down stiffly in his chair at the desk. He doesn't offer me a seat, so I'm forced to stand before him. I see him glance at the letter in my hand and I put my hand out of sight behind my back.

'Well?' he asks.

I can feel hatred and anger churning inside me. I make an effort to master it, to speak calmly, but I don't succeed. I've been rehearsing what to say to him all afternoon, but now the words desert me. After a moment's painful silence, I end up blurting out: 'Why do you hate me so?'

Even in my own ears it sounds childish and petulant.

Christensen observes me narrowly before replying. 'You are mistaken,' he says heavily. 'I don't know you.' His voice hardens as he continues: 'But it is quite natural that I should object to a Frenchman's whore as company for my son.'

'That's a lie,' I cry passionately.

Christensen looks at me almost triumphantly, and I sense that I won't get anywhere with anger and indignation. I need to be as cool as he is. I clench my trembling hands into fists and try to bring my temper under control.

'Do you believe all the gossip you hear?' I ask with a creditable attempt at calm. I force myself to look at him. 'No. In fact, I expect you helped make those stories up.'

'Nonsense,' he snaps dismissively, but I can see a slight flush under his tan, and I wonder if I've hit home. He gets up and walks to the window and back. Then he leans on his desk watching me.

We both stand in silence for a moment, and I try to find the words to say what I really came to say. And I pray that I'm doing the right thing. In the end I come straight out with it: 'I think we both know the truth about my parentage,' I say.

Christensen sits down abruptly in his chair. He's gone as white as a sheet.

'You know who I am, don't you?' I ask. 'You don't dislike me because of any connection I had with Perroy. It started long before that. As soon as I arrived in Skagen. You were shocked at the very sight of me. I suppose your brother must have . . .'

'My brother?' Christensen gasps. He clutches the edge of the desk and leans forward, a look of painful intensity on his face. 'What do you know of my brother?'

'That he was my father,' I say, and I'm surprised how calmly I'm managing to speak. This feels unreal, like a dream. The truth is out. There's no going back. 'Which makes me your niece, doesn't it? Why would you hate your niece, Hr Christensen? Hate her so much that you would pay someone as unreliable as Perroy to take her off to Paris?'

'That's a lie,' Christensen gasps. 'You can't prove it.' His eyes dart about unsteadily.

I shrug. I can't prove it, but I don't need to. We both know.

'I can prove I'm who I say I am,' I tell him. I produce my mother's letter from behind my back and lay it on the desk in front of him. 'This is a letter my mother wrote to your brother before she died,' I explain. 'I don't know what it says. You'll see it's still sealed.'

Christensen stares at the letter without touching it. He looks almost afraid of it. I see a muscle below his right eye twitch. I still don't know how much he knows.

261

'Did my father write to you?' I ask. 'Did he tell you about my mother?' There's a long pause.

'Yes,' Christensen croaks at last. 'That's right. He wrote me a letter before he . . . died.'

I nod, but I'm not satisfied. 'But you seemed to recognize me, that day on the west coast.'

'No. How could I have done?' His voice is stronger now. 'I did not know you existed. But I deduced from your name who you might be.'

'Then why did you not speak to me about it?'

'Why did you not come to me?' Christensen counters. I stare at him perplexed, trying to fathom his behaviour. None of it quite adds up.

'Perhaps I should have come sooner,' I admit. 'But I had seen you, and heard a little about you, and I was afraid.'

'Afraid?' Christensen looks shocked, but he can't possibly be surprised.

'Yes, afraid. You looked so stern. And the Anchers told me, you see, about your strict views. My childhood in England was . . . difficult. Because of my birth. I didn't want the same thing to happen here.' I'm aware my voice sounds constricted. I'm finding this subject really difficult to talk about. Especially to this man whom I dislike so intensely.

Christensen makes a strangled sound in his throat and gets to his feet. Instinctively I take a step back, but he merely begins to pace the room, his face working soundlessly.

'So why are you here now?' he demands abruptly. 'What is it that you want from me? Money?'

'No!' I cry indignantly. 'I came because Mikkel is un-happy. You are being cruel to him. Because you're angry that Perroy let you down.' There are so many thoughts in my head and I struggle to put them into words. 'You can't punish me, so you punish him. It's not fair.'

Christensen turns on me: 'Don't tell me how to raise my son,' he shouts furiously. 'Don't tell me . . . ' his voice trails off unexpectedly. My heart is hammering with fright.

I'm shaking now. My whole body is trembling. The man who is my uncle merely sits down heavily at the desk again, and stares into space. I don't know what I expected from him. I certainly didn't expect him to welcome me into his family with open arms. But this silence is dreadful.

'Was my father anything like you?' I ask. 'Because if he was, I'm glad I never met him.'

Exhausted, I turn towards the door. I've taken far more than five minutes of his time, but I'm not sure I've achieved anything. Then I hear his voice, 'Marianne, wait . . . ' Christensen is standing bowed over, one hand stretched out. He looks different all of a sudden. Older, more vulnerable. I pause. It's the first time he's used my name. But then he draws himself up again.

'Nothing. Go. Just go,' he mutters.

I push the door open and leave, walking past Mikkel and his family who are sitting quietly together in the parlour. I send Mikkel an apologetic look as I pass. I let myself out. I've gained nothing except possibly to get Mikkel deeper into trouble.

Instead of walking back to the hotel, I turn my steps towards the beach. The air is like soup, thick and heavy. My clothes and hair stick damply to me, and I feel as though I might suffocate any minute.

TWENTY-EIGHT

I glance behind me as I walk down to the beach. A huge storm cloud is gathering in the west. Out to sea it still looks like a warm summer's day, the sun sparkling on the water. But as I turn and begin to walk south along the coast, I can see the cloud piling up, drawing closer. It's inky black, tinged with yellow. Jagged bolts of lightning flash across it. The air is heavy and still.

Only a part of my mind is interested in the storm. The rest is busy puzzling over Christensen's behaviour. I feel there's something that's eluding me, like a piece of the jigsaw that's gone missing. If I had it, if I could see the whole picture, I'd be able to make sense of it. As it is, I don't understand. I'm also bitterly disappointed. I suppose despite everything, I hoped for a warmer reception from the only family I have.

A small voice to my right disturbs my thoughts.

'Marianne?' A small, grubby child emerges from behind an upturned boat. She stands sucking her thumb, watching me. Her dress is a dirty rag, her hair a tangled mass.

'Lise?' I can hardly believe my eyes. Three months ago, I left her clean and tidy, with a ribbon in her hair. I can hardly see it's the same child.

'Lise, look at you, what's the matter?'

She shakes her head and doesn't move. I can hear the first rumbles of thunder in the distance.

'I miss you, Marianne. You promised to come and see me, but you never did.'

A feeling of guilt creeps over me. She's right, I haven't been back once. I've been too busy, too selfish.

'Come here, Lise. You've found me now.' Taking her grubby hand, I lead her down to the water's edge. The water is silted and sluggish today. I scoop some up and wash her hands and face. Close to, I can see her hair is crawling again, but there's nothing I can do about that.

'You're not wearing your ribbon.' I don't know what else to say.

'Mother took it away. A long time ago.' Lise says this simply, accepting it. My own problems recede as I look at the lost little girl before me and grieve for her happy chatter and bright looks. They are gone now as though they had never been. I resolve not to neglect her again, but I don't say it aloud this time. She might not believe me.

'And how are your brothers and sisters?' I ask her. She doesn't understand the question, so I ask: 'Do Jakob and Morten go fishing?'

'Jakob does, he brings food home for us most days,' she nods. 'But Morten gets drunk, and gets mad at us all.' She says this quite artlessly, but also sorrowfully.

There's a crack of thunder, and the heavy, hot air stirs languidly. I feel my hair move. The storm cloud reaches the sun and covers it, like a lamp being blown out. We both shiver.

'Lise, there's a storm coming. You should get home now.'

Lise shakes her head. 'No, I want to stay with you.'

I don't have the energy to argue. My limbs feel weighed down and my head hurts. I walk on along the beach and she follows me, slipping her hand in mine. Not surprisingly, the beach is almost deserted. A few children have been bathing, but are leaving now, with anxious glances at the storm clouds inland. One boy keeps looking out to sea as well, as though searching for something. I follow his gaze, but can't see anything. No boats or ships.

Further down, some men have been hauling their boats high up onto the beach, in case the storm stirs up the sea. They too are leaving. Only one man remains. He has his back to us, working on his boat. It's unusual to see anyone breaking the Sabbath. As we come closer we can see he's scraping at the upturned hull with a tool of some sort.

A stronger gust of wind blows across the beach, and this time the air is colder. It also brings a few heavy drops of rain with it. I look up. The cloud is almost upon us. The day has darkened as though it were evening. The weather suits my mood. I'd like to stay on the beach throughout the storm, but I know I should take Lise home.

We're almost level with the man working on the boat. My stomach drops sickeningly as he turns and I see it's Peter. It's too late to turn away now, he's seen us. A huge flash of lightning flickers, reflecting on his face.

'*Dav*, Marianne,' he says coldly. No doubt he thinks I've thrown myself in his way on purpose. I'm mortified. Peter turns away from me, but then hesitates and turns back. He looks at me more closely, and his face is no longer hostile.

'So, you didn't . . . you didn't go away with them after all. The French people.'

He seems to be struggling to find the words, but I'm delighted that he's speaking to me at all.

'No. I never had any intention of leaving with them. They invited me, but I preferred to stay in Skagen. Besides,' I give a shaky laugh, 'they don't pay very well. Not at all in fact.'

Peter nods gravely. 'So I heard,' he says, and I'm not surprised he already knows. Skagen is a small place.

Another bright flash of lightning is followed by a loud crack of thunder right overhead. It makes us all jump. The rain begins to fall in earnest, and a squall of wind makes my skirts flap and whips some strands of my hair out of its bun. I feel Lise shiver again. Peter looks up at the sky.

'You should both go home,' he says. 'It's going to be a bad storm.'

'You're right.' I tug on Lise's hand. 'Come on, Lise, I'll take you.' But she's looking out to sea.

'Why's that boy still swimming?' she asks, pointing.

Peter and I both look out to sea, sure she must be mistaken. 'No one's swimming now, Lise,' I tell her. 'They've all gone home.' But the words are scarcely out of my mouth before I spot a white arm flash some distance out.

I screw up my eyes and can just make out a head. It looks like a child.

'The fool!' exclaims Peter. He glances up at the sky again. 'What the devil is he doing right out there?' He hesitates only a moment and then throws his tools aside and turns his boat back over. Throwing its small anchor and both oars in, he begins to drag it down to the water.

'Let me go with you,' I beg at once.

'Of course not,' Peter says firmly. 'Get that child home. I'll fetch the lad in.'

But I help him push the boat down to the water, and then out some distance until she floats. Waves are rushing onto the beach. He grasps my hand briefly. 'Thank you, Marianne. Now go.'

I don't answer him. I just stand there, knee deep in the water, watching him as he takes the oars and begins to row out.

'Marianne?' calls Lise from the beach. 'I'm getting all wet.' It's raining hard now; the drops are landing on my head, running down my face and neck. My skirts are swirling unheeded about my ankles in the sea. I wade back to Lise and kneel down, putting my hand on her shoulder.

'I'm going to stay here, to make sure Peter's safe. But you must go home now.'

Lise pouts. 'I'm not going home, everyone's cross there. I like being with you.' Another crack of thunder, like an explosion, makes her shriek and throw her arms around me.

I disengage myself, and stand up, my eyes seeking

Peter's boat. I can't see the boy any longer. It's raining in great sheets. The wind is buffeting us. Lines of waves are tearing inland, marking each of the sandbars. Water is streaming down me. My hair has come down but I don't care. I feel a fierce exaltation in being out in the elements like this.

We're both watching the boat, now far out in the surf, when a huge jagged flash of lightning reaches down out of the sky towards it. There's a huge bang, followed so immediately by a crack of thunder that it sounds almost like an echo. We both jump, and scream with fright. When I recover, and search for Peter's boat, I can see only an upturned hull. I dash the rain out of my eyes and look again.

'Oh, what's happened? Did the lightning strike the boat?' I stare through the rain and murky light, desperate to see some sign of Peter, but I can see nothing except the hull, bobbing in the swell.

'We must get help.' I begin to run up the beach, pulling Lise with me. 'Come on!' The wind is driving the raindrops straight into my face and tearing at my wet hair. I can hardly see where I'm going. I almost fall over another small rowing boat. The next flash lights it up, upturned on the sand, its oars neatly stowed beneath it. It's clear to me at once what I must do.

First I kneel down beside Lise again. Taking her by both shoulders, I shout to her urgently, fighting to be heard above the waves and wind.

'Listen to me. I need your help. Peter's in danger and I can't leave him. Do you understand?'

She nods.

'Good. This is what I need you to do.' I smooth back her hair that the rain has plastered to her face. 'Run to the nearest house. Bang on the door until someone answers. You have to find grown-ups. Tell them Peter Hansen's in trouble. And that Marianne is trying to help. Can you do that?'

'Yes.' Lise nods bravely. 'Will you be safe, Marianne?'

'I will be,' I promise. 'As long as you fetch help.'

But I'm not as sure as I try to sound. I'm shaking as I pull the small boat down to the sea and push it into the waves. The strong offshore wind helps me. With my usual inelegant scramble, I haul myself into the boat and fit the oars into the rowlocks. I've never rowed on the open sea before, and this is a really bad time to start.

I fight with the waves as they try to push me off course, but the wind helps me onwards in uneven jumps. The water is slapping against the sides of the boat. The effort steadies my nerves. It's better to be doing something than standing helplessly on the beach.

Every few strokes, I look anxiously over my shoulder to check I'm on course for Peter's upturned boat. It's still there, rocking. Eventually I reach it. I hear a weak shout over the noise of the wind. A pale skinny arm waves to me from the far side of the upturned boat. As my own craft bumps into the hull, I ship my oars and grab hold of it. Hand over hand, I pull myself around.

'Peter?' I cry.

'*Her er han!*' Here he is, calls a faint voice. The two

271

boats are bumping and knocking against one another in the turbulent sea. I hang on grimly, leaning over the side of my own boat, pulling it around Peter's, until I see the boy. He's clinging to the edge of the boat with one hand, trying to hold on to Peter's limp body with the other arm. He's not managing to keep Peter's head out of the waves, which wash right over him from time to time. His eyes are closed, and he's as pale as death.

'Is he alive?' I gasp, anguished.

'I don't know,' splutters the boy. 'Help!'

I reach down into the water and take hold of Peter under his arms. I try to pull him up into the boat, but he's far too heavy for me. I can't do more than lift him a short way, rocking the boat precariously.

'Help me!' I order the boy. He tries to push Peter, but it doesn't make any difference. He just disappears under the water himself.

'I can't,' he gasps, coming up again. His skin has a bluish tinge, he looks exhausted.

'Can you climb in?' I ask. He pulls himself around to the opposite side and tries. He's so weak it takes him two or three goes to get over the side. As the boat lurches, I cling desperately to Peter.

The boy is skinny and small, he can't be more than ten years old. He's also completely naked. He sits in the boat, shivering in the wind and the rain. The lightning and thunder continue around us.

'What are you doing out here?' I demand angrily.

'It was a stupid bet,' he says, shamefaced. 'I went out further than I meant to. I didn't see the storm coming

272

up behind me. He came out to get me,' he says, pointing at Peter. 'Is he all right?'

'I don't know. Help me get him in.' He leans over the side of the boat next to me and takes hold of Peter as well. Together we pull with all our strength. The boat tips, slopping water over the side. Even between us, we can't pull Peter high enough to get him aboard. We just bang him against the edge of the boat.

I can feel hot tears of fear and frustration running down my face, mingling with the rain and the salt sea-water. 'I'm sorry, Peter,' I say, as I hold him tight. Every lurch bruises my ribs as I lean out over the edge of the boat, but I hang on. I slip one hand inside Peter's shirt, to where I think his heart should be. His skin is cold and slippery like a corpse. But as I hold my hand against his chest, I think I can feel a faint heartbeat. It gives me hope.

'What's your name?' I shout to the boy.

'Jesper,' he shouts back.

'Look towards the beach, Jesper. Can you see anyone?' He stares inland, shielding his eyes against the lashing rain.

'I'm not sure,' he shouts at last.

'Then you'll have to row us in. I can't let go of Peter.'

Shivering, Jesper reaches for the oars and fits them into the rowlocks. He pulls feebly on them, but he's rowing against the wind now and we don't make any progress.

'Row harder!' I yell.

'I'm too tired,' he pleads.

My arms are aching, I'm chilled and bruised and terrified for Peter. I've no patience left, and lose my temper completely.

'None of us would be here if it wasn't for your stupidity,' I shout. 'Do you want him to die for rescuing you? It's up to you to get us back to the beach!'

In reply, he sets his teeth and pulls with all his might, fighting the wind. The waves are with us at least. Now I can feel the boat moving. I hang on to Peter, my arms numb, and murmur words of encouragement that he can't hear. 'We'll soon be safe, you're going to be all right,' I tell him. 'Just don't die, please don't die. We're nearly there.'

The rain lessens gradually, and it's no longer quite so dark. All of a sudden, Jesper ships the oars, and turns around.

'Here! Over here!' he yells, waving his arms.

A boat emerges out of the rain, four men on board. Strong hands take Peter from me and haul him out of the waves. Jesper too, is lifted across and wrapped in a blanket and an oilskin. One of the men reaches out for me. With a shock, I recognize Christensen. Instinctively, I push him away.

'Don't you touch me!' I shout at him furiously.

'What do you think you're doing out here?' he cries in a hoarse voice. 'You could have got yourself killed!'

'What do you care if I drown?' I yell.

'Så så,' says a soothing voice, and another man puts Christensen out of his way and helps me across into the bigger boat.

'You've had a fright, but there's no need for heated words or blame,' he says kindly, wrapping me in a blanket. Christensen secures the small rowing boat so it can be towed ashore. A man is pouring *snaps* into Peter's mouth. He chokes and stirs, but doesn't recover consciousness. He's so pale.

'He's alive,' I hear someone say. They lay him down in the bottom of the boat. I can't bear to see his head against the boards. I scramble across to him, lifting his heavy head and cradling it in my lap. As the men row with strong strokes towards the beach, I stroke Peter's wet hair out of his face, and allow a small measure of relief to wash over me. He's alive, surely that means he'll be all right. The rain has almost stopped now, and the storm is heading out to sea. We reach the beach in no time.

The three of us are lifted out and carried onto the sand one by one. One man asks me briefly what happened, and I explain as best I can. In return, he tells me how Lise raised the alarm for us.

Once they've hauled the boats up onto the beach, two men set off with Peter, carrying him home. I want to go with him, but I don't know what sort of reception I'd get from his family. Jesper is led off by another man, and I'm left alone on the beach with Christensen. The last man in the world I want to be with.

Weak and trembling, I turn and begin to walk towards the hotel.

'Marianne!' calls Christensen. I ignore him, but he follows me. 'Wait! Are you well enough to go by yourself? I'm sorry I scolded you . . . '

275

I turn on him. 'Leave me alone, I hate you,' I say fiercely.

'You don't understand. Marianne, I must speak with you once more.'

'I don't want to hear anything you have to say!' I spit the words out, glaring at him. This time he flinches and takes a step back.

I turn and stumble away from him as fast as I can. All the way back to the hotel, I'm aware of him following at a distance, but he doesn't attempt to speak to me again.

TWENTY-NINE

August 1886

I t's been a long day. I wanted to make up the time I missed yesterday. Fru Brøndum said I didn't have to. When I insisted on being allowed to work, she gave me light duties such as setting tables and blanching almonds. She praised me for my bravery. Everyone is making far too much fuss about what I did. Anyone would have done the same.

A note was brought to me by an errand boy an hour ago. Sitting on my bed, I break the seal and spread the paper open on my lap. Although I've learned spoken Danish, and can read some of my hymn book, written Danish is still a struggle for me. I need to spend some time over it before I'm sure I understand it all:

My dearest Marianne,

Peter has a concussion and must remain quietly in bed for several days at least. The doctor has good hopes that he will make a complete recovery.

It is thanks to you, Marianne, that he is here for us to nurse. Words cannot express our gratitude. We hope that you are none the worse for your exposure to the storm.

With all good wishes,

Annette Hansen

Impulsively, I decide to run over there at once. I hope they won't mind. It's only early evening after all. I quickly wash my face and hands and change my dress. I run all the way to Peter's house, stopping only to pluck a bunch of rosebay willowherb on the way. The tall pink flowers grow in patches around the houses at this time of year, their fluffy seeds blowing in the wind.

The back door is open, a couple of hens scratching in the sand outside. I slow down in order to catch my breath, and then walk in through the workroom. Peter's father is sitting on a stool, mending the nets. His face lights up when he sees me. He gets to his feet, calling for his wife. Annette comes out of the kitchen, wiping her hands on her apron. She embraces me warmly.

'Dear girl,' she murmurs. Her coldness of the last month is apparently in the past, and I'm more than happy.

'Christensen told us what happened,' she continues. 'You saved Peter's life.'

'It wasn't just me.' The mention of Christensen has unsettled me. What has he been saying about me? 'If Lise Jakobsen hadn't run for help, we might never have reached the beach,' I explain.

'She's a good girl too,' Annette agrees. 'Come in and sit down, my dear. Can I get you anything? A glass of ale? Or a cup of coffee?'

I shake my head. 'No, thank you. You don't want to be bothered with visitors. I just came to hear how Peter is. And to bring these.' I offer her the bunch of wild flowers.

'*Tak!*' says Annette, and begins hunting distractedly for

a vase or a pot to stand them in. 'Sorry if I'm not quite myself,' she says, emerging from a cupboard. 'It's been a shock, you understand.' She stands still a moment, her hand to her head. I take the vase from her and pour some water into it. Then I put the flowers in, trying to arrange them so they sit prettily.

'We all know, of course,' she continues, watching me, 'that while the sea provides our living, it can also take our husbands, brothers, and sons from us at any time. And when they carried Peter in yesterday afternoon, I thought at first . . .

'He was limp and so very white. But they assured me he was only unconscious. My husband went straight for the doctor. He has a huge bruise on the back of his head. That's what caused the harm. Luckily it's summer, so he wasn't exposed to severe cold in the water.'

'The bruise must be from when the boat overturned,' I explain.

'Come and have a glimpse of the patient,' Annette begs. 'Then please sit down and tell me exactly how it all happened.'

Peter is very pale, lying on his back, breathing heavily. His head is bandaged, and it gives me a fright to see him like that. I long to sit by him and talk to him, hold his hand, but his mother ushers me anxiously back out again.

'He needs rest,' she whispers. I understand that while I'm forgiven, while they are grateful to me, she doesn't want me too close to Peter. Perhaps she still believes the rumours about me.

We sit and talk while dusk creeps into the corners of the house. The days are already drawing in. It's difficult to relive the events of yesterday, and embarrassing to be treated like a heroine. I try to play down my own part in the rescue, but Peter's parents have heard a glowing report from Christensen. It seems strangely unlike him to speak well of me. I mistrust his motives.

It's late when I return to the hotel. I feel happier than I've felt for a long while, optimistic that Peter will recover. My happiness is further increased by the sight of an easel, oils, and a bundle of brushes in the corner of our attic room. Someone has carried up Perroy's things for me. I run my hands over them longingly, before pulling on my nightgown and climbing into bed. Hannah is already fast asleep beside me.

It's my last day in the hotel today. My things are packed and ready to go to Hannah's house where I'm to stay through the winter months. I'm leaving in the morning.

In the middle of the afternoon, Hr Brøndum calls me down to the office and pays me the last of my wages. It's not a large sum, as most of my money was to have come from the Perroys. But together with the money I earned sewing for Annette, it should see me through the winter.

I'm about to leave the office, when Hr Brøndum asks me to sit down again.

'There's a visitor here for you, Marianne. He's asked to see you in private, so I've shown him into the far sitting room. Will you go to him now?'

'A visitor? For me?'

I can't imagine who would come and see me at the hotel. As I follow Hr Brøndum through the first two sitting rooms, I run through all the possibilities in my mind.

In the last sitting room, standing looking out of one of the windows, hands clasped behind him, is Christensen. As we enter, he turns. He nods his thanks to Brøndum, who withdraws, pulling the door shut behind him.

'You,' I state baldly, not bothering to conceal the dislike I feel.

'Please.' Christensen holds up a hand briefly in a supplicating gesture. 'Allow me to explain. Take a seat.'

I hesitate a moment and then sit down on the very edge of an upright chair near the door. I'm as far away from him as possible without actually leaving the room. Christensen watches me and shakes his head a little. He looks sad.

'I've made you hate me,' he says heavily. 'It's hardly surprising.' He pauses, and sits down, but then stands up again. 'I don't know where to start,' he says, his eyes on me. 'Perhaps I should tell you, first of all, that I read your mother's letter.' His voice shakes. I wonder what was in the letter. 'I realize I have a great deal of explaining to do, Marianne. I do not think what I have to tell you will make you like me any better. Where to begin? I suppose it began the day when my son came home and told me a young English girl had arrived in Skagen, with the name of Marianne Shaw on her trunk.'

Christensen stops and shakes his head again: 'No. It

starts further back than that. Much further back. With a shipwreck, in fact. And yet that's not the right place to start either.'

Christensen sits down again, and stares at his hands, clasping and unclasping them. I stare at him in surprise. He is so far from his usual stern, self-contained self that I can scarcely recognize him. His hair is windblown, his face pale, with dark shadows beneath his eyes. He's wearing his Sunday best, though it's a weekday, but he looks as though he's dressed all by guess. Everything is slightly creased and crooked.

'When you came to see me last Sunday,' he begins, 'you were honest and courageous enough to speak of the relationship that . . . exists between us.'

There's a pause while he looks out of the window. The only sound I can hear is the faint buzz of a fly against the windowpane.

After a few moments, Christensen puts his head in his hands and gives a small moan. Then he stands up abruptly and paces the room. 'I need to go back to that shipwreck I mentioned after all. We were two brothers. Lars and myself. My name is Per. We ran away from home together. Did you know that much?' I nod, and he continues. 'Our father was a stern man. Prosperous by Skagen standards, but miserly. He worked us hard, beat us often, and gave little reward. We were sure we could do better elsewhere. So we left.'

He pauses. How closely he's describing himself when he speaks of his father. I wonder whether he's aware of it.

282

'We were young and foolish. We soon found, of course, that we could only get work doing what we'd learned: fishing. And there was no family standing by to make sure we were paid fairly. We got as far as Ribe before we found work on the freight ships which sailed to and fro to England back then. Ribe is right down in the south of Jutland in case you don't know. It's all changed now. Esbjerg is the biggest harbour, but that's by the by.

'It was on a trip to England that we ran aground. The tides and the sandbanks of the Humber estuary can be treacherous, as I'm sure you know. We were caught in a summer storm. My brother and I were sleeping below deck when the ship ran into a sandbank. We felt the tremendous lurch, the groaning and shrieking of the boat. Water began rushing in at once. We struggled up on deck to find the crew had already taken the lifeboat and left us.'

Christensen pauses in his narrative, and paces the room a few times. He picks up a napkin from the table and begins twisting it in his hands. He seems agitated. I wait for him to continue his tale, curious to hear what he has to say.

'There are two occasions in my life when I acted neither honourably nor bravely,' he continues. 'And both occurred during that ill-fated England trip. I've worked hard throughout my life since, to atone. I've been stern and severe with others, but hardest of all upon myself. But I've never told anyone the truth as I'm about to tell you, Marianne.

'The ship was sinking fast, listing heavily to one side

and taking in water. We had only one life ring between us. My brother went below in search of the spare life-jackets we knew were stored in the hold. But while he was down there, the ship, with a great screech and groan, began to break up. Huge waves broke across the stern, pouring water over us. The ship was slipping down off the sandbank into the deeper water, and I knew she was lost.'

Christensen looks wild-eyed as he tells me this, and I realize he's reliving the experience he has kept a secret for so long. Despite myself, I've become involved. I ask breathlessly: 'What did you do?'

'At that moment I had a choice,' he tells me, and walks to one of the windows to look out. I wonder whether he's seeing the garden outside or the storm of long ago. 'I could have gone down and tried to help my brother out. Or I could have waited for him. Either would have been braver than what I did do. Taking the life ring, I jumped into the sea and struck out for shore.' Christensen glances briefly at me, perhaps trying to gauge my reaction. I remain silent and he sighs.

'I've gone over that moment so many times. If only I'd waited a little longer, if only I'd gone down for him. But I didn't. As a member of the lifeboat crew I have helped save dozens of lives since then. But it doesn't matter how many people I save: it will never be enough. Because I left my brother to drown.'

'But . . . how can he have drowned? That doesn't make any sense.' I'm bewildered suddenly. 'You left my father to drown?'

284

'No,' he says quickly. 'Let me explain a little further. I barely survived the swim myself. It was summer, so the sea wasn't cold. But I was caught by a current or the tide, I never knew which, and swept helplessly for miles. The wind was strong, and the waves huge. I often couldn't even see the shore, and when I tried to swim towards it I made little progress. I have a vague memory of seeing the beach before me at last, and of being swept onto the sand by the surf. I was beyond exhaustion.

'The rest I know because I was told rather than because I can remember it. I was found unconscious on the beach by a gentleman who was out for an early morning stroll on the sands. He had me carried home to be nursed. His name was Edward Shaw. Your grandfather, in fact.'

'*You* were?' I gasp. I know this part of the story from my mother, but it doesn't match. 'No, you can't have been. It was Lars.'

Christensen shakes his head sadly and continues.

'His body was never found. The bodies of the rest of the crew were however. They were less lucky than me. Their lifeboat overturned and they were all drowned. I have always seen it as a judgement on them for abandoning us.

'I was in a fever for several days. When I came to myself, I found I'd been identified as Lars Christensen from the only document they had found on me that was still legible. I could have corrected them, of course. I should have done. But I was weak after the fever. I had no strength and little English for explanations. And it gave me some comfort at the time to be called by my brother's name. Later, of course, I hid behind the name.'

He pauses for a long moment. 'I'm afraid I'm the man your mother knew as Lars. I am your father.'

'It can't be true,' I whisper, appalled. Whatever I had expected to hear from him, it wasn't this. How can this possibly be the man my mother loved so devotedly all these years? My overriding emotion is one of sick disgust. 'You *lied* to me,' I accuse him. 'And you lied to my mother.'

Christensen sits down opposite me. He scans my face searchingly, but I don't want to look at him. 'I did lie, Marianne. I was a coward,' he admits. 'God will punish me for it.'

'So you've known all this time? And said nothing? Treated me like . . . ' It's my turn to jump to my feet. I, too, walk to the window. My eyes look out, but my gaze is inward, seeing the scenes he's described, trying to fit all the information together. And it does fit, I realize reluctantly. Abruptly I turn back to face him. 'You have more to explain,' I say harshly. 'You promised my mother you'd return. Why didn't you?'

Christensen buries his face in his hands again, his fingers clutching at his hair.

'I meant to,' he cries in a muffled voice. 'God be my witness, I intended to return.' He pauses, and then raises his head. 'Your grandfather threw me out of the house. Did your mother tell you that? I would have married her there and then. I wanted nothing more. But he refused. A great many hard words were said. He blamed me for engaging her affections.'

'He didn't know she was with child though, did he?' My tone is hard and bitter.

'How could he have done? I didn't know myself.'

'But you must have realized it was possible.'

'I didn't think . . . I was very young, Marianne.'

'My mother was even younger,' I say angrily. 'You promised her you'd come back, you promised to write, and you never did. She had to cope with the consequences. And still she loved you. All her life. She trusted you'd come for her as you promised. She even sent me looking for you after she died. Looking for the wrong man, as it turns out.' I'm furious, shaking with rage. All those years of hardship and loneliness are his fault. He did it to us.

Christensen—I can't think of him as my father—is weeping now. Tears are trickling down his weather-beaten cheeks into his beard. They don't move me in the least.

'When I reached Esbjerg,' he continues, his voice unsteady, 'there was a letter from my mother. It had been waiting for some time. She wrote that my father had died. She begged me to return. So I did. With my older brother dead, I was suddenly the heir to everything. The house, the boat, the land my father had owned.'

'So why didn't you write to my mother then?'

'I meant to. From day to day, I put it off. In the end I thought perhaps she would have forgotten me, living in her grand house in Mablethorpe. I thought I might just have been a passing fancy for her . . . '

'As she was for you?' I demand, horrified.

'I didn't say that,' Christensen countered swiftly.

'You didn't need to. I see it all now. Meanwhile my

287

mother was turned out of the house for expecting your child and spent the rest of her life in a shabby tenement room in Grimsby, working for her living. I never even saw this grand house you're talking about. Meanwhile, you just happened to make a very advantageous marriage here yourself, didn't you?' I don't try to hide my bitterness and anger. On the contrary, I take pleasure in lashing him with my words. He deserves it all. He looks both shocked and embarrassed. I look at him, bowed and tearstained, and wonder how I could ever have found him frightening.

'Did you ever really love my mother?' I ask him. 'Even for a moment?'

'Of course I loved her. I've had a lifetime to regret my decision. But it was too late. All too late.'

'I don't believe you,' I say. There's a long silence. He makes no attempt to convince me. 'Shall I tell you something of my mother's life after you left?' I ask. He turns anxious eyes on me. I suspect he'd rather not know, but I tell him anyway.

'Her father gave her an hour to leave the house when he discovered her condition. She was only able to take one bag and one trunk with her and was forbidden ever to communicate with her family again. The coachman had orders to drive her to a destination of her choice and leave her there. She only had money because her mother managed to disobey her husband and give her some before she left.

'I don't know where she went first, friendless and ashamed as she was, but I know that she ended up at

Hope House in Grimsby. I don't suppose you know it, do you? No, of course not. You could have no reason to go to such a place. It's a house of Christian charity. They rescue "fallen women" and try to turn them to a better way of life. That's where I was born. In a house full of prostitutes.'

Christensen is silent. I can see a dawning horror in his face. It's clear he never considered this possibility. I feel a savage pleasure in his unhappiness.

'I don't know how mother managed in the first years, but in all the years I can remember, we moved from one sordid tenement building to another. We were reviled and despised. An unmarried mother and her illegitimate child. We made our living from sewing, which I learned as soon as I could hold a needle. We had no friends, we went nowhere. While you lived here in comfort, honoured and respected, my mother was called a whore, and grew sick in the smoke and dirt of Grimsby. You broke her heart.'

'You are breaking mine now,' Christensen replies hoarsely. He's no longer crying his tears of self-pity. He's pale and still.

'Good.' The word hangs in the air between us for a moment. The room is vibrating with my pent-up anger.

'When I first saw you on the beach that day,' he says quietly, 'I had the chance to begin to repair the damage I had done.'

'Did you know who I was, even then?'

He nods.

'How could I not? For a moment I thought it was

Esther standing before me. The years vanished in a flash. Then I saw your fair hair, your surprised look. I had heard your name. I suspected who you must be.'

'But you said nothing.'

'Another wrong decision. I denied the truth to myself. And I was afraid. I had built my life on my guilt. Buried it deep in reckless bravery and a reputation for stern morals. How would that look if the truth were known? I asked myself. For a time I believed you were waiting to expose me. Every day I awoke with a dread of what the day might hold. If someone spoke under their breath, I believed they must be discussing me. I thought I was standing in a trap that might snap shut at any minute. But gradually I came to realize you didn't know. I decided you had to be discouraged from settling here. Then the truth could remain hidden. I could continue my life as before. And having once started down that route, it was hard to turn back. I saw you as a threat. In so doing I managed to forget you were my daughter. Esther's daughter. Can you forgive me, Marianne?'

'Forgive you?' I ask, astonished. 'My life was empty when I came here. The only good thing in it, my mother, had been taken from me. Then even my hope of finding my father was dashed. But despite this, I found some happiness. For the first time in my life, I found friends. You tried to part us. I found acceptance. But you spread lies about me. I found a place I love, and you tried to have me taken away. And then, just like that, you want me to forgive you?'

'I'm truly sorry,' he says humbly.

'Words,' I say scornfully. 'They are so easy. You'll have to show me you're sorry before we can talk about forgiveness.' I pause, still feeling angry. Something at the back of my mind is bothering me. I realize what it is: 'You weren't sorry when I came to speak to you last Sunday,' I remind him.

'I was taken by surprise. Later, when I had time to reflect, I admired your courage. I've watched you all year, Marianne. I've seen you grow in confidence and make a life for yourself. Heard you learn Danish. I saw your drawings when Mikkel brought your sketchbook home. I detested the part I played last Sunday, even as I did it. After you left, I couldn't sit still. I was so ashamed. And then I finally plucked up the courage to read your mother's letter. Dear God . . . I've never known such shame as her gentle words of reproach brought me.' A dry sob escapes him, as though torn from his chest. 'Poor Esther. She trusted me and I abandoned her. I have not acted honourably, Marianne. I am a scoundrel, a blaggard, a deserter . . . all the names you can think of: none of them are too harsh for what I did to her. But I never truly knew it till I read her letter.

'I had barely had time to take it all in when they came to tell me you had rowed out to sea in the storm. The realization that I might have lost you too was truly appalling. I had had no chance to repair the dreadful harm I had done. No chance even to try and explain. On the way to the beach, I promised God that if He let me find you alive, I would make amends. So tell me, Marianne. What can I do to prove to you that I'm sorry

291

for what I've done? How can I help you? You need money perhaps. A new start somewhere?'

So he still wants to be rid of me. I glare at him in disgust. 'I wouldn't touch an øre of your filthy money. I want nothing from you.'

'What can I do then?' he pleads.

I'm surprised at the depth of my loathing for him. I wonder whether I'll ever be able to overcome it. I think he wants me to feel sorry for him, but I don't. I had somehow expected that if I ever found my father I would love him. How wrong I was.

'You can do something for someone else,' I say at last. An idea is taking shape in my mind. I like it very much indeed.

'Someone else? Who?' asks Christensen, sounding surprised.

'Mikkel,' I tell him. My half-brother, I realize suddenly. For the first time in this conversation, a wave of pleasure sweeps over me. A brother to be proud of, I think.

'He wants to study. He's not suited to fishing. You know that better than I do. He'd be wasted. I want you to let him go. More than that. I want you to support him. Stop persecuting him. He's the cleverest person I ever met. You should be proud of your son.'

Christensen looks at me, and at first he's scowling. This isn't at all what he'd expected. Then, with an effort, he smiles and agrees. 'Very well. I'll try and do as you ask.'

'Then we have nothing more to discuss,' I say, and stand up. My legs are unsteady under me, and I feel light-headed. I want to be alone to think.

'One more thing,' I hear him say. I stop, my hand on the door handle. 'I would prefer it . . . that is, I can't see there's any need for anyone to know what we've spoken about today. If you remember, I promised you confidentiality.'

'Yes, *you* did. I did not.' I stand for a moment, thinking, and then I shake my head. 'No. My parentage has been a source of secrecy and shame all my life. The time for that is over. I don't want to live out my life with people and keep such a secret from them. It would be living a lie.'

Christensen bows his head, as if accepting the inevitable.

I leave him and go up to my room in the attic. I sit on my bed and stare at my trunk without seeing it until Hannah joins me.

'Marianne? Are you all right?' She takes my hand. 'You're cold. What did Hr Christensen want? You were with him for so long. Everyone's been wondering.'

'He came to tell me he's my father.' I'm surprised how easy it is to say. Hannah looks utterly confused, as though she hasn't heard me right.

'What do you mean, your father? He can't be.'

'It's rather a long story.' Slowly, with pauses and explanations, I begin to recount the essential points of the tale. It seems to gain in shape and substance as I talk. It becomes real. It's my history. My narrative is punctuated by cries of wonder and sympathy from Hannah. I tell her everything except the bargain about Mikkel. Time enough for her to hear of that if it happens.

THIRTY

I t's warm and pleasant on the bench outside Hannah's mother's house. I'm making the most of the mild weather to sit outdoors and sew a grey flannel dress for Lise. It'll keep her warm through the winter. She's my near neighbour now. It's taken me a few days to grow used to being so much alone again. I'll be glad when Hannah finishes work for the season too.

Peter is recovering. I haven't seen him, but I've heard from others how he's doing. And folded neatly on the table inside is a pile of work for Annette. I intend to start on that when I've finished Lise's dress.

I'm just finishing a hem, when Mikkel appears. He runs towards me with a look of great excitement on his face. I put the sewing aside, and wait eagerly to hear what he has to say.

'*God morgen*, Marianne!' he says merrily, shaking hands and taking a seat next to me in the sun.

'You look very pleased with yourself,' I remark. It's a week since I spoke to Christensen, and I've been expecting every day to hear something from Mikkel. He laughs, and it's good to hear him so happy.

'Yes, I've had some good news. I can hardly believe it

myself yet.' Mikkel shakes his head in wonder. 'My father's arranged for me to resume my studies with Mogens. And as soon as I can get a place at a school, he's promised to pay for me to go. I can hardly believe it. He even said he would consider allowing me to go to university afterwards, if I work hard. I'm going to get away, see some more of the world. I'm going to *study*, Marianne!'

'I'm so pleased for you!' I say warmly. 'Are you very happy?'

'Yes, of course I am. I'll be even happier presently, when I've had a chance to take it in. I always thought father was so hard and uncaring, especially towards me. And recently he's been worse than ever. I can't understand what's brought about such a change.'

'Did he seem different?' I ask cautiously. 'Apart from this sudden decision?'

'No,' says Mikkel, shaking his head. 'Not really. Perhaps less harsh. It was more what he was saying that was different.'

I take a deep breath. 'I have something to tell you too,' I say, suddenly a little shy. I don't know how he'll feel about hearing I'm his sister. 'You might not like it,' I warn him.

Slowly, haltingly, I retell my story, glossing over the parts that show his father in too bad a light. Mikkel listens in growing astonishment. He doesn't interrupt.

'My father?' he demands at last, bemused. 'My father had an illegitimate child? And he abandoned you and your mother? But you should hear what he says about men who do such things.'

'I think that was his guilt speaking. Though it seems to be the case that neither he nor my mother knew she was expecting a child when he left.'

'So . . . you're really my sister?' Mikkel asks.

'Half-sister, yes.' I grin at him, as he sits there lost in wonder. After a moment he grins back.

'And you really didn't know? All this time?'

I shake my head. 'No, I think I must have been stupid not to guess. Now that I know, it seems so obvious. And yet, how could I have worked it out? I had the wrong name. I thought my father was dead. It did confuse me that your father seemed to hate me so. But I drew all the wrong conclusions. I realized that you might be my cousin.'

'But you didn't say.'

'I was ashamed to. At first I was afraid you'd turn your back on an illegitimate child. My birth has brought me so much trouble and shame in my life.'

'So that's why you never talked about your life in England.' Mikkel moves closer and gives me a hug. '*Hej, søster,*' he says. 'You're my friend. I wouldn't have cared. Do I care about Hannah's birth?'

I don't want to cry, but I can't quite stop the tears from filling my eyes. I brush them away quickly, and Mikkel gives me another hug.

'No, I know you don't. If my father had been anyone else, I might have told you at some point,' I say.

He sits in silence for a few minutes, and I can see he's thinking it all over.

'My father must have married very soon afterwards, because there's not much difference in our ages.'

'Yes, I'm glad my mother never knew how quickly she was forgotten.'

Mikkel grins ruefully. 'I'll tell you what: I don't think I'll ever be as much in awe of father again.' Then he asks in a would-be casual voice: 'Does Hannah know?'

'Yes, I told her as soon as I knew. Have you told her your news yet?'

'No. I promised to fetch her this afternoon when she finishes at Brøndum's and help her carry her things home. I think she'll be pleased for me, don't you?' He doesn't meet my eyes as he says this.

'She'll miss you when you go,' I tell him truthfully.

When Mikkel brings Hannah back, she's pale and strained. She is bravely trying to be pleased for Mikkel and to be cheerful, but as soon as he leaves, she goes inside and throws herself on the bed, weeping unrestrainedly. I hold her, stroke her hair, and whisper words of comfort.

'He's not going immediately, Hannah. And besides, you know that if Mikkel was kept here against his will, he'd become bitter and frustrated. That wouldn't do either of you any good in the long run. Let him go, and he may come back.'

'With a wife and five children,' sobs Hannah. She's inconsolable. I haven't the courage to tell her I'm to blame. I just hug her closer, tears of sympathy in my own eyes.

'Hannah, I do understand how you're feeling,' I tell

her. 'Really I do. I've lost Peter too. I pushed him away with my stubbornness, my pig-headed determination to paint at any cost.' Hannah catches her breath on a sob, and squeezes my hand.

'Don't you think you'll make it up now that Perroy has gone?' she asks.

I shake my head sadly. A stray tear makes its way down my face. 'I really don't think so,' I say quietly. 'I've heard nothing from him.'

'But you saved his life!' cries Hannah indignantly, her eyes red-rimmed and swimming with tears.

'Yes, but that doesn't mean I win him. I'm not the prince in a fairy tale. And there's my background to consider. He didn't know about that before. No. It's all in the past. I expect nothing.'

'Do you regret it?' asks Hannah.

I hesitate. 'I don't regret learning to paint. But perhaps I wish I'd been more cautious. I certainly wish things had been different.'

'At least you have your painting. I have nothing.' Hannah begins to sob afresh, and I hold her tight once more.

I stay with Hannah until her mother returns. Leaving her in safe hands, I gather up my brush, palette, and my easel, and walk down to the beach. I feel shaken by Hannah's distress. It has also reminded me of my own loss. I hope to find some calm and peace in my work.

I've been studying the gulls: herring gulls, black-headed gulls, and arctic terns. I have a number of sketches. Today I want to try painting them. The late afternoon sunshine is just right.

It's beautiful on the beach. The sun is sparkling on the sea, as it often does at this hour. The sky above seems infinitely huge. I remember the enclosed room in Grimsby, the smoke and the noise, and take a deep breath of the pure, clear air. How I wish my mother were here to see and enjoy it all.

The beauty around me calms and soothes. I try to soak up the feeling of the light and the colour and the warmth of the sun to sustain me through the long, dark winter when it comes.

I paint steadily, slowly, losing myself in my attempt to capture the birds and the sea. It's very difficult, and I don't get on well. But I love it nonetheless. Unlike my sewing and embroidery, which are merely work, this is a deep pleasure. It's a part of me.

The sun sinks slowly behind me, altering the light. The sparkle fades from the sea and, reluctantly, I put down my brush. I can do no more today. Wiping the paint from my hands with a rag, I turn to look inland at the sun setting behind me. Before I can really take in the gold and orange of the sky, I realize, with a small shock, there's someone sitting quite close by, watching me.

'*God aften*, Peter,' I greet him. I'm surprised and delighted by his presence. 'I didn't know you were there.'

He gets to his feet and walks towards me. 'I saw you, and I wanted to speak to you. I could see how occupied you were, so I waited. How is it going?' He indicates my painting. I shrug.

'I'm making progress. But I have so much still to learn. Anna Ancher has kindly offered to continue teaching me through the winter. I can't believe how lucky I am.'

He smiles at me. I can see he's still not completely well. He's pale under his tan, and doesn't yet move with his usual strength and confidence.

'How are you feeling?' I ask.

'I'm recovering, but too slowly for my liking. I'm not made for idleness. I'm going to try a few hours work tomorrow. Do you have time for a walk with me now? Have you finished painting?'

'Yes, I have. A walk would be lovely.' Leaving the easel and palette where they are, we walk down to the water's edge and head south.

'I must thank you for saving my life,' Peter says.

I smile. 'Please, don't,' I beg. I feel a moment's disappointment. That's all he wants, I think. Just to thank me. Then he'll go.

'You were very brave,' he says softly.

'So everyone keeps telling me. I didn't feel brave. I was scared,' I admit.

'That's what bravery is. Do you think when the lifeboat goes out in a storm, that the men aboard are not afraid? Myself included.' He pauses, and we walk in silence for a while. When he speaks again there's constraint in h' voice.

'I also want to apologize. For what I said at midsur mer. I was worried for you. But I was also jealous an hurt, and it made me unkind. I know there was nothin between you and that Frenchman. I'm sorry that I ev believed there could be. I see how important your painting is to you and I'm ashamed that I tried to interfere.' He picks up a pebble from the water's edge and throws it. It skips twice before disappearing with a small splash. We walk on. When he speaks next, his tone is lighter.

'I'll be happier knowing it's Anna Ancher teaching you than that damnable Frenchman, all the same.' We both laugh. The implications of what he's saying fill me with hope and pleasure. But I'm curious too.

'So what makes you believe all of a sudden that there was nothing?'

'Your father came to see me the day before yesterday. We had a long talk.'

I'm completely stunned. I don't know how to reply, so I say nothing for a long while. Finally I ask: 'My father? So you know . . . '

'He told me a great many things.'

'I was going to tell you . . . about my parents,' I say in a low voice. I hardly dare look at Peter now, terrified I might see something different in his eyes. But to my surprise, he takes my hand.

'I'm sure you would have done. But perhaps it came best from him. Especially the truth about some of the lies he's told about you.'

Holding hands, we continue to walk along the sand. The waves hush at our feet. I'm both nervous and happy all at once. The sun sinks below the dunes to our right, and the light changes again. There's a deep luminous blue glow around us: the Skagen light. I look around me in awe.

302

'Isn't it beautiful?' I ask Peter.

But Peter is looking at me, drawing me closer. He puts his arms around me. Anxiously, I look up at his face. The love and warmth I see there makes my heart beat faster. I reach one hand up and tenderly touch his cheek, and then his fair hair. He smiles down at me, his eyes shining in the blue dusk.

'*Jeg elsker dig*, Marianne,' he whispers. I love you.

I shiver with pleasure, and it's a moment or two before I realize he's waiting for an answer.

'*Jeg elsker også dig*,' I assure him.

All these months, we've loved one another and not known how to say it. How uncomplicated it seems now.

Peter bends his head down and kisses me. His lips and his tongue are soft and warm. As we kiss, I stroke his hair and then his neck, and forget everything except the moment.

Eventually Peter lifts his head and looks down at me again. His arms are close about me in the growing chill of the evening.

'Do you remember when I carried you across the stream, the day you arrived?'

'How could I forget? I was so embarrassed.'

'I know you were. You blushed so red I thought you might catch fire. Such a pale, timid thing you were back then.'

'It's not quite a year ago,' I tell him, but he's not listening. He's kissing my forehead, my eyelids, and my cheeks. I close my eyes and lean against him. His lips find mine again.

'You'll marry me, won't you, Marianne?' he murmurs in my ear.

'Marry you?' I say unsteadily.

'I know it's too soon to ask you. But you see, I have no doubt in my mind at all,' he says seriously. 'I'll understand though, if you're not sure. Or if you think you're too young, I'll wait.'

'I could never love anyone like I love you,' I tell him. 'And I'd love to marry you, only . . .'

'Only what?' Peter asks, and his voice is gentle.

'I want to carry on learning to paint.' It's almost dark now, but I can see the flash of his teeth as he smiles.

'I expected you to say that. You can carry on painting.'

'Even go to art school if I can get a place?' I ask daringly. This time it's Peter who hesitates. 'I think I could pay for at least some of it myself, by selling these.' I reach under the neckline of my dress and pull out the pearl necklace that's hidden there. The pearls glow blue-white in the dusk. I hear Peter catch his breath.

'I've never seen you wear those,' he says.

'No, they're too fine for me.'

Peter shakes his head: 'Not at all.' He touches the pearls lightly, arranging them more becomingly. 'I hope you won't need to sell these. They look beautiful on you. I can help you pay for art school if that's what you want to do.'

I'm touched by his response. I'm asking so much, and he's offering more.

'Thank you,' I say softly. He draws me closer.

'How about a wedding next summer? Then I'll have the winter to finish the house.'

'*Det vil være dejligt*. I should like that very much,' I tell him. I've never meant anything more in my life. I'm overflowing with happiness. We seal our engagement with a kiss, and I can feel my body responding to his, full of pleasure and longing.

Then, holding hands, our fingers laced together, we turn and walk slowly back the way we came.

Marie-Louise Jensen (née Chalcraft) was born in Henley-on-Thames of an English father and Danish mother. Her early years were plagued by teachers telling her to get her head out of a book and learn useless things like maths. Marie-Louise studied Scandinavian and German with literature at the UEA and has lived in both Denmark and Germany. After teaching English at a German university for four years, Marie-Louise returned to England to care for her children full time. She completed an MA in Writing for Young People at the Bath Spa University in 2005. Marie-Louise reads, reviews and writes books for young people. She lives in Bath and home educates her two sons.